...rfect Stranger

"...tale of young newlyweds parted and reunited after nearly two years engages readers' emotions...a touching, heartwarming story."

—*RT Book Reviews*, 4 Stars

"Marvelous...the perfect blend of interesting, emotionally complex, and openhearted protagonists... In a story of personal growth and excited rediscovery, both characters must overcome scorn and opposition from their family and colleagues in order to come into themselves, appreciate each other, and turn a naively arranged marriage into a passionate partnership."

—*Publishers Weekly*, Starred Review

"It's a pleasure to have Ms. Ashford writing books again. Regency fans can look forward to an author who knows her period."

—*Fresh Fiction*

"Ashford's latest flawlessly written love story is a quietly compelling tale... The author's ability to create truly memorable characters while getting all the historical domestic details exactly right ensures that romance readers picky about authenticity will be well rewarded."

—*Booklist*

Praise for *Once Again a Bride*

"A near-perfect example of everything that makes this genre an escapist joy to read: unsought love triumphs despite difficult circumstances, unpleasantness is resolved and mysteries cleared, and good people get the happy lives they deserve."

—*Publishers Weekly*

"A bit of gothic suspense, a double love story, and the right touches of humor and sensuality add up to this delightfully fast-paced read about second chances and love's redeeming power."

—*RT Book Reviews*, 4 Stars

"Ms. Ashford has written a superbly crafted story with elements of political unrest, some gothic suspense, and an interesting romance."

—*Fresh Fiction*

"Well-rendered, relatable characters, superb writing, an excellent sense of time and place, and gentle wit make this a romance that shouldn't be missed... Ashford returns with a Regency winner that will please her longtime fans and garner new ones."

—*Library Journal*

"Mystery entwines with the romance, as Ms. Ashford leads us astray... *Once Again a Bride* is great fun."

—*Historical Hilarity*

Also by Jane Ashford

Heir to the DUKE

JANE ASHFORD

sourcebooks
casablanca

Published by Sourcebooks Casablanca, an imprint of Sourcebooks,
Inc.
P.O. Box 4410, Naperville, Illinois 60567-4410
(630) 961-3900
Fax: (630) 961-2168
www.sourcebooks.com

Printed and bound in Canada.
MBP 10 9 8 7 6 5 4 3 2 1

One

NATHANIEL GRESHAM, VISCOUNT HIGHTOWER, stirred in his sleep. His hands groped for bedclothes, found nothing. Sensing wrongness, his consciousness rose through layers of befuddlement and wisps of dreams. He opened his eyes to find a gaping maw of three-inch fangs inches from his throat.

"Aah!"

Nathaniel threw up his arms to shield his face and twisted to the side. The convulsive movement brought him right to the edge of a large four-poster bed, and he scrambled to avoid falling three feet to the floor. He twisted in the opposite direction and struck out at the sharp, yellowed teeth. They did not snap shut on his forearm or lunge into his face once more. Indeed, they did not move at all, except sideways under his blow. There was no snarl or slaver, no spark of rage in the shiny eye behind the fangs. Nathaniel shoved them farther away and sat up.

He was stark naked, on a large bed stripped bare of linens, covered only by a moth-eaten gray wolf skin. The wretched thing's head had been carefully placed on his chest, to ensure the rude awakening. His hips still rested under its hindquarters. Molting fur peppered the bed. The mere sight of the ancient pelt made his skin itch. Revolted, he pushed it all the way off and moved to the foot of the bed, struggling to get his bearings. This wasn't his bedchamber. The blue-striped wallpaper was alien, the furnishings unfamiliar; the windows with their slant of early morning light were in the wrong place. Then he remembered. He was staying at the Earl of Moreley's country house, because tomorrow—no, today—he was to marry the earl's daughter at their local parish church.

Nathaniel glared at the wolf skin, then rubbed his hands over his face. This was what it meant to have five brothers—five younger brothers—on one's wedding day. Or rather, on one's wedding eve, a night they'd insisted upon marking with bowls of rack punch. Had it been three? Or had he lost count? No wonder they'd kept filling his glass, if they had this prank planned. Where the devil had they found a wolf skin in a strange house? And hadn't he told his father, when Robert was born in his sixth year, that four sons were quite enough? Even for a duke, six sons were excessive. At this particular moment, Nathaniel thought that his parents might have been content with just one.

He rose, stretching stiff limbs and marveling that he had only a mild headache. Revenge on his brothers would have to wait for another day. Today, he was getting married. He was doing his duty to his name and his line, pledging himself to a woman who would be an admirable duchess when their turn came—may it be far in the future. The match was eminently suitable. All society acknowledged its rightness. And despite Violet's irascible grandmother, the occasional bane of his existence, he could have no complaints.

Indeed, why had the word even occurred to him? No one had rushed him into marriage. He had enjoyed a plenitude of seasons in London and a number of agreeable flirtations and liaisons with delightful females. Though they had never spoken of it, he was aware that his parents had given him every opportunity to fall in love. But the passion that had overtaken them in their young days had not befallen him. He wasn't sure why, but once he'd passed thirty he concluded it never would. He'd had more than enough time to observe that such a bond was rare in the circles of the *haut ton*.

Nathaniel stretched again, his bare limbs a bit chilly. This marriage was certainly not a penance. He liked Violet very much. They'd been acquainted for years. He did not know whether she'd had other offers, but he supposed that she too had waited for love to find her. They had that in common. They were also well suited by background, had similar tastes, and enjoyed the same even temperament. When he'd decided that the time for marriage had come, he'd simply known that she was the proper candidate. He expected their union to be gracious, harmonious, and ideal for the significant position they would someday be called upon to fulfill. And now it was time to stop woolgathering, put on his dressing gown, and begin this momentous day.

Nathaniel walked over to the oaken wardrobe on the far wall and opened it.

It was empty. All his clothes had disappeared.

He stared at the bare hooks. This part of the prank would be Sebastian's doing, he imagined. It had his next younger brother's touch. Nathaniel met his own gaze in the mirror set into the wardrobe door, and acknowledged the spark of amused annoyance in his eyes. His brothers had a fiendish facility for complicated jests.

The figure in the glass shook its head. All the sons of the Duke of Langford were tall, handsome, broad-shouldered men with auburn hair and blue eyes. Sebastian was the tallest. Robert the wittiest. Randolph was acknowledged as the handsomest, James the most adventurous, and Alan the smartest. But he was the eldest, and the heir.

For as long as he could remember, Nathaniel had felt the weight of his destiny. The others said it was a burden to have everything done ahead of them, but he'd felt the onus of being the pattern, setting up the expectations, being the son visitors scrutinized the most. He would be the next duke; he must show he was worthy. Thus, he kept a tight rein on his wilder impulses. Instead, he was the one who came to the rescue when one of his brothers went too far, kicking up a lark.

And so now, he did not slam the empty wardrobe shut, but simply closed it. He would leave it to his valet to straighten this out. He wanted hot water for washing, and then clothes, and then breakfast. He went to ring for Cates, and discovered that the bell rope had been removed. He could see the wire to which it had been connected, near the ceiling, twelve feet up. It must have taken two or three of his brothers to reach so high.

For a moment he just stood there, staring at it. This final touch would be Robert's idea, no doubt. He'd always been the most ingenious, the brother who added the crowning climax to a prank. Robert would be the one to set the others guffawing—describing their elder brother slinking through the corridors of the Earl of Moreley's house wrapped in a wolf skin, like some sort of demented ancient Celt. Even Nathaniel had to smile at the picture. How would Violet's fierce stickler of a grandmother like that? And all the other near and distant relations visiting for the wedding? He'd barely met most of them. Perhaps he'd twine some ivy from outside the window in his hair and attempt a Gaelic war cry.

Nathaniel laughed. Truth to tell, it was a splendid prank, unfolding like a puzzle box upon its hapless victim. All that remained was for him to wiggle out of the trap so cunningly set.

He eyed the windows and considered pulling down some of his almost-mother-in-law's elaborate draperies to wrap about himself. But one panel would trail behind him like a coronation robe. The picture was little better than the wolf skin. Perhaps he would just wait until Cates arrived on his own. It couldn't be too much longer. In fact, judging by the sunlight, his valet ought to have appeared well before now. Where the devil was he?

As if in answer to this thought, there was a knock at the door.

"Nathaniel?"

The voice was the last he expected. "Violet?"

"Are you all right? James said you needed to speak to me most urgent—" The door opened, and Nathaniel's promised bride looked around the panels. "Oh!" Her mouth dropped open.

Nathaniel—stark naked, next to a bed sporting only a rumpled wolf skin—braced for a shriek, a shocked retreat, babbled apologies. But Violet just looked at him. Indeed, it seemed as if she couldn't tear her eyes away. He could almost feel her gaze traveling along his skin, as if it left trails of warmth. He saw something stir in those gray eyes, something he'd never observed before, and his body began to respond to the possibility of much more than he'd expected from his suitable marriage. Respond all too eagerly.

Nathaniel moved over behind the bed. "My brothers' idea of a joke," he said with a gesture toward the wolf skin.

Violet blinked. Color flooded her cheeks, and she looked away. "How did they…?" Her voice was rather choked.

"They are endlessly inventive. They stole my clothes as well. Would you have someone send Cates to me? I would ring but"—he pointed to the bell wire—"they were quite thorough."

Violet glanced at the denuded wire, swallowed, and gave a quick nod. "Of course." In the next instant, she was gone.

"Well, well," murmured Nathaniel to the wolf. "That was interesting."

His days of being capable of interest long past, the wolf made no reply.

❧

Outside the closed door, Lady Violet Devere put her hands to her blazing cheeks and took a moment to recover her breath before going in search of Nathaniel's valet. She'd never seen a grown man totally naked before. Half-naked, yes. Perhaps three quarters, if you counted…? What was wrong with her brain? It was jumping about like a startled grasshopper.

It was just… Nathaniel had seemed so *very* naked. She hadn't been able to look away; she hadn't even been able to think that she should avert her eyes. The sight of him—so tall and handsome and…naked had been riveting. And tonight she would be his wife, granted the…freedom of all that…nakedness. She had married friends; she knew what that meant.

Of course she had married friends. She was twenty-six years old! Which explained why she'd opened his bedchamber door. When she shouldn't have. It was quite improper. But his brother James had sounded so odd when he spoke to her. She'd leapt to dire conclusions and rushed in, fearing that the wedding was to be put off, that her grandmother had said or done something outrageous. The thought was insupportable. Her future was settled at last. She would grow no older waiting to marry. She would *not* watch yet another crop of debs enter society and pair off.

It was all very well for Nathaniel. He was a man, free of the countless idiotic strictures that beset an unmarried "girl" with an iron-willed grandmother who was absolutely devoted to the proprieties. He could do whatever he liked with his…really gorgeous body.

Violet took a deep breath, and then another. She stood straighter, consciously relaxed tense muscles. All was well. It had merely been a prank. She knew about pranks; she had two much younger brothers, welcomed with relief after her disappointing female birth, and rather spoiled by their parents. A belated laugh escaped her. The sons of the Duke of Langford must be masters of the art to have somehow stranded Nathaniel, naked, with the skin of the wolf her grandfather had shot in the wilds of Russia. Wasn't it kept in a locked cabinet?

Violet started for the servants' hall, slightly hampered by the cascade of ruffles at the hem of her white dress. She jerked the fabric out of her way. She hated white, and was all too aware that the hue did not flatter her. It washed out her pale complexion, her sandy hair and gray eyes. Put her in white—in any pastel, really—and she practically faded into the wallpaper. Of course, this didn't matter to Grandmamma. An unmarried girl wore pale colors, and that was that. The rules were not to be questioned, even when they made one look a complete frump. And Violet's mother existed firmly under *her* mother-in-law's thumb.

Catching movement in the corner of her eye, Violet paused before a long mirror on the corridor wall. Her features were good, if she did say so—straight nose, well-shaped lips, eyes a lucent gray. If allowed to make something of them, with a more fashionable haircut and perhaps just a touch of color for her cheeks…? Violet imagined her grandmother's horror at the latter idea. She imagined it for several seconds.

How she hated ruffles. And this dress had far too

many, cluttering the silhouette, obscuring the lines of her form. She'd seen gowns at London balls that would have accentuated the subtle curves she definitely possessed, in colors and fabrics that would flatter rather than subdue.

The question popped into her mind: what would Nathaniel think if he came upon her naked?

Violet flushed again. The rosy hue was quite becoming. She stared at her reflection and acknowledged that it was going to be quite…interesting to see what Nathaniel thought. Their match was the union of two great families. And as Violet's grandmother never tired of repeating, it wasn't about her. Nathaniel needed a wife who could be a proper duchess. But perhaps he needed other things as well. Violet watched her mirror image smile in a quite unfamiliar way.

She scarcely recognized herself. It was as if impulses long stifled were surfacing in the mirror, summoned by the sight of her almost-husband. Violet blinked. If her grandmother, or her father, or her mother came along now, she'd be in for a scold. Fierce, cold, fearful—they each had their way of pointing out her shortcomings. Of which she seemed to have a never-ending supply. At times, it had even seemed to Violet that her family valued their criticisms more than her future prospects.

She was crushing the hated ruffles in both hands, she realized. She opened them.

It didn't matter. Nathaniel had offered for her. In a few hours she would be a married woman, and everything would be different. She could do as she pleased. She would no longer live with her grandmother.

She would not be told what to wear and whom she could see. She would not be scrutinized for flaws at every turn. In her own household, she would be the arbiter. In fact, she had a list of things Grandmamma had forbidden, and she intended to indulge in them as soon as might be. Violet nodded at her reflection with a steely gaze that would have startled those who thought they knew her.

A footman appeared at the end of the corridor. Violet dropped her eyes and moved away from the mirror, resuming her mantle of sweet compliance. "John, would you tell Cates that his lordship wants him? The bell is…broken." Violet wondered what that prim valet would think when he found Nathaniel naked with a wolf skin? But perhaps he was used to pranks; he had been with Nathaniel for a long time, and it seemed the Duke of Langford's sons were addicted to them.

"Mr. Cates seems to be out this morning, your ladyship," replied the footman, his face stiff with disapproval.

"Out? Where?"

"No one seems to know, your ladyship."

That was odd. Or… It must be part of the prank. Violet nodded to the footman and walked farther along the corridor until she heard male voices from a small parlor on her right. Taking another step on paths forbidden by her grandmother, Violet eased the door open a crack and peeked through. All of Nathaniel's brothers were gathered around the hearth, a very handsome conspiracy. Shamelessly, Violet eavesdropped.

"This has gone far enough. We should take him some clothes," said Alan.

He was the youngest brother, and the only one married so far, Violet recalled. He lived in Oxford and did something at the university. Violet thought she might like his wife, Ariel. She hadn't had a chance to find out, because Grandmamma didn't approve of her for some reason. She added an item to her list: get to know Ariel Gresham.

"Nonsense," said Robert. "It's a challenge to his ingenuity."

Violet was well acquainted with both Robert and Sebastian. They were extremely fashionable young men and fixtures of the *haut ton*. Robert was known for his wit, and Sebastian for the exquisite cut of his Guard's uniforms.

"He's getting married in three hours," Randolph pointed out.

Thank you, thought Violet. Randolph was the clergyman. His parish was somewhere up north, and he was rarely in town. Violet had met him only twice before. Should a man of the cloth be pulling pranks involving nakedness and wolf skins?

"Plenty of time," said Sebastian.

Who was notorious for being late to social engagements, Violet thought.

"No, it isn't," said Alan.

"I sent Violet to him," said James.

This fifth-oldest Gresham brother had just returned from a three-year naval mission that had taken him right around the world. Violet didn't know him at all.

The rest of them turned on him in a general babble of, "You what?"

"I passed her on the stairs and told her Nathaniel needed to speak to her. Most urgently." James grinned.

Violet blinked. She had thought James the least striking of the brothers. His smile changed her opinion. It was full of vitality and perfectly charming.

Randolph sank into an armchair. "What have we done? To expose a gently reared young lady…"

Alan let out a long sigh.

"She will have a nervous collapse," said Robert, sounding rather awed. "She will fall into a fit of the vapors and never come out. Why have we heard no shrieks or running footsteps?"

Was this what they thought of her? Violet was mortified. Her grandmother would say it was what she got for listening at doors. The same grandmother who had ensured that people saw Violet as a prudish, missish stick.

"They're getting married," James said. "Whatever she sees…well, she's going to see it anyway."

"With a wolf skin?" said Alan.

Randolph made a choking sound.

"If the old lady finds out…" began Sebastian.

"We flee the country," responded Robert. "James will find us a ship to the antipodes."

Violet had to stifle a laugh. She hadn't realized how much she was going to enjoy being a Gresham. Suppressing a smile, she pushed the parlor door open and walked in. "What have you done with Cates?" she demanded.

She was met with silence and a circle of staring blue masculine eyes.

"Cates?" said Robert.

"Nathaniel's valet? He appears to be missing."

"Missing?" said Randolph.

Violet turned to him, and he took a step back. "So I am told. Am I not speaking clearly? Perhaps if you returned our bell rope…?"

"You know about the…" Alan's voice trailed off.

Violet raised her eyebrows. "I was just speaking to Nathaniel and—"

"Nathaniel? In his room?" interrupted Robert.

"In his room," she confirmed. "With his lupine companion."

Robert's mouth fell open. James burst out laughing. "I locked the valet in the garden shed," he admitted.

From the babble that broke out, Violet concluded that this had not been part of the plan. Pitching her voice to cut through it, she said, "You will release him immediately and send him to Nathaniel." She fixed each brother in turn with a stern look. "Yes?"

"Yes," said Alan. The others nodded.

With an answering nod, Violet turned and went out.

Silence followed. Finally, Robert spoke in hushed tones. "She sounded just like her grandmother."

This elicited another round of solemn nods. Except from James. "What's wrong with you?" he said. "She seems like a capital girl to me."

Two

THE MARRIAGE OF NATHANIEL GRESHAM, VISCOUNT
Hightower, and Lady Violet Devere took place later
that morning at the village church near the Deveres'
country home. His wardrobe returned from its hiding
place, the viscount was handsome and composed in a
dark blue coat. No one, seeing him stand so calmly
before the altar, would have imagined him waking
naked under a wolf skin a few hours earlier. The bride
looked resolute, and slightly washed out, in a gown of
pale pink. Those present were too accustomed to her
wan appearance to wonder at the wardrobe choice.

The simple ceremony was witnessed by the couple's
families and close friends. On one side of the church,
the elder Langfords exhibited more genial dignity than
visible joy. Indeed, the duke, a tall, spare, handsome
man of sixty or so, exchanged at least one unfathomable look with his duchess. Adele Gresham, though
well past fifty, was exceedingly striking in a blue
ensemble that complemented hair of a deep, rich color
between chestnut and strawberry. She sat very straight.
Tall, angular, with arching brows and an aquiline nose,

she was known for not suffering fools, and the one glance she let slip to the opposite rank of pews suggested that this ability was under considerable strain.

For their part, the bride's parents seemed oddly subdued. They looked more often to the earl's formidable mother than to their marrying offspring. The Dowager Countess of Moreley glowered in the front pew, bent a little forward, both hands resting on the head of her ebony cane. At seventy-six, with her prominent features accentuated by age, her once fine figure sabotaged by gravity, she'd been compared by one quaking sprig of fashion to a cathedral gargoyle. If she had ever exhibited an errant sense of humor, her gown of stone-gray sarcenet might have been seen as wry defiance of this characterization. But no one had ever accused Violet's grandmother of whimsy. Next to her the stocky, sandy-haired earl and his plump, anxious wife were obviously mere retinue. Only Violet's younger brothers, sixteen and fourteen, added vitality to the Devere pew.

To those who knew them, the groom's bevy of brothers seemed a bit subdued as well. They put it down to the solemnity of the occasion, unaware of Nathaniel's mustering of the troops once he was dressed and breakfasted. He'd lined them up in a vacant parlor like a company of soldiers, acknowledged the depths of their ingenuity and the hilarity of the results, and informed them that the remainder of his wedding day was to be prank-free. Walking down the row, he'd fixed each brother with a stern eye, and received solemn promises in return. When he cared to exert it, Nathaniel had a natural authority that could not be denied.

Sebastian stood up with the viscount at the altar. Alan sat next to their parents with his lovely wife Ariel at his side. The rest filled the second pew with three sets of wide shoulders, and there was not a peep from any of them, not even James.

Afterward, guests and prominent neighbors joined the family at the house for a celebration of the wedding. Reception rooms filled with a buzz of conversation, and chattering groups spilled out into the beautiful June day through French doors open to the gardens.

"Oh, my," declared one lady as the Langford brothers paused on the terrace for a brotherly toast. "I must say that the sight of them all together is quite breathtaking."

"It's the first time they've all been gathered in some years. Lord James has been at sea," responded her friend, who prided herself on knowing every tiny tidbit of gossip.

"And only the eldest married?"

"And the youngest, Lord Alan."

"How odd."

"Oh, it was quite the mystery. Some country nobody called Bolton, from Cornwall." She bent closer to murmur in her friend's ear. "Though some say her mother was an actress."

"No!"

The other nodded. "And a dear 'friend' of the Prince Regent."

"Ah. So that's how it came about?"

The gossip looked frustrated. "The details of the match are unclear. But Lord Sebastian, now, he is recently engaged. Announced in a perfectly straightforward way."

"He's the taller one, with the side whiskers?"

"Cavalry regiment," was the laconic reply. "He snagged Georgina Stane."

"The heiress?"

"Indeed. Lord Sebastian beat out a whole crowd of suitors."

The second lady looked impressed, but dubious. "Has he met her family?"

"He must have. They courted through most of the season."

"Oh, her family does not go up to London. I believe Lady Georgina was staying with her aunt. Or her grandmother?" At her friend's inquiring look, the lady added, "I've heard the Stanes are rather…eccentric."

"Indeed?"

Eyes bright, the lady bent closer to whisper.

On a sofa in the largest parlor, Violet's grandmother was holding forth to a captive audience. "Of course, the Devere family goes back to the Conqueror on both sides. The Langford dukedom was only granted in 1683. Charles II, you know. Not what you would call…really sound."

Passing behind her, Nathaniel wanted to mutter that his ancestor had already been an earl at the time, but he didn't. Arguing with the dowager countess of Moreley was useless. She could never be convinced that her opinions were wrong, and she was only too delighted to explain the stupidity of those who didn't share them.

Nathaniel moved on, conscious of glances following him and remarks being made. He'd attended scores of parties since his early youth, and attracted notice at many of them, for the sake of his rank and position. He'd never come to enjoy it, and today was worse. As the groom, he was the continual center of attention.

He paused in a doorway between rooms, looking for Violet, and heard his brother James's voice from one side. "I put away a goodly bit of prize money during the war, and I'm thinking it's time to find a nice English girl and get leg-shackled."

"If you think of it as 'shackled—'" began Alan's wife Ariel.

"Just an expression," James interrupted. "I've heard you're quite the matchmaker."

"Well, when you come to visit us next month, we shall see," said Ariel. "I can introduce you to some young ladies."

"Not bluestockings, mind," said James. "Alan's the one for books and such."

Nathaniel grinned as Ariel agreed, and moved on into the crowd.

❧

Violet wondered if the toasts and congratulations and evaluating glances would ever end—particularly those from the people who clearly wondered how she'd managed such a match. Those made her want to pour red wine down the front of her wretched pink dress until it turned a more flattering color. Except she also wanted to drink the wine—lots of it. And from the way her grandmother occasionally frowned at her, she probably knew it. Violet was surprised Grandmamma hadn't marched over and taken her glass away from her.

Looking happy, making happy meaningless

conversation, was exhausting. Not that she wasn't happy. She was. Of course she was. Or, at least, she was very glad the wedding was done. She was excited to get on with her new life. She appreciated Nathaniel's steady presence and the good wishes of her real friends. But how she longed to get away! None of these people could imagine the pressure that had been building up in her over all these years of being the good girl—even years after she didn't feel like a girl at all. They had no notion of the familial conspiracy that made certain every hint of rebellion was squelched. She'd been part of it; she knew that. She'd given in to the frowns and orders.

But that was over now, and with freedom so near, the desire for it was pushing at her like floodwater straining at a dam. She hadn't understood precisely what it would be like once she was actually married. She was afraid something would burst out before all these wedding guests, and she would go whirling and chattering among them like a bedlamite. The image called up the memory of Nathaniel naked with the wolf skin. Here were scenes to set all of society on its ear. The idea had a strange attraction. She could almost wish to see the faces of Nathaniel's brothers, who thought her such a buttoned-up miss. But it wasn't going to happen. She retained more self-control than that.

The minutes and hours dragged interminably, but finally they were going out to the carriage. People followed to wave and call farewells. The door was shut, the horses given their heads, and they were off on the three-hour drive to the manor where they were to spend the first two weeks of their marriage. Violet watched until the gates of her old home disappeared around a bend in the road. "Thank God that is over," she said then, referring to the entire chapter of her early life.

Nathaniel looked a bit surprised at her vehemence. "Are you worn out? Your mother thought a country wedding would be less tiring…"

"No, Grandmamma would not be so unfashionable as to remain in London an instant after the season ended," she corrected.

"Ah."

There was no need to say more. Her grandmother was an established sore point. She had found things to criticize even in the estimable Viscount Hightower. "And I'm not tired. Except of…" Violet let the sentence die. There was no need to burden Nathaniel with complaints about her endless "girlhood." Particularly now that it was over.

After waiting politely to see if she would continue, he said, "I think you will like Hightower. The countryside thereabouts is thought to be very beautiful."

"Your title comes from there?"

"Yes, the manor was one of the earliest Gresham land holdings."

"Before Charles II?" When Nathaniel looked startled, she smiled. "Yes, I heard Grandmamma disparaging the date of the dukedom."

Nathaniel smiled back. He had a wonderful smile. She'd noticed that before, but not quite so vividly. When he truly smiled, his handsome face gained warmth and depth, and she felt as if she could fall forever into his blue eyes. As they shared a moment of conspiratorial glee, Violet's heartbeat stuttered. She saw her new husband smiling before her, and standing ruefully naked in his empty bedchamber this morning. Something in his gaze suggested that he might be thinking of that moment too, when she had been unable to tear her eyes away from his sculpted form. Violet felt bits of her body tighten in response to the notion.

They were alone together. For hours. Quite close together, really, in the confines of the traveling carriage. They hadn't been alone before, not for more than a few minutes, due to her grandmother's antiquated notions. Violet felt as if the air was thickening around her. If he wished to touch her now, he could. She wished he would. And yet, she had made a plan for their first moments of intimacy. She'd seen each step in her mind's eye a hundred times. Should she throw it to the four winds? Should she cast herself into his arms, here in the moving carriage? Part of her cried out, "Yes!" But Violet found she was not quite that daring. She wished she was. Perhaps she could become so?

The silence had begun to seem long. She should say something. "Is there actually a tower?" It came out breathless. Nathaniel's smile broadened. Could he read her mind?

"Yes, indeed," he said. "A ruined one. It's said to be quite ancient. Hightower is not far from Chichester, you know, which is full of Roman remains."

This bit of geography steadied Violet's senses as it reminded her of other plans. "It's not too far from Brighton either, is it?"

"About fifty miles."

About what she'd estimated; not a difficult journey.

"You know that the house isn't grand," Nathaniel added. "Nothing like Fairleigh."

Violet nodded. Fairleigh, their eventual home, was just five miles from Langford Abbey, the duke's main seat. She had visited it, and approved some renovations that were in train. She knew that Nathaniel needed to be nearby to help his father administer the ducal lands. She also knew that the duchess hoped to enlist her in a variety of charitable ventures. She and Nathaniel had a host of duties laid out for them that would last the rest of their lives.

Violet suppressed a sigh. She didn't object to responsibility. She'd known full well that it lay ahead. She only wanted a little time before all those duties descended. She deserved it. Nathaniel did too. Surely he would enjoy a bit of freedom? The pent-up energy that had surged in her at the wedding breakfast swept through her again—that fierce longing to make her own choices, plunge into experience. "I should so like to spend the summer in Brighton!" The words had escaped her, unstoppable, propelled by that energy. She hadn't meant to bring this up so soon. But she'd waited so long!

"Brighton?" Nathaniel looked surprised.

"I've always wanted to go."

"I didn't realize you were fond of the seaside."

"I love it." Violet actually had no idea if this was true. She'd never spent any time by the ocean. But she knew she wanted balls and excursions and bride visits and... She reached out and put a hand on his arm. "It would be such fun!"

Their eyes met, and intense awareness filled the carriage once more. His coat sleeve seemed hot where her fingers rested.

"I don't know," said Nathaniel slowly. "The good places will all be leased by now."

"Surely something could be found?"

Nathaniel blinked at the hint of a snap in her voice. For a moment, he seemed to hear an unsettling echo of her grandmother's steely tones. But that was ridiculous. No one could be less like the dowager than his gentle bride. "I'll have some inquiries made," he conceded.

"Wonderful." Violet smiled, and sternly repressed a desire to insist. She mustn't let her longings get out of hand. There would be plenty of time to convince him in the days ahead.

❧

They arrived at Hightower in the golden light of early evening, which gave the house of mellow red brick, built in Tudor times, the look of a painting. The building was set on a gentle rise in the middle of a wide valley. Below lay a small lake, shimmering with reflected reds from the sunset. A little sailboat was tied to the dock there, and sheep and cattle grazed in nearby fields. The ruined tower that Nathaniel had mentioned crowned the farther rim of the valley, as if placed there by a discerning artist, its fallen stones and empty windows silhouetted against the banded sky.

Nathaniel pointed it out to Violet as their carriage wound its way up to the front door. His memories of this place were fond, though not lifelong. Ownership had come to him on his majority, and he had used the house as an informal respite in a formal life, visiting now and then with a few good friends, sailing and fishing and riding in the countryside. Here he had a good steward and no particular duties. He could set aside responsibility in simple pleasures. He had chosen it for the first days of marriage because he had always felt easy and contented within its walls. There was no crowd of onlookers to scrutinize and evaluate, no pressure to be a worthy representative of an ancient line.

They were welcomed by the housekeeper and their personal servants, who had come ahead in another coach with their luggage. Cates had hot water and towels ready in his dressing room, and Nathaniel supposed Violet's maid, Renshaw, did in hers. He washed off the grit of the journey and went back downstairs to await his bride.

As he'd ordered, a light supper was laid out in the main parlor, with champagne and a bowl of strawberries. The food was plain, so that there was no need for attendants. A small fire burned in the hearth, more for coziness than warmth on this mild June night. Nathaniel had tried to anticipate every awkwardness associated with the new intimacy of marriage, and ease it. Although, after Violet's frank gaze this morning—had it really been this same day that she opened his bedchamber door?—he wondered if he had been too scrupulous.

On that thought, Violet appeared in the doorway. She had changed into a gown he had never seen before. He knew this because it was so unlike her usual pale raiment. Its sweep of deep rose silk whispered and clung along the length of her body. Its neckline dipped in a way that insisted he notice the soft curves of her bosom. Her cheeks had more color; her gray eyes sparkled. Altogether, she was more alluring and vibrant than the young woman he thought he knew so well. More and more interesting, he thought. "Would you care for champagne?"

"Oh, yes, please."

He opened the bottle and filled a slender crystal goblet. Smiling at him, she drank it down and held it out for more. He'd never seen her indulge in more than one glass of wine, and he wondered if she was bolstering her courage. "A bit of chicken?" he offered, to reassure her that she would not be hurried. "Or strawberries?" He found his gaze following the tantalizing line of her bodice, and forced it upward.

"Strawberries," replied Violet. She walked over to the table and dropped three of the tiny fruits, one by one, into her glass. "People do that, don't they? Put strawberries in champagne?" She tilted the goblet, caught one of the berries with the tip of her tongue, and ate it.

Momentarily, Nathaniel was transfixed. "I…believe they do."

"Do you want some?" She picked up another strawberry and held it out like a challenge.

Nathaniel moved two steps closer, grasped her extended wrist, and took the fruit with his lips. He saw as well as heard Violet's indrawn breath. The dip of that neckline made it thoroughly visible. For one hopeful moment, he thought it was going to slip and reveal more of what he so wished to see. But of course it didn't. They made gowns that way, somehow. So that they teased. Once again, he pulled his eyes away. Noting a tiny tremor in her hand, he let go.

"Do you…do you want another?" she breathed.

Meeting her wide gaze, he nodded. Violet picked up a strawberry and fed it to him. As the sweet taste burst in his mouth, he took one and offered it. Violet's lips parted. He ran the berry slowly along her lower lip, leaving a crimson trail of juice, before popping it into her mouth. Violet didn't move. He bent nearer. When she showed no signs of withdrawing, he leaned in and licked the stain away.

She shivered. And then she set her champagne down with a sharp click, made a kind of lunge, and crushed her lips to his. Nathaniel's arms slid automatically around her as they swayed with her onslaught. He pulled her close even as he eased the kiss into something softer and slower. His new wife's inexpert enthusiasm made him want to smile, even as desire spiked in him at the feel of her under his hands. He let the kiss go on. And on.

"Oh," said Violet when they parted at last. "Oh, that was nothing like when we kissed before."

There had shared a very few decorous embraces, when they could snatch a moment away from her chaperones. "It's helpful not to feel that your grandmother is just around the corner waiting to pounce," Nathaniel pointed out.

"Yes." Violet laughed. It sounded a little wild. She laced her arms around his neck. "She can't do that anymore. Ever. Will you kiss me again?"

"With pleasure, Lady Hightower." And he did.

This time he let his hand drift up to that tantalizing bodice. And when her breath caught, he pushed the small sleeve of her gown down her shoulder in order to touch her more directly.

"Keep doing that," she demanded when the kiss at last melted away.

"This?" As his fingertips teased, his body strained with arousal.

"Yes!"

"I'd be delighted to do so. But we should go upstairs before we…make a spectacle of ourselves before the servants." He drew her toward the door of the room.

Violet blinked, her gray eyes going from blurred and dreamy to sharply aware. "Upstairs. Yes. I'll go. You can come in ten minutes."

"Ten…?" No part of Nathaniel wanted to wait even three.

"I have a plan."

"A…plan?"

"Ten minutes," Violet repeated, and rushed out. Nathaniel was left startled, perplexed, and almost too taut with desire to acknowledge a thread of amusement. But he obeyed his bride's commands, and waited.

When he entered her bedchamber at the appointed time, he discovered Violet standing in the center of the room, illuminated by three large branches of candles. She wore a nightdress of whisper-thin gauze. The candlelight shone right through it. It fastened with ribbons at the shoulders in the same shade of deep blue. His fingers itched to untie those bows.

"I bought it secretly," she said.

He thought her voice trembled just slightly. He reminded himself to go slowly, even though desire was beating in him like a hammer on an anvil.

"Most of my bride clothes are dreadful, because Grandmamma insisted. Like all those…those sacks of ruffles she's made me wear."

Nathaniel's mind grappled with the phrase "sacks of ruffles" and came up blank.

"But I managed to get a few things." Violet took hold of the ends of the ribbons and pulled. The bows unraveled. The nightgown slithered softly to the floor. "I saw you naked this morning," Violet said. "Turn about, fair play."

Nathaniel scarcely heard. He was dimly aware that he had gasped. He'd thought of Violet as suitable and intelligent and perfectly pleasant to look at. How could he have failed to notice that she had a glorious body? The curve of breast that her dress had revealed was only the beginning. She also possessed a narrow waist, a beautiful flare of hip, long, lovely legs.

"You look as if someone had hit you over the head," she said. Violet hid a quaver of nerves. Nathaniel's eyes looked as if they might burst into flame. The astonishing sensations she'd experienced downstairs receded a bit as inner voices scolded her for being inexcusably brazen. She looked down. "Isn't it…? Aren't I…?"

"You are exquisite," her new husband said.

She let out her breath. This was most satisfactory. She reminded herself that she had prepared for this moment. What she'd had to go through just to get the nightgown! "I've heard the first time is likely to be... difficult." Indeed, two of her married friends had seemed to relish sharing harrowing tales of their wedding nights. "I...I expect to benefit from your expertise."

Nathaniel blinked. Some of the—slightly intimidating—fire went out of his gaze. "My expertise?"

"You've had plenty of time to learn all about it," Violet pointed out. "And society positively...encourages you to do so."

"It?"

Was he smiling? Was she making a fool of herself? Marianne had said the best thing was to keep quiet and endure what was soon over, but Jane had sworn there could be much more. And when Nathaniel had touched her downstairs, Violet had realized she must be right. "You know what I mean," she said.

"Because of my expertise."

Part of Violet wanted to snatch up the nightgown and shield her nakedness. But another stubborn part made her stand taller and say, "Yes. And if you are laughing at me, I swear I will—"

"I am not laughing at you."

"Prove it!"

"How can I do that? I fear you must take my word."

His voice was like warm honey. It made her knees feel wobbly. "You can... You can take off your clothes too," she heard herself say.

"A capital idea," Nathaniel replied, already pulling his coat from his wide shoulders.

Violet watched as he threw the garment over an armchair. His neckcloth followed, revealing the strong column of his throat. He sat briefly to pull off his boots, then rose and began to unbutton his shirt. "Perhaps you would like to help me with these?"

"What?" Violet's mouth felt dry. She swallowed.

"Buttons. Pesky things." He beckoned.

Feeling as if a taut string was pulling her, Violet moved toward him. When she was close, he caught one of her hands and placed it on…a button.

Briefly, she fumbled. Then she used both hands to undo it, and the next, and so on down his chest. Nathaniel's breath caught when her fingers brushed the hard muscles of his stomach. So she did it again, experimentally, as she pushed the shirt off. He grasped her upper arms and pulled her into another amazing kiss. Her bare skin burned against his.

And then he let her go. Violet stared up at him, bereft. But he paused only to skim out of the rest of his clothes, pick her up, and lay her on the large four-poster bed. "Alas, no wolf skin," he murmured in her ear as he joined her.

Violet was surprised by a gurgle of laughter. She was also aware of a—rather large—change in his body from what she'd seen this morning. "Is it time?"

Nathaniel smiled down at her. Heat simmered in his blue eyes again, but also, she thought, great kindness. How odd. "Time for me to demonstrate my 'expertise,'" he replied, and set his lips and fingers roving over her. They teased and caressed and coaxed until Violet thought she would drown in the shivers of sensation coursing through her. And then his attention centered in the tightest, most insistent spot, and she did. She was swept away entirely on a breaking wave of pleasure.

"So, you see how it can be," he murmured as he held her through it. "But now, I fear I cannot wait any longer."

There was some pain, but Violet didn't care. She'd seen how it could—would—be.

Three

VIOLET WOKE UP THE MISTRESS OF HER OWN HOUSEHOLD.

She didn't think of it right away. She opened her eyes as usual, alone as usual, and stretched in the snowy, lavender-scented linens, blinked at the golden swath of morning sunshine. Where was her nightgown? Oh. She wriggled as memories of last night surfaced, in body and mind, and wondered dreamily where Nathaniel was right now.

And then the entirety of the change hit. She was Lady Hightower, in charge of this house and several others. The routines of the day were hers to order. No one would be frowning at her for sleeping past a certain hour, criticizing her every move, nagging at her over strict notions of propriety. Or, if they did, she could ignore them, contradict them even. She could have whims and crochets. Or...perhaps she was too young for crochets. But she could certainly consult her own tastes and desires and make her own decisions.

The bedroom door opened, and Renshaw bustled in, setting down a jar of hot water and throwing back curtains. "Are you *still* abed, my lady? Do you mean to sleep the day away?"

And all in an instant, Violet's mood darkened.

Renshaw picked up her gauze nightdress from the floor and held it out. Morning light filtered through the delicate blue fabric. "Where did this come from?" she asked in scandalized tones.

In a moment's cowardice, Violet thought of saying that Nathaniel had given it to her.

"Disgusting." Renshaw crumpled the delicate garment into a ball. It looked so fragile in her square hands. "Only an abandoned hussy would wear a wisp like this." The lines of disapproval in her face were only too familiar.

But seeing the lovely gauze crushed galvanized Violet. "Don't do that," she said.

"It's going straight into the rubbish bin," Renshaw continued, showing no sign of having heard her. "Before any of the servants here see it. Why, their tongues would be wagging from here to Berkeley Square."

Violet started to sit up, recalled that she was naked, and ducked back under the coverlet. "No, it isn't! It's beautiful."

Renshaw fixed her with the stern gaze that had intimidated Violet since she was fifteen, when her grandmother had assigned her a personal maid of nearly forty—one thoroughly in tune with Grandmamma's outlook on life. "It most certainly will, my lady. We will not have this sort of scandalous garment in the house. What will his lordship think?"

He'd seemed to think it was perfectly delightful last night, Violet almost said. But she noticed that

Renshaw was laying out one of her old dresses. "I don't want to wear that one," she said.

Renshaw ignored her preference, as she had every objection Violet had ever made. Shaking out the mass of pale pink ruffles, she merely replied, "This is very suitable for a day in the country."

If you meant to spend it sitting in a parlor with an embroidery hoop, Violet thought. Fading into the wallpaper and looking quite colorless. Which she did not! She would not! But despite her inner vehemence, futility descended on Violet like a smothering blanket. She'd long ago given up arguing with Renshaw. Whenever she did, the case was submitted to her grandmother, who always agreed with the maid. Violet's mother was never any help at all, and of course her father took no part in decisions about gowns or the proper pursuits of girlhood. And so it was no use even trying...

She clenched her fists under the sheets. That era was over. She was the mistress of the house now. There was no higher authority. Violet threw back the bed linens and stood up, stark naked.

Renshaw's tight, downturned mouth fell open. "My lady!"

"I will wear the green walking dress." The pale color was not much better than the pink, but at least it had fewer ruffles. Violet had been able to sneak only one vivid silk gown into the orders for her bride clothes. As soon as possible, she meant to replace her entire wardrobe.

It was difficult to carry off nakedness in the face of such simmering disapproval. Though she wanted to rush, Violet made herself walk slowly over to the wardrobe. She took her dressing gown from a hook and slipped it on like armor. "The green," she repeated, and held Renshaw's outraged gaze, pretending she was staring down a yapping pug. Finally, rigid with outrage, the maid turned to fetch her choice.

It was a tiny victory. And it left Violet roiling with emotion as she went downstairs. The staff's eagerness to provide her with a fresh pot of tea and hot toast was somewhat consoling. She told herself to be patient. Changing one's life took a bit of time.

"What would you like to do today?" Nathaniel asked Violet half an hour later, when he found her in the breakfast room. He'd thought she might be self-conscious after last night, and indeed she did not exhibit her customary cool composure. She looked more like herself, however, in a pale green dress that gave little hint of the enticing body he'd been so delighted to discover.

"I would like to have fun!" she exclaimed.

Nathaniel blinked in surprise. *Fun* was not actually a word he associated with Violet. She'd always seemed so serious. Indeed, it was not one that entered into very many of his busy days. His brother Robert had once accused him of having no idea how to have fun, which was nonsense, of course.

What would Violet consider fun, he wondered? He was about to ask her when he noticed movement in the branches outside the window. "There's a good wind. We might go for a sail on the lake. Do you like sailing?"

Violet looked at the swaying trees, then back at him. "I've never been."

"Oh, you must try it then." Sailing was definitely fun. Nathaniel loved the breeze in his face, the skim of the boat over the water.

"Well…all right." Her hands fluttered in the ruffles of her gown.

"Don't worry, you won't get wet. The boat and I are old friends." He smiled at her.

She'd be delighted to get this dress wet, Violet thought. To ruin it entirely, in fact. Could she somehow manage to rip it to shreds on a boat? Or perhaps lake water left indelible stains. There was a thought. Could she find activities in the next two weeks that would destroy all her hated old gowns? Berry picking. Berries left stains, and thorns could wreak havoc on muslin and cambric. But no, it was too early in the year for berries.

"You should fetch a bonnet," Nathaniel said.

She didn't want to go upstairs and engage in another battle of wills with Renshaw. No doubt her maid would disapprove of sailing. Right now, she would disapprove of anything Violet wished to do. "Are you going to wear a hat?"

"Well, no…"

"Then I shan't either."

"Your hair will be blown about. And it will be cool out on the—"

"I don't care!"

For some reason, she said it as if she was ready to defend her position to the last ditch, so Nathaniel merely offered an arm. He wondered what could have caused this militant mood? She seemed a different person from the sweet experimenter of last night. But then, that enthusiastic wife had been quite unlike the Violet he'd thought he knew. Clearly marriage offered a host of new perspectives on character.

He looked down at Violet, who seemed to have drifted off into some distant realm of thought—one that gave quite a stern set to her mouth. No, there was no hint of the sultry creature in the gauze nightgown. But then, they'd been alone. Now, they walked through a landscape peopled by the curious eyes of various servants. She was, quite sensibly, presenting a dignified facade. Perhaps, like him, she often felt like an actor on the stage. Not merely Nathaniel, but The Duke's Eldest Son, The Heir, The Hope for the Future. He nodded to himself. Of course the impeccably reared Violet would not expose private feelings in public any more than he would.

He led her out the back way, so that he could snag a worn shooting jacket from the row of hooks by the rear entrance to the house. With it folded over his free arm, he escorted her across the lawn and down to the lake.

It was lovely June day, mild and sunny with a few clouds floating in the blue sky. The gardens were splashed with red and yellow blooms, and the scent of flowers rode the freshening breeze. Birds called from the trees. The landscape offered everything he loved about the country.

On the dock where his small boat was tied, Nathaniel took Violet's hand. "Step toward the center," he told her. "And sit in the bow—the front."

She did as he said, making a small sound when the
boat rocked under her feet. When she was settled,
Nathaniel handed her the shooting jacket. "It can
be much cooler out on the water." Then he stepped
aboard himself.

It was a nice little craft, sixteen feet long with a
mast in the center, already rigged and waiting. He
raised the sail, letting it flap in the breeze as he loosed
the mooring lines and took the rudder. Gauging the
wind, he tightened the sail and eased them away from
the dock. When they cleared the end, he pulled the
sheet tauter. The boat tilted and sped up, water hissing
along the wood. He saw Violet grip the gunwale and
lean away from the side skimming nearest the water.
He kept them steady, not letting the craft heel over as
much as he would have if alone.

His reward was to see her gradually lose her ner-
vousness. Slowly, her grip eased. She sat straighter. She
raised her head to the wind. Finally, she turned and
smiled at him. "It's like flying."

He nodded, smiling back, and their gaze held.
He was delighted that she shared this pleasure with
him. And how lovely she looked, out here on the
water. The wind had whipped color into her cheeks.
Her sandy hair leaped and curled around her face.
And her gray eyes shimmered and sparkled. Violet's
beauty—for it was undoubtedly beauty—arose from
animation, he realized. When she was subdued and
distant, as she'd always been when he saw her before
their marriage, it was hidden. A secret, like the flower
she was named for, obscured by broader leaves in
the forest. But now, and last night, he'd discovered

a different Violet—vibrant, responsive. Watching her laugh as spray spattered her sleeve, he felt extremely fortunate. His instincts had somehow led him to a prize. He'd chosen Violet, married the proper young lady in good faith. This vital woman was an unanticipated bonus.

Violet noticed that Nathaniel's blue eyes were flaming again, as they had last night. Sailing rather reminded her of that marvelous interlude in the bedchamber. They were together, skimming along in a breathless balance. He handled the boat with easy mastery. She could let go and revel in the pleasure of it. It was glorious. If only they could be transported from here back into the bedroom, all in an instant. Even though it was midmorning and quite an improper time for... Her cheeks grew hot. His gaze seemed to reach into all her most tender places. She couldn't look away. How glad she was that her friend Jane had been right about the delicious possibilities of marriage.

A puff of wind rattled the sail and pushed the boat farther over. Violet gasped and clung to the gunwale again. Nathaniel corrected course, and the tilt eased. The wind was a bit stronger out here in the center of the lake, where it was quite deep. He needed to pay attention. "Don't worry," he said as he loosed the line and shifted to a different tack. "We're quite safe."

The boat bucked, and she laughed. "I'm not worried. I was just...startled." She rubbed her arms.

"Are you cold? Put on the shooting jacket."

She did so. It was much too large for her. She rolled back the sleeves to free her hands. Her hair whipped across her face, and as she pushed it back, she laughed again. Nathaniel's heart lifted at the sound.

"You're very good with the boat," Violet said.

"I learned to sail as a boy, at Langford. Father taught us all."

"All of your brothers?"

"Yes."

"Did you have a larger boat?"

"What? Oh." Nathaniel laughed. "We couldn't all go out at once. Indeed, as soon as we were all old enough, it was a regular melee vying for a turn. I had to set up a rota—"

"You did? Not your father?"

"He was rather busy. And I'm the eldest."

Violet nodded. He automatically took the responsibility, she noticed.

"They would try to sneak around it," Nathaniel reminisced with a smile. "Once, Robert slipped out after dinner and sailed all the way to the center of the lake—the one at Langford is much larger than this. Then the wind died and left him drifting far from shore. It was hours before anyone heard him shouting."

Violet looked around. The breeze seemed steady. "If the wind dies…?"

"It won't," Nathaniel assured her. "Not today. And we have oars with us." He pointed to a pair lashed near his feet. "Robert did not. I had to row out and fetch him."

"You did? Why not some servant?"

Nathaniel looked confused for a moment. "Well, I had set up the schedule."

It didn't occur to him to push the task off on someone

else, Violet realized. Duty was simply engrained in him. She found it admirable, but…did he take it a bit too far?

They skimmed across the water, occasionally veering from one angle to another. Violet enjoyed the dip of the boat and the speed, but after a while she began to tire of the sun and the wind in her face. It made no sense. She was only sitting. But still she felt weary. "Shall we go back?" she asked finally, when it seemed that Nathaniel could sail all day.

He started, as if he'd been far away. "Of course."

He turned the boat, but not toward the little dock, now some distance away. When Violet wondered at it, he explained that they had to "beat against the wind." This appeared to mean that they could not go directly back. They had to sail far to the left of the dock, and then to the right, and then back again, moving only marginally closer with each sweep. So while they had raced out, they crept back. And Violet began to be a little bored, as well as tired, and hungry. "Must we return to the dock?" she asked after another long diagonal run. "Couldn't we just land anywhere?" She gestured to the closest curve of shore.

"You'd be up to your knees in mud if you tried to step out there."

Violet thought she could endure muddy shoes to be back on the dryish land a tantalizing fifteen feet away. She was already blown to pieces, with a touch of headache from the sun. "Perhaps I could jump over it," she suggested.

"When one takes out a boat, one must return it to its mooring," her new husband replied.

It sounded like a quote—like a rule from above. Like the sort of thing Violet's grandmother might say, had she ever said anything about boats. Violet subsided in defeat as the craft turned again in what seemed a nonsensical direction.

When at last Nathaniel tied the lines and offered her a hand to step out, the romance of sailing had diminished in Violet's mind. And it seemed as if she could actually hear her grandmother's sarcastic voice, informing her that the headache was her own fault. She wouldn't have it if she'd worn a hat. "Yes, all right!" she said.

Nathaniel looked up from securing the sail. "What?"

Violet flushed, embarrassed that she'd spoken aloud. "Nothing." She turned and started toward the house. The next time she went out sailing—if she did—she would suggest turning back a bit sooner.

❧

To crown it all, Renshaw had a great deal to say about the state of her hair when she reached her room, and Violet came back downstairs full of vexation. The wild desire to make a change beat in her once again. She went to the back parlor to work on her lists, but couldn't settle to it. Instead, she stood by the window and looked out over the lush gardens. When Nathaniel came in sometime later, words burst from her. "We should make plans." It came out far too abruptly.

Nathaniel looked at the pile of papers on the writing table. "Plans?"

"We are embarking on a whole new stage of life. There are so many things to decide."

That sounded like more duties and tasks piled onto those already on his plate. "There's plenty of time for that."

It wasn't new for him, Violet realized. His life would be much the same. It was she who had been magically transformed from an "innocent girl" to a married woman with far greater social freedom. People would tell her the juiciest gossip. Once she'd acquired a new wardrobe as flattering as the gown she'd worn last night, everyone would see her differently too. Of course, if she was ever to be free… "I am going to dismiss Renshaw."

"Really? I thought she had been with you for many years."

"She has. That's the problem. She argues with me constantly."

Nathaniel looked concerned. "Still, old family retainers—"

"I shall give her a very generous pension." She had the power to do that now. And clothes, Violet thought. She would give Renshaw all the horrid dresses that Grandmamma had forced her to buy and Renshaw had forced her to wear. Let her don those shapeless masses of ruffles and see how she liked it. Or Renshaw could sell them. Even with their dowdiness, they were worth a good deal. Violet didn't care. And if Renshaw wished to continue in service, no doubt Grandmamma would find her a position, or give her one. They agreed on everything. "I want a proper dresser, someone younger, who knows all the latest fashions."

"I didn't think you cared very much about fashion," Nathaniel replied.

How could a perfectly nice man be so heedlessly cruel? Violet wondered. Did he not see what this simple question implied about her appearance? The threat of tears burned in her eyes, and she ruthlessly suppressed them. She supposed it was some consolation that he saw it as a choice. She dressed like a frump because she cared nothing for fashion.

Violet took a deep breath. She couldn't actually blame him. Why would anyone think she cared for fashion when they observed the clothes chosen by her grandmother? It was all part of the false persona enveloping her like an oppressive mask. Nobody knew what she really cared about; sometimes it was hard to know herself. "We should go to Brighton," she said. She hadn't meant to push for it again so soon. It had just popped out.

Nathaniel gazed at her as if trying to puzzle something out. "We'd just be on display there. It's much more relaxing…"

Violet wanted to display a whole new character. She couldn't wait to do so. "There's so much going on in Brighton. Dances and evening parties and sea bathing." She wanted to try everything—savor and indulge and discover why certain activities were thought to be so improper. Not that she would stray far beyond the line, of course. But her grandmother's idea of improper was obviously antiquated.

"The best lodgings will all be taken," Nathaniel pointed out.

"I know. You said that before. It doesn't matter. Any place is fine."

"You can't really think that any—"

"Oh, Nathaniel, don't you want to enjoy every moment of life?" She had to throw out her arms. She barely kept herself from spinning in a circle.

His answering look was bemused; his reply remained noncommittal. How would she convince him that they simply *must* go?

❧

A packet of letters arrived later that day, and Nathaniel retreated to a small sitting room to read them. As he'd asked not to be disturbed, he was surprised by a knock on the door. And even more startled when Renshaw entered without waiting for his reply. The lady's maid didn't apologize for the intrusion. Indeed, she looked quite truculent as she stood before him, hands folded at her waist. "Her ladyship is attempting to dismiss me," she said.

She seemed to expect a particular response. Nathaniel didn't know what to say. It was natural for her to be upset, he supposed, but it wasn't really his affair. And what did she mean, "attempting to"?

"That is out of the question," Renshaw continued. "Lady Violet—Lady Hightower, I should say—is wayward and flighty. She requires mature guidance. Which I have always provided to her. I cannot be spared."

Despite his noble birth, Nathaniel was by no means high-nosed. He rarely thought about his social position. But now he was stunned. He couldn't believe a servant was speaking to him in this way about his wife. "I beg your pardon?"

Renshaw looked at him as if he were slow. "You need to tell her that I am staying on, my lord."

Even more astonished by her commanding air, Nathaniel shook his head. "I shall do no such thing. Why would I?"

Renshaw's lined face creased further in a frown. "Then I'll go straight to her ladyship's grandmother," she replied. "I'll be obliged to tell her the whole."

She said it as if it were a practiced threat. And in a way, Nathaniel felt the force of her words. Violet's grandmother was formidable. She'd been a burden on their courtship in many ways. But now they were married. The old woman lived far away. She wasn't a significant factor in their lives any longer.

"She will be quite angry," Renshaw added, with a kind of gleeful malice.

And all in a moment, Nathaniel got a deeper sense of Violet's previous life. She'd lived—all the time—with the dowager countess, not simply encountered her now and then. And it appeared that she'd been saddled with a personal servant devoted to her grandmother's interests rather than her own. Sympathy rose in him at the thought of this petty domestic tyranny. It became obvious why Violet wished to dismiss the woman. "It is completely up to Lady Hightower who serves her," he answered. "I have nothing to say in the matter."

Renshaw blinked as if she couldn't believe what she was hearing.

"I will arrange for a carriage tomorrow to take you—"

"Directly to Moreley, to her grandmother," Renshaw put in, as if this might change his mind.

Nathaniel had never been interrupted by a servant

in his life. The experience silenced him for an instant. Then he considered withdrawing the offer of a carriage, which was actually quite generous. Most employers would have merely paid for a ticket on the stage. "If you like," he said coldly then.

"She'll hear all about this," Renshaw repeated. She couldn't seem to comprehend how little he cared.

Nathaniel nodded. "You may go," he said.

Renshaw looked positively grim. Clearly she was not accustomed to being treated as a…servant. She swept out in a swirl of black skirts.

If Violet wanted to go to Brighton, Nathaniel thought when the sour maid was gone, then by God they would go to Brighton. After living for years with that harpy—and her grandmother—she should have something she wanted. He remembered the way her eyes had flashed when she spoke of enjoying life—so urgent, so animated. He understood it far better now. Nathaniel rose and fetched pen and paper to compose a note to his father's man of business about finding lodgings in the seaside town.

When it was written and sent off, he looked for Violet to give her the news. The way her face lit confirmed his decision, though he was startled when she twirled in a circle in full view of one of the footmen. "We'll have such a splendid time," she said. She was like a child granted some unexpected treat. Her gray eyes positively sparkled.

Nathaniel eased her into a nearby parlor, closing the door on the young servitor, who appeared to be fighting a grin.

"When will we go?" Violet asked.

"As soon as Herndon finds us rooms."

"Will that take a long while?" She felt suddenly anxious. "You thought there would be none left."

"He is extremely efficient. He will discover something."

"Of course he will." Violet threw out her arms, unable to stay still. She couldn't remember an occasion when one of her wishes had been so easily granted. "I feel like Cinderella," she said. As a girl, she'd never tired of the transformation—from despised slavey to adored princess.

"Just for a trip to the seaside?" Nathaniel looked amused.

Abruptly, Violet felt foolish and, oddly, more naked than when she'd shed her gauze nightdress last night. "Oh, well…" She fumbled for the cool persona that had long shielded her from hurt. How had she allowed it to slip so far?

Nathaniel's expression changed, and she couldn't interpret it, which was worrisome. "What…what is your favorite fairy tale?" she blurted out, and then nearly buried her face in her hands. Why had she said something so idiotic?

"Ah…hmm…perhaps…Bluebeard," said her new husband.

"What?"

Nathaniel wiggled his eyebrows like a stage villain, then spoke in a deep, ominous tone. "Have I told you about the tower chamber at Langford that you must never enter?"

A gust of laughter dissipated Violet's unease. "No, you haven't."

"Not something to mention *before* the wedding," he intoned.

"Also, there is no tower at Langford."

Nathaniel cocked his head and shrugged. "Ah, true. Cellar chamber, I should have said."

"Should you?"

"Down the darkest, dankest corridor. Where the black beetles, er, flourish. And the ring of keys, which you must never touch, hangs—"

"In the housekeeper's room. She's shown them all to me. And she would never tolerate even one black beetle."

"Unless she is…" Nathaniel paused, shrugged again, and looked rueful. "No, she wouldn't. My imagination doesn't run that far."

Violet smiled up at him, grateful for the diversion. "I begin to see where your brothers learned to play pranks, 'my lord.'"

"Hardly learned. Where is the finesse in a molting wolf skin?"

"Well, I shall always remember it with fondness. When I opened that door…"

Their eyes met, and Violet could see that he too was recalling the moment when he'd stood naked before her. It burned in his blue eyes. "I do owe them a debt of gratitude for that," he murmured, stepping closer.

Four

THE VISCOUNT AND VISCOUNTESS HIGHTOWER arrived in Brighton two weeks later. This late in June the summer season was well under way, and the news was duly conveyed to the Prince Regent via the daily list he received, alerting him to any additions to society in the enclave he had done so much to make fashionable. It spread from there around the town, and a number of summer denizens noted that bride visits were in order. Tradition and politeness and sheer curiosity mandated such visits, though not much was expected from the newly married pair, both well known to the *haut ton*. Emily Cowper had once described Nathaniel as "so terribly worthy," and many thought Violet insipid and possibly a bit stupid. Still, it was the done thing, and servants were dispatched to discover the Hightowers' Brighton address.

The Langfords' canny man of business had managed to find them a set of apartments, though they were well back from the sea. As Nathaniel had warned, all lodgings on the fashionable Marine Parade and in the Steine were long since taken. But Herndon had unearthed a pleasant spot on the upper floor of a spacious dwelling, high enough to catch breezes from the water and much less noisy than the more coveted locations. Nathaniel and Violet found themselves with a large parlor and two commodious bedchambers separated by a dressing room, with servants' quarters at the top of the house. The rooms were decorated in light blues and greens, with airy draperies and comfortable furnishings. Their landlady occupied the first floor and basement and provided meals for an extra charge.

Nathaniel enjoyed Violet's excitement at the prospect of seaside society. How often had he watched one of his brothers throw himself into a new interest or pursuit? Watching her examine their new surroundings and make plans, he felt a familiar warmth, and concern. His brothers' enthusiasms sometimes led to difficulties, and appeals for help, which of course he gave. They relied on him when they didn't wish to go to their parents. Not that they had ever done anything very bad, but no young man wished to appear foolish before elders as assured and capable as the duke and duchess. From the news in recent letters, Nathaniel feared some such problems might be looming.

Violet's first wish, her burning desire, was to visit a dressmaker, and finding a good one in Brighton was quite easy. Several of the finest London modistes set up shop in the seaside town in the summer, following their customers to the shore. Indeed, one she had marked down as particularly skilled at the sort of dashing styles she wanted was in town. Violet lost no time in making an appointment to see her.

While still at the manor she had written to London

about a new lady's maid, and the agency sent three candidates to see her in their first days at Brighton. All of them were eminently qualified, but one seemed perfect to Violet. Miss Catherine Furness had previously served a lady known to be in the first stare of fashion who had died unexpectedly. The maid had an impressive list of skills and sterling references. And she was about Violet's age, which definitely appealed. Indeed, when the woman let slip that several of her former mistress's friends had expressed interest in employing her, Violet exerted herself to lure her in. By the end of the interview, she almost felt like a petitioner rather than an employer. She emphasized that she wished to make a splash in society and offered a very good salary, and finally Miss Furness accepted the position. Even a blistering letter from her grandmother about Renshaw's dismissal didn't dent Violet's triumph over this, though she did tremble a bit when she first read it. Then she put it away and didn't look at it again.

With these two things accomplished, Violet's preparations to attend their first major outing in Brighton, a ball at the Castle Inn, were quite different from any earlier in her life. For one thing, the dress shimmering on the bed was a vision of sapphire silk. For another, her maid was determined to make her look beautiful, not relentlessly dowdy. "When one's hair is not a striking color, it requires an arresting style," Furness declared. She was wielding a curling iron like a magician's wand, and transforming Violet's sandy locks into a profusion of curls.

"Will they stay in?" she wondered.

"For the evening, my lady," was the confident reply. Furness finished and put the last iron with its fellows on the hearth, then proceeded to thread a deep blue ribbon through Violet's tresses. "And I think just a touch of color," she added.

"Oh." Despite her errant imaginings, Violet drew back at the sight of the little pot of rouge, her grandmother's blistering comments echoing in her head. "I don't think I can—"

"Your grandparents painted their faces," Furness pointed out. "Men as well. All sorts of powder and patch. They wouldn't venture out of their dressing rooms without it."

Surely the dowager hadn't been among them, Violet thought. Yet it had been the fashion in her youth. She tried to imagine Grandmamma in such a toilette, and failed. "Yes, but now people consider it quite—"

"No one will know it's there. Let me just try a bit, my lady, and if you don't like it, we'll wash it right off."

And so Violet did. And found she looked so much better with Furness's touch of color that she was sorely tempted. Even with her grandmother's cries of horror echoing in her brain, she admired the woman looking back at her from the mirror. She had a polish, a sophistication, that fulfilled Violet's secret dreams. That woman might be as daring as Violet had often wished to be. No, she wasn't going to wash it off.

When Nathaniel knocked at the door a bit later and was invited to enter, he was dazzled by his wife's transformation. Violet wore a gown that glinted in the candlelight. Its scooped neckline and clinging cut flattered her form more than any ensemble he had ever seen her wear. Her hair looked different as well, and her cheeks glowed. The new lady's maid stood beside her, somehow looking like an artist revealing her masterwork despite her bent head and folded hands. Indeed, under the sidelong glance of this slender, dark-haired servant, Nathaniel almost questioned his own appearance. Yet he knew Cates had turned him out in his customary style. "You look lovely," he said.

Violet smiled. Her gray eyes sparkled. When she took his proffered arm, she looked so happy that Nathaniel was again glad that he'd given in to her wishes and brought her to the seaside.

They arrived at the inn as the dancing was beginning, and their entrance attracted a good deal of notice. Nathaniel didn't care for the stares and murmurs, and he hoped that Violet wasn't too uncomfortable, as most eyes seemed to be on her. When he looked down at her, however, ready to shield or reassure, she was positively glowing.

They were greeted by a variety of acquaintances as they moved deeper into the room, though Nathaniel didn't encounter any of his close friends. Most of them had gone into the country, either to attend to their own estates or join house parties.

"Oh, there's Marianne," said Violet.

She tugged at his arm and led him toward the far corner of the chamber, to a group that included an attractive young woman Nathaniel recognized as one of her friends. "You look stunning," she said to his wife when they reached her.

Violet couldn't help but preen a little. She and

Marianne Fanshawe—now Marianne Norton, Lady Granchester—had been friends since they were presented in the same year. People often wondered at it, she knew, because the contrasts between them seemed far greater than the similarities. Marianne had married following her first season, contracting a brilliant match to one of the Marriage Mart's most eligible bachelors, while Violet remained a spinster. Marianne was strikingly beautiful, with red-gold hair instead of sandy, eyes of a vibrant blue instead of gray, and classic features. She had been a little thin, but motherhood had remedied that. Violet had actually overheard acquaintances wondering why Violet would spend time with a female who was so much prettier than she. Despite passing pangs of envy, she did it because Marianne was also intelligent and understanding and funny.

"You're doing it," Marianne said to her. "Breaking out at last."

Violet leaned closer and murmured, "I dismissed Renshaw."

"You didn't!" When Violet nodded, Marianne added, "Good for you." They had often discussed Renshaw's tyrannical ways.

Her friend looked a bit tired, Violet thought, and there was a discontented droop to her full lips. She looked around the room for Marianne's husband, Anthony, but didn't see him.

Violet was aware that she had confided more deeply in Marianne than vice versa. She hoped that might change now that she was also a married woman, and thus no longer to be "shielded" from the realities of life. She'd gathered from a few hints that Marianne's marriage was not a happy one, and she would have been glad to help her in any way she could. Violet drew her away from Nathaniel, who obligingly began to chat with others in the group. "Are you all right?" Violet asked.

"Of course," replied Marianne.

The words sounded automatic. Violet examined her friend's pretty face. You did not tell someone you cared for that she looked fatigued and sad in the middle of a ball. "Is Anthony here?" she ventured.

Marianne laughed without humor. "As he much prefers, he is at the pavilion, playing whist with the Regent and the Duke of York."

Even Violet had heard of these high-stakes games. Cronies of the Prince Regent won and lost sizable sums over whiskey and cards. She hadn't realized that Granchester formed part of that set. He was fifteen years older than Marianne, but still a good deal younger than the Regent. "I didn't know he was fond of cards," she said, and at once felt the remark to be silly.

Marianne shrugged. "Fond?" Her gaze drifted off over Violet's shoulder. She eyed the crowd as if they were an unbearably tedious sight.

Violet puzzled over what she had meant by that one sarcastic word, and over what she might say to comfort her friend. And then, all at once, Marianne's face changed. The fatigue lifted. Her lips turned up. Her blue eyes lit with their former allure. The alteration was so marked that Violet turned to discover what had sparked it. But she saw only chattering groups of partygoers and the dancers beyond.

"There is someone I must speak to," Marianne said.

She slipped past two nearby gentlemen and around a cluster of young ladies. In a moment, she had disappeared into the crowd. Though she craned her neck, Violet couldn't see where she went.

"The next dance is a waltz," Nathaniel said behind her. "May I have the honor?"

Violet turned to find him looking down at her with warmth in his eyes. He held out a hand. Violet took it, and set aside the question of Marianne's odd behavior for another time.

They joined the other dancers as the music began. Nathaniel held her closer than he had when they'd danced before, and she let her fingers caress the nape of his neck. All else fell away as her consciousness of his body, inches away from hers, demanded her total attention. His hand on her waist seemed to radiate heat through the silk of her gown. His smile bewitched her. The dance steps felt like floating. Violet's pulse accelerated with the sheer bliss of knowing that here at last was the freedom she'd yearned for—in her glorious dress, with a forbidden touch of color in her cheeks, enclosed in the embrace of her handsome husband. She'd done it! She'd escaped into a new life. She was the sovereign of all she surveyed. Looking around the ballroom as they spun through a turn, she became aware of eyes on her from every direction, and she reveled in it. The glances were surprised, admiring, speculative; a few were sour and spiteful. But Violet didn't even care about those. Whatever their attitudes, the onlookers were not seeing a dowdy, missish female without style or wit. She had unmistakably declared her liberation from her grandmother's rule.

During the remainder of the evening, Violet received more invitations to dance than she had during the last two seasons in London. She put it down to the improvements in her appearance, and it was true that they had a great influence. But the happiness and assurance radiating from her added an element that mere prettiness could not provide, and drew the interest of men and women alike.

Nathaniel made sure he had Violet's hand for the set before the interval, and they went in to supper together. He looked around for her friend Marianne, to ask her to join them, but he saw no sign of her. So he steered his wife to a table occupied by three couples they knew, and they were warmly welcomed to the remaining chairs.

"The men must fetch us food," said one of the ladies, fanning her glowing cheeks. "I declare, these new shoes pinch my feet like medieval instruments of torture."

"You must be the mighty hunters of the buffet tables," another said with a laugh. "And bring us what we most desire or—"

"Or?" replied one of the gentlemen with a raised eyebrow.

"Or suffer dire consequences," was the arch reply.

"Champagne," said the third lady.

"Oh, yes!" said Violet. "We must have bottles and bottles of champagne."

Her enthusiasm drew amused looks.

"I was never allo…" She faltered, briefly embarrassed, and then hurried on. "I love champagne!"

Nathaniel met her eyes. Memories of their first night together drifted in their locked gaze.

"Oh, lud, we're in the presence of newlyweds," said the first lady.

There were smirks and even a giggle. All three of these couples, like most people their age, had been married for some years. Nathaniel moved to shield Violet. "Shall we go in search of sustenance?" he asked, and led the men off to raid the buffet.

They ate lobster patties and luscious cakes and lemon ices. Whenever the champagne bottle was offered, Violet held out her glass.

"You may regret that tomorrow," Nathaniel murmured in her ear with the fourth.

"Have you never been foxed?" Violet replied, a bit too loudly.

"Well, I—"

"Thoroughly foxed? Bosky, dipping deep? Drunk as a wheelbarrow?"

The others were listening now, greatly diverted. Nathaniel winced inwardly at their amused looks. "I have, but not very oft—"

"And why a wheelbarrow?" Violet wondered more loudly. "What do wheelbarrows have to do with it?"

"It's what you load your drunken friends into to get them home, my innocent," said the man who had been most assiduous in filling her glass.

"I am not an innocent," declared Violet. She drained her glass and held it out for more, which she was promptly given.

She wasn't the age of an innocent, Nathaniel thought. But her grandmother's iron hand had left her seeming far younger than twenty-six. And tonight was making it abundantly clear that it had also left her champing at the bit to break free. He hadn't bargained on that.

Nathaniel surveyed their companions. Their amusement was good-natured. Indeed, two of the women seemed benevolently delighted by Violet's antics. One of the gentlemen caught his gaze and offered a comradely grin. Clearly, they liked this new Violet. But Nathaniel remained off-balance, all too aware of the many other eyes upon them. Of course there was no harm in a few glasses of champagne. It was just— this wasn't the sort of behavior he'd expected from his utterly suitable future duchess.

After supper, during their second waltz, Violet missed a step. He caught her. "Are you all right?"

"I'm fine. I'm wonderful!" was the reply. She gave a joyous little skip that nearly jostled them into a nearby couple. "Don't be stodgy, Nathaniel. I can't bear stodgy."

A bit insulted, he guided her through a turn. He was not, and never had been, stodgy. It was not stodgy to worry about her. That was the function of greater experience. If she would drink far more champagne than she was used to and then dance… A fine spectacle it would be if the new Viscountess Hightower fell down drunk at a Brighton ball.

Nathaniel caught himself, wondering at the tone of that last thought. It was not so bad as that.

But his concern for his wife added a measure of tension to the rest of the ball. As he watched her go down the line of a country-dance with another partner, he thought he saw her wobble. He didn't believe anyone else noticed, but his fears for her made it difficult to engage in light conversation or invite other ladies to stand up with him.

He suddenly remembered an evening during his brother Robert's first season in town. Robert, just nineteen, had insisted upon joining one of the high-stakes tables—peopled by much older, hardened players—at a card party. With no way to remove him without humiliation, Nathaniel had been forced to watch Robert lose a large sum of money. His anxiety tonight was quite similar—a queasy feeling of teetering on the edge of disaster.

Fortunately, none occurred. But Nathaniel was glad when the evening ended, and relieved that his town carriage had arrived, brought in easy stages from London. For although it wasn't far to their lodgings, he judged that Violet was too…tired to walk.

She was laughing as he handed her into the carriage, and the carefree lilt of it lifted his spirits. "You enjoyed the ball?"

"Tremendously!" As he sat beside her and the horses started up, Violet threw her arms around his neck and kissed him. "It was beyond anything." She kissed him again.

His arms full of enthusiastic wife, Nathaniel responded in kind now that they were alone. Heat rose in his veins. He scarcely noticed when the carriage stopped after their short journey. Only the driver's eventual query of, "My lord?" from the box restored him to his surroundings. Quickly, he untangled himself. "We're back," he said to Violet. "We must go in." And up to the bedroom, he added silently, as soon as may be.

"Back?" Violet gave a great sigh. She stretched, which did marvelous things to the thin silk of her gown.

"At our lodgings. Come." He opened the carriage door and stepped down, turning to offer her a hand.

Violet blinked and gave him a dazzling smile. She took his hand and joined him on the street. When he opened the door, she practically danced up the stairs. Once in their parlor, she threw out her arms and whirled round and round, sapphire silk belling out, and said, "Oh, Nathaniel, life is going to be glorious from now on!"

He caught her as she reeled past and waltzed her around the sofa, down the big room and then up again. Violet giggled as he steered them through the doorway and into her bedchamber.

Five

RATHER THAN WAKING, VIOLET CRAWLED BACK UP TO consciousness the next morning. She was ill. Someone seemed to have filled her head with hot coals, and the heat was boiling her eyes in their sockets. Though she hadn't moved from her bed, her pulse was pounding. Her mouth was dry as dust, her stomach roiling. The narrow beams of light escaping the closed draperies seemed like actual spears, lancing through her. When she struggled to sit up, she felt briefly dizzy.

Oh.

This was what Nathaniel had meant when he said she would regret drinking so much champagne. This was "paying the price" for overindulgence. She'd heard the condition spoken about, but knowledge of its existence was not the same as experiencing it. Not at all. Not in the least. The actuality was perfectly wretched.

Violet swallowed to moisten her throat and tried to be philosophical. Was she not determined to have all sorts of new experiences? Obviously, not all of them would be as joyous as last night's ball. Life had its ups and downs. Clearly, there were some ventures into the unknown that one did not need to repeat. Ever. And here was one of them. Violet nodded, and suppressed a moan at the resulting stab in her head.

With a soft knock, the landlady's serving maid entered. She carried a tray holding a large pot of tea and a plate of dry toast. "His lordship told me to bring this up, my lady. When you didn't come to breakfast." The girl set the tray over Violet's knees and went to open the draperies.

"Leave them closed!"

The maid froze in place, then let her arms drop. "Yes, my lady." With a sidelong look at Violet, she went out.

There was a twist of paper on the tray too. A headache powder, Violet realized with a surge of gratitude. God bless Nathaniel. Moving with great deliberation, she poured tea, sipped, nibbled on a slice of toast, and swallowed the remedy. Thankfully, her stomach tolerated the lot. She emptied the cup of tea and poured another.

She was going to stay in bed. For as long as she wished. Until she felt better. There was no one here to tell her that this was evilly slothful. Her grand-mother could not descend like the wrath of the Lord and scold her about the champagne. She was mistress of the house—the lodgings—and she would do as she pleased.

Gradually, her pains eased. Her head cleared. By the time the teapot and the plate were empty, Violet was once again able to consider all the outings she planned to savor in Brighton.

She would call on Marianne as soon as she found

her direction. It was a delight to know she had a close friend in town. One of the ladies at supper last night had proposed an expedition to Donaldson's Library later in the week. And she would certainly go. The same woman had also been full of advice on how to make the best of the Brighton season.

Thus, Violet now knew that the fashionable hour to stroll along the Marine Parade—to see and be seen by the leading lights of society—was nine o'clock in the evening. There was a theater in the New Road, and a regular program of balls and card assemblies at the Ship and Castle Inns on alternate evenings. She had hopes of an invitation to the pavilion as well; she'd been introduced to the Regent at her presentation in the Queen's drawing room, as had Nathaniel. The Regent had never taken any notice of her after that, but technically they were acquainted.

Nathaniel had expressed interest in the race meetings held on the Downs just outside town. And of course, there was sea bathing. Violet was determined to try it, although the idea that she must prepare for her dip by drinking seawater for several days was a bit off-putting. Still, sea bathing was known to be healthful. And it was another of the many things that she had never done.

Finally feeling ready to face the day, Violet rose and rang for Furness. Here was another cause for cheer, she thought, as the new lady's maid entered with a smile rather than a sour glare—and not the least thought of berating her. Instead, they conspired together to create a fashionable ensemble.

When she had washed and donned another of her

new dresses, Violet felt thoroughly renewed. When she discovered Nathaniel in the parlor reading a letter, she gave him a grateful smile. "You were right about the champagne," she admitted. "I won't be drinking so much again."

Nathaniel smiled back. He was glad to know that, like Robert at the gaming table, she'd had a salutary lesson.

"Is your letter interesting?" Violet asked, sitting down opposite him on the sofa.

He looked back down at the scrawled page. "That's just the word for it. Sebastian seems to be having a rather odd time."

"Isn't he visiting Georgina Stane's family in the country?"

Nathaniel nodded. When his next older brother had become engaged at the end of last season, it had seemed a very good match. Well, it was. But his letter was a puzzle.

"So what is odd about that?"

Nathaniel reread a paragraph. "Sebastian has never been the most lucid writer, but it seems there was an uproar involving a Hindu and a pack of lapdogs."

"A Hindu?" Violet raised her eyebrows. "You mean a person from India? At the Stanes's?"

Nathaniel nodded. "Sebastian's handwriting is a disgrace. I thought at first he was talking about a hindrance of some kind, but later in the letter the word is definitely Hindu."

"Who has lapdogs?"

He frowned at the page. "I don't think the Hindu fellow has them. Sounds like they belong to Georgina Stane's mother."

"It must be that," Violet said. "Ladies often have a lapdog. And Hindus…" She trailed off with a shrug.

"I know. But Sebastian seems to say that there are sixteen."

"Sixteen lapdogs?"

Running his finger down the length of the letter, Nathaniel read, "A 'deuced sea of furry, yapping little rats' assaulted this Hindu fellow's ankles and tripped him up. Apparently, he fell on his face on the drawing-room carpet."

Violet laughed, then put her hand up to her lips. "I'm sorry, but it's such a ridiculous picture."

Nathaniel had to agree, although he was soon back to frowning over his brother's missive.

"Is there something else?" Violet asked. "You look worried."

"I'm just not sure what he expects me to do."

"You? Why should you do anything?"

"If he's in a scrape…"

"It sounds to me like the Hindu man is the one in trouble. If you can even call it that. Was he hurt?"

Nathaniel shook his head. "No mention of it."

"Well then, Sebastian is just sending you news of his visit. Perhaps he thought to amuse you." Violet smiled.

"My brothers don't send news. They…report in… call for the troops to ride to the rescue." Nathaniel turned over the pages to make certain he had read the entire letter.

Violet's laugh trailed off. "Rescue?"

"When they're in a fix."

"But Sebastian is past thirty, isn't he? And a cavalry major?"

"Yes." Nathaniel wasn't certain what these bare facts had to do with the case.

"Isn't he well able to get out of his own fixes?" Violet cocked her head. "He seems quite a capable person to me."

"He is," Nathaniel replied.

"Well then?"

"I'm the eldest. My brothers look to me." It seemed a self-evident point. He turned back to the letter. "If I can make out what he wishes me to do."

There was a short silence. After a while Nathaniel looked up and met a quizzical gaze. "I suppose you must answer Sebastian's letter and ask him," Violet said.

"Yes." He rose and went to the writing desk for pen and paper.

Violet watched him, thinking of the tray brought up to her room earlier. Nathaniel had analyzed her likely state and taken steps to ensure her comfort. He'd made certain she was...tended. And now he was determined to do the same for his brother, even though it was not at all clear—to Violet, at least—that any action was needed. This was part of his character, it seemed. Curious to learn more, she asked, "What do you do when you have, oh, a whole afternoon to yourself? Time for whatever you wish. No one else to consider."

He turned from the desk and gazed at her. "What?"

"All the world before you and only yourself to please?" she added with a teasing smile.

Nathaniel frowned. "An afternoon?"

It was hardly a difficult question, Violet thought. She'd meant for him just to throw out an answer.

"In town, or the country?" he said.

She started to say, "either." But he was already making heavy work of his choices. "Country."

"Um. Good weather or bad?"

"Splendid weather, a glorious day."

"And is it hunting season, or—"

"Is there nothing that simply—pops into your head?" Violet said. The query had been half a joke, and he was taking it so seriously.

"Pops?" The concept appeared alien to him.

"Apple tart or lemon ice?" Violet said then.

"What?"

"Just pick. Don't think about it." This was a game she and her friend Jane used to play, years ago. They tossed choices back and forth, vying to reply faster and faster. Violet smiled at the memory. Those contests were among the few times when she could be herself, without fear of censure. And they'd discovered interesting things about each other as well.

"Don't think?" Nathaniel frowned. "I'm not terribly fond of sweets."

"Roses or lilies then?"

"They each have their attractions…"

"No, you mustn't consider," Violet repeated. "Just choose in a flash."

"Why?" He looked as much amused as puzzled.

"That's the game."

"And you win by answering quickly?"

"Not win, no."

"But if you give the right answers?"

"There aren't any 'right' answers."

"Then how is it a game?"

Violet had to laugh. But she wasn't willing to give up just yet. "It just is," she insisted. She needed to think of choices more familiar to him, where he would have a distinct opinion. "Shooting pheasants or hunting rabbits?" she tried.

"Ah. Well, with the beaters and dogs you get more pheasants, of course. But it can be a greater challenge to—"

Violet waved her hands at him.

"Oh. Rabbit hunting," he said. "But doesn't one explain why one chooses—"

"Watch fob or tie pin," Violet interrupted.

"Both," he replied promptly, as if he was getting the hang of the thing.

Violet shook her head. He was right. That had been a poor pairing. "*Morning Chronicle* or *Morning Post*?" she tossed back.

"*Chronicle*."

She congratulated herself on giving him a simple choice. The Langfords were known as solid Whigs. "Whist or billiards?"

"It rather depends—" He caught himself with a smile. "Billiards."

"Newmarket or Ascot?"

"No, I cannot favor one or the other. They each have their distinct attractions."

"White's or—"

Nathaniel shook his head. "You must know the answer to that. And I do need to get back to my letter, Violet."

He turned to the desk again, leaving Violet feeling that she'd been silly. She didn't know him well enough to pose revealing choices, she realized. Their long social acquaintance had brought familiarity, but no true knowledge. So she'd appeared childish, not at all the way she wished him to see her. Her cheeks heated with embarrassment. Should she apologize? No, that would just make it worse. And there was nothing to apologize for, in any case. This was a distance that only time would cure.

⁓

Before Violet managed to catch Marianne at home, or further her scheme of sea bathing, the hoped-for royal summons arrived. The Viscount and Viscountess Hightower were invited to attend a reception at the Prince Regent's pavilion. Violet took this as the final stamp of approval on her Brighton season. So far, it had been all she could wish for in terms of society's attention and admiration. Her plans for a new sort of life were unfolding wonderfully.

Accompanied by Furness, who had an acute eye for fashion, Violet visited the dressmaker again. She wanted a special sort of toilette for this occasion. Between them, they settled on a daring style with swathes of gauze cut on the bias, rippling down her body in varying shades of sea green. Like clinging waves; *not* like ruffles! She would wear only one petticoat under it, though that garment was to be sewn of sturdy satin. She did not wish to be quite transparent to the world. In a hushed little shop on the Steine, she and Furness found a hair ornament with a spray of tiny emeralds. It would rest in the cloud of curls that was becoming her signature look.

In the meantime, the Hightowers went to the theater and to another of the local assemblies. Several times, Violet persuaded Nathaniel to join the evening promenade, strolling along the seaside, nodding to acquaintances and stopping to chat with those they knew better. "Everyone walks so slowly," he complained. "In fact, everything in Brighton seems to move at a dawdle."

"There are the race meetings," Violet pointed out.

"Where you stand and watch the *horses* run," he replied. "This seems to be a lazy place."

"It is summer."

He gazed up at the scudding gray clouds, then back at her.

"You could sail," Violet said, remembering how much he'd liked it. "I believe there are boats for hire."

"Ocean sailing is quite a different matter from tooling about a small lake. The skippers won't be giving the wheel to a stranger. I would be a mere passenger."

As he seemed determined not to be pleased, Violet let the matter drop. But she moved closer, pressing the curve of her breast against his forearm, reminding him that Brighton included at least one delightful physical activity. Nathaniel looked down at her. Violet's breath quickened as he slowly smiled. Their nights together remained a delicious shared secret, a hidden adventure of trailed fingertips and pounding pulses that underlay every other activity.

❧

Nathaniel fidgeted on the parlor sofa, waiting for Violet to be ready to go out. It would not do to arrive too late at the pavilion. Whatever one might think privately of the Prince Regent, he was still royalty, and his invitations were not to be taken lightly.

Violet seemed to take longer and longer to dress as the days passed. Admittedly, the results were striking. Indeed, he wondered whether people who had not seen her since their wedding would easily recognize her now. As for her grandmother... Nathaniel almost winced as he imagined the old woman's reaction to the change. He could practically hear that booming voice of hers deploring and condemning. He began to calculate when they would have to see her again. Not until the spring, surely, in London, if they went to town for the season. Perhaps they need not? But he knew Violet would wish to go. He decided that he would arrange to avoid the first encounter of his wife and her family.

"Nathaniel?"

He started. Violet stood before him, glowing and expectant. She wore some kind of green concoction that fell in curves and whispered around her, emphasizing the lovely lines of her body. Green and gold glittered in her hair. Her gray eyes held a vivacity that was equally alluring.

He was on his feet, with no memory of standing. He caught a hint of the flowery scent she always wore, and it transported him to other moments, of tantalizing touches and murmuring darkness. He offered his arm, and she took it with a saucy smile. It occurred to him that he was rather fortunate in his marriage, even though he had not been swept away by passion like his parents.

Nathaniel had visited the pavilion once before, years ago, in the company of his father. Since then, the famous building had become even more ornate and fanciful. Each year, demands on the nation's treasury showed that the Regent would never finish embellishing the place.

Everywhere one looked in the succession of hot, crowded rooms there were lavish chandeliers and tented fabric and mirrors, many featuring coiling dragons. The reds and purples and yellows were almost an assault. It amused him to watch Violet try to keep her mouth from hanging open.

"Oh," she said finally. "I know people say the decoration is overdone and…and excessive. But it's rather magnificent, isn't it?"

"Do you think so?"

His wife nodded. She gazed from side to side, seeming to drink in the lavish decoration. She appeared quite unconscious of the many pairs of eyes observing them, cataloging the demeanor and behavior of the Langford heirs. Nathaniel nodded to an acquaintance as they passed, his face showing nothing of his thoughts. Three months ago, he would have vowed that Lady Violet Devere hated being on display quite as much as he did. More so, even, with her tendency to fade into the woodwork at large gatherings. He'd seen her as overly self-effacing. He'd even looked forward to bringing her out of her shell a bit, as he now remembered. Had he not been surrounded by the chattering crowd, he would have laughed at the idea. She'd brought herself out quite thoroughly. And surprised him in other, more…intimate ways as well. He had no complaints about that. None at all. It was just… Sometimes it was disconcerting to have been so wrong about a person he thought he knew.

The portly Regent greeted them in the archway of the farthest chamber with his customary jovial ease. "Hightower, ain't it? Langford's son?"

Nathaniel bowed. "Your Grace."

"And who's this?" Their host eyed Violet with blatant appreciation.

"My wife."

"Ah yes, I heard about that. Moreley's daughter, eh?"

"Yes, Your Grace." Violet sank into a curtsy.

With no pretense of restraint, the Regent looked down the bodice of her dress. His gaze was assessing, admiring, not too subtly lascivious. Suddenly, the gown seemed a little too daring to Nathaniel. "You're a lucky man, Hightower," the Regent said as she rose. Nathaniel didn't appreciate the knowing look that accompanied the compliment. "Enjoying Brighton, Lady Hightower?" he added.

"Very much. There are so many amusements and such interesting people."

"Amusements, hah. I'd be happy to show you some of the…best of them." He waggled his eyebrows at her, chubbily suggestive.

Other people were arriving, waiting their turn to greet their host. Nathaniel urged Violet onward on the heels of her murmured acknowledgment. He noticed the Regent's eyes following her as they moved into the crowd, and he didn't like the leer in them. "The Regent…ah…" How to put this, here in public?

"He sometimes takes a…strong interest in attractive women. His…attentions can be a trifle excessive."

"He behaves that way to everyone," Violet replied.

"Not quite everyone."

Violet smiled. "It was mere reflex. I believe he may even see it as a sort of politeness." Violet had heard her friend Jane say this. And she couldn't believe the Prince Regent had any real interest in her. Looking around the room she could see a dozen women younger and prettier than she. She had new clothes, and a more fashionable air, but she would never be a Beauty.

Nathaniel shook his head. Clearly, he wasn't convinced, and she rather enjoyed that fact. His little bit of jealousy was terribly flattering, and rather exciting.

They moved through the party, talking with friends and surveying more of the lush surroundings. Violet had one glass of champagne, no more, saving her indulgence for the luxuriant buffet. After supper she joined a group of friends who were admiring the music room, a brilliant red-and-gold chamber in the Chinese style. "Look at that," said one of their party, pointing at the winged dragons hovering above the curtain pelmets. Chandeliers like giant water lilies hung from the high, vaulted ceiling and lit the space almost like daylight. At the top of the room was a tentlike octagonal cornice.

Through the milling and exclamations of her friends, Violet noticed Lord Granchester standing on the other side of the room. When she went over to say hello, he reacted with cool surprise and had to be reminded of her identity. Told she was a good friend of his wife, he showed no interest. "Is Marianne here?" Violet asked. She hadn't seen her.

"I haven't the least idea," was the bored reply. "If you will excuse me." With no effort at all to be polite, he walked away.

Watching his tall, athletic figure pass under the arched doorway, Violet remembered how romantic it had seemed when Marianne caught the eye of this noted Corinthian. Scores of young ladies had set their caps at Granchester and been disappointed. When he offered for Marianne, it had been hailed as such a triumph for her. Violet knew Marianne had been dazzled. Granchester was handsome, assured, slavishly admired, and wealthy, of course. To find that such a man had succumbed to your charms… She'd been envious; she admitted it. It had been obvious even then, in her first year out, that she would never achieve such a coup.

Now, seven years later, she stood in the pavilion's gaudy precincts and wondered about the aftermath of their whirlwind courtship and swoon-worthy love match. Granchester's behavior did not suggest a happy partnership. And Marianne had definitely looked downcast when Violet encountered her at the assembly. Violet remembered her friend's advice about simply enduring the intimacies of marriage. The implications of that hadn't really sunk in until now. She realized that she'd seldom seen the pair together during the last two London seasons. Violet's face heated with chagrin. Had her sour thread of envy blinded her to a friend's unhappiness? Had she been too self-absorbed to notice

Marianne's situation? That was a lowering reflection. Violet thought of herself as a good friend. She prided herself on it.

Nathaniel appeared under the archway that Granchester had passed through. As he approached, Violet was struck by the contrast between the two men. Granchester had the subtle swagger of a leader of fashion, the certainty that he was the sinecure of all eyes; he pretended to ignore all that attention while actually savoring it. Nathaniel dressed and moved quite differently; everything about him seemed designed not to draw undue notice. Yet he was quite as handsome and well set up, as elegant in his own way. Marianne's husband had an edge, an air of...not danger precisely, but it was obvious you'd be unwise to cross him. Violet's husband was...safe as houses.

She'd had a wistful moment or two about the nature of her marriage, Violet thought. She'd compared it unfavorably to Marianne's. In this moment, she wondered why.

"It's getting late," Nathaniel said when he reached her. "Are you ready to go?"

"Yes!"

He looked surprised at her vehemence. "Is anything wrong?" he asked.

"Nothing. Nothing at all."

Back at their lodgings, she took his hand, led him into her bedchamber, and threw herself into his arms. Nathaniel staggered slightly as he caught her, but he responded at once to her raised lips. She never got enough of his kisses.

When, after some time, he drew away, Nathaniel

smiled down at her. "You're lively tonight, and it can't be put down to champagne this time."

Rather than answering, Violet loosened first one, then another, of the fingers of her long kid glove. Slowly, she pulled off the left-hand one, did the same with the right. She loved seeing Nathaniel's blue eyes begin to burn. She turned around. "Will you undo the buttons of my gown?"

"With pleasure."

Violet had a brief qualm. "Do be careful. It's so beautiful. I know I will wish to wear it again."

"I'm always very careful with beautiful things," her husband replied.

And he was.

Six

"I SCARCELY SEE YOU THESE DAYS," SAID NATHANIEL as Violet hurried through the parlor toward the stairs.

She paused. "That's not true."

He eyed her frogged and tasseled walking dress, no doubt in the first stare of fashion, like her tilted confection of a hat. It wasn't true, precisely. But in their third week in Brighton, she seemed to have a great many engagements. She was always rushing off to meet an acquaintance at the library, or shop in the Steine for…who knew what. She had masses of new clothes. She'd established herself in a group of dashing young married women. Indeed, one or two of them were a bit more dashing than Nathaniel would have preferred. And she was always on the go, and seemingly delighted to be.

He hadn't found any similar mooring. He'd joined Raggett's Club on the Steine, even though he didn't care for high play, and attended two race meetings with groups of other gentlemen. But he'd found no particularly congenial companions. On the contrary, he'd discovered that he actually missed his duties around Langford. Riding about the estate conferring with tenants or the steward could get tedious, but at the end of the day he would have accomplished necessary tasks. There was satisfaction in that. Here in Brighton, there was none. There was only the continual social round and the never-ending sense that he must embody his position. "Where are you off to now?" he asked Violet.

"I'm going sea bathing at last."

Nathaniel looked out at the gray day, heavy with the threat of rain, and shivered at the thought of cold seawater. "Why not choose a sunny afternoon?"

"They say one must bathe in chilly weather, when the pores of the skin are safely closed."

"I beg your pardon?"

"If you plunge in when heated by the sun, you risk a severe chill," Violet informed him. She gazed out at the lowering clouds. "That is what I was told."

"I should think there was a danger of that in any sort of weather. We aren't in the tropics, you know."

"Sea bathing is a very healthful practice," Violet said. "Lady Hartwood swears by it."

Nathaniel snorted. He had been tossed into cold water a time or two when sailing, and it had not felt especially salubrious. "Is that the Lady Hartwood who walks all bent over, leaning on two canes?"

A giggle escaped Violet. "Oh, don't be a stick in the mud."

"It is you who are likely to be knee deep in cold mud."

"Sand, not mud, silly." Violet had been checking the contents of her reticule. "Oh, I forgot my hand-kerchief." She turned back to her bedchamber.

Wondering what good a scrap of lace-edged linen would be against the rigors of the English Channel, Nathaniel opened one of the letters that had been delivered a few moments ago. Just as Violet returned to the parlor, he leapt to his feet, clutching the single page.

"What is it?" she exclaimed.

"James has been shot. No, shot at. What the deuce?" Quickly, he ran his eye down the rest of the—lamentably short—message.

"Is he all right?"

"Apparently. He says he is only writing in case I might hear the news from someone else. He seems to think it a great joke that some…person fired a revolver at him at one of Ariel's garden parties."

"What?"

"Precisely." Nathaniel read the whole letter again.

"At a garden party? But who…why?"

"I can't understand who it was. First he says 'he' and then 'she.'"

"A woman shot at him?"

"I tell you, I don't know." Nathaniel gripped his hair, then resisted pulling on it. How dare his brother send news like this in such an uninformative way?

"Your family just grows more and more interesting," Violet remarked.

Nathaniel turned to stare at her.

"No one in mine meets Hindus with lapdogs or is shot at. At least, perhaps when out hunting they might have been? No. I never heard of any relative of mine being shot at. And if they were, I should think they'd be prostrate with anxiety. James really treats it as a joke?"

Nathaniel nodded. The one clear thing in his brother's message was the amused tone.

"He must be very brave."

"I suppose he is," replied Nathaniel slowly. He hadn't really thought about it before. "James has been in the navy for nine years, and has been in several large battles." He looked down at the letter. "I know him the least well of all my brothers. I was sent off to school when he was still a toddler. And then he joined up at sixteen."

"And he's sailed all around the world," said Violet. "It must have been thrilling."

Nathaniel snorted. "It seems to have turned his brain. I'm going to write Alan and get the real story."

"Not James?"

He shook his head. "Alan is the most sensible of us all, and the clearest writer. It comes of being a scholar, I suppose. Oh…" Could that have been what happened?

"You've thought of something," Violet said.

"No… I just wondered…"

"What? I can see that it's important." She moved closer, looking at the letter in his hand.

"I don't know whether it's… It just occurred to me that Ariel might be…up to something."

"Alan's wife? Why would you think so?" Violet's eyes widened. "You don't think *she* shot at him?"

Nathaniel's brain filled with wild surmise. Could gunfire be part of some scheme? But no, that was too fantastic. "No, of course not."

"Then what? What should she be 'up to'?" Violet cocked her head. "Is she often up to things?"

"She has a most…active mind," Nathaniel allowed.

Violet eyed him as if trying to decipher his expression. "I am so sorry I've had no opportunity to get to know her."

"You'll like her," Nathaniel replied, as a diversion.

"I'm more and more sure I shall," his wife answered. "But what did you mean?"

"Mean?"

"Nathaniel!"

It was said in a tone that surfaced occasionally in her voice, the one that straightened one's spine and made information just burst out. "Ariel helped with, er, gave some advice to Sebastian and Robert about…women."

"Women?" Violet looked intensely intrigued.

"Sebastian wasn't getting anywhere with Georgina Stane, and Ariel suggested that he should—"

"What?"

"I beg your—"

"Should what?" Violet demanded.

"Ask her questions, and be sure to listen to the answers." Nathaniel had not entirely understood this advice, but he couldn't deny that it had served the purpose.

"Indeed?" Violet's expression as she considered this made him wary. "What sort of questions?"

Nathaniel searched his memory. He hadn't paid close attention. He'd been focused on his own concerns. "About her opinions," he recalled finally. "And her experiences."

"So he was to pretend to be interested in these things?"

Just now and then, for a sentence or two, Violet could sound rather like her grandmother. It was…unsettling.

Nathaniel was actually relieved that he remembered the answer to this. Ariel had made a particular point of it. "No, he had to be—or become—truly interested. Otherwise, it was no good."

"I see. Did he?"

"I…I suppose so." He had no idea.

"Did she advise you as well?" Violet inquired.

"Me?" He did not bleat it. He had never been anything resembling a bleater. "No."

"No?"

Nathaniel felt as if she saw right through him. "Not…as such."

"As such?"

"She had a few thoughts on how to handle your grandmother."

Violet's pale eyebrows went up.

"The old lady was forever keeping us apart," he reminded her.

"I know!"

"Ariel suggested that if I dropped a few hints to your father about how it was putting me off the match…" He stopped as he saw her frown.

"That's what happened," Violet said. "I couldn't understand why Grandmamma was suddenly more lenient."

"If you call it lenient," complained Nathaniel. They'd never had the freedom granted most other engaged couples.

"Well, for her," Violet conceded.

"Thank God we don't have to worry about her any longer," Nathaniel said with perfect truth, and a hope that the subject was exhausted.

Violet nodded. "I must become *well* acquainted

with Ariel as soon as may be. We should invite them to visit Brighton."

Nathaniel didn't want to imagine the mischief that such collusion might bring. "Won't you be late for your sea bathing?" he said.

Violet's eyes flew to the clock on the mantelpiece. "Oh, I must go!"

She hurried out. Nathaniel let out a long breath and turned to begin his letter to Alan.

≈⁂≈

As agreed, Violet stopped for Marianne on her way to the seaside, at the Granchesters' very desirable lodgings on the Marine Parade. She had, with difficulty, convinced her friend to join the sea bathing expedition. Though they were staying in the same small resort town, it had proven hard to see much of Marianne. She claimed to be continually occupied, but never said with what. Twice, when Violet had called on her friend, Marianne was out. Yet she never saw her on the promenade, and only rarely at one of the assemblies.

Today, however, she had persuaded her, and they walked together toward the ladies' side of the beach. It remained a chilly, gray day, with clouds streaming above the treeless coast. The Channel was also gray, with lines of pale foam farther out. Some bathing machines were already in the water. Others awaited their next customers at the edge. By inquiring, Violet found Mrs. Crane, with whom she had made the appointment.

This sturdy woman stood by her machine like a superior sort of washerwoman. The sleeves of her gown were rolled above her elbows, and the skirts kilted up high enough to reveal her knees. Heavy wooden clogs sheathed her feet. "Up you get then, my ladies," she said when Violet identified herself.

The bathing machine before them was like a miniature house—wooden walls and a peaked roof— mounted on four large wheels. There was a horse tethered to the front and a set of three wooden steps leading up to a door at the back. This stood open, revealing a wooden bench fastened to one wall of the interior, empty except for a pile of fluffy towels.

Mrs. Crane handed each of them a bundle of gray flannel. "Once you're safely in, undress and put these on," she instructed, as if she had said it a thousand times before.

Violet and Marianne carried the cloth up the steps and into the apparatus. Mrs. Crane shut the door behind them. Violet hadn't realized how cramped they would be. Though they'd been friends for years, their association had not included disrobing together.

After an awkward moment, they turned their backs on each other and began to undress. To make things more difficult, the bathing machine lurched into motion, throwing off their balance. They bumped and jostled. Violet could hear the splash of water made by the wheels as she untangled her feet from her petticoat.

"Did you, umm, did you drink the prescribed glasses of seawater?" Violet said as she slipped off her underthings.

"No, I didn't," said Marianne. "I tried one, but it was too nasty."

"They say bathing won't do you as much good if you have not."

"Do you really believe that?"

"Well…"

"What is this thing she's given us?" Marianne went on.

Unfolding the bundle of flannel, Violet found that it was a wide, shapeless smock. She raised it over her head and let it fall around her bare body, wiggling her arms into the long sleeves. The garment had a high neck and fell down to her ankles, with no tailoring whatsoever. It was like wearing some sort of tent. "It's a bathing costume," she replied. Peeking to be sure Marianne had donned hers as well, she turned around.

As one, they burst out laughing. Marianne pointed at her, then raised a fold of her own smock to point at that. "This is the ugliest garment I've ever seen, let alone worn," she said when she could speak.

The floor lurched again, and the two women caught each other to keep from falling. "Whatever have you gotten me into?" said Marianne.

"An adventure," Violet replied. As she was perfectly healthy, sea bathing had the appeal of a novelty rather than a cure. "What can it hurt?"

They came to a stop. A brisk knock on the door heralded the round red face of Mrs. Crane, peering around the edge. "Ready, my ladies?" she asked. When Violet nodded, she opened the door wide.

The horse had pulled them some distance away from shore. And then it had apparently been turned round again, because Violet faced a wide expanse of heaving water, stretching off to the horizon. There was no sign of the bustling town or the safe, dry countryside that lay behind.

Standing on the bottom step, Mrs. Crane held out a helping hand. Which seemed hardly necessary, Violet thought. She was well capable of managing three stairs. She stepped down once, twice, a third time, and then dropped into cold water up to her bosom. She gasped with the shock. Her smock puffed up around her like an errant balloon. "Oh, oh."

"How is it?" Marianne asked.

The icy seawater had invaded every crevice. Violet swallowed. "Bracing."

Marianne looked doubtful. But Mrs. Crane had hold of her hand and was urging her onward. So she too stepped down, and gave a little scream as the sea took her. "Violet, you wretch! It's freezing!"

"It's not that bad." The cold seemed a little less as she adjusted.

"Are you mad? It's horridly cold."

They stood facing each other, two heads bobbing above inflated bubbles of flannel. Violet pushed at her smock, watched the cloth dip and wobble. She felt another laugh rising in her chest.

"What are we supposed to do now?" Marianne asked. She wrapped her arms around her chest, shivering. "I didn't know it would be like ice."

"We should, er, absorb the healthful properties of the sea," Violet replied.

Marianne's lips twitched. "How exactly do we do that?"

"Well, I'm not entirely cer—"

And then Mrs. Crane, crouched on the lowest step

of the bathing machine like a cathedral gargoyle, put her hands on Violet's shoulders and pressed very firmly down. "Not my hai—" Violet began. But it was too late. She was under the water. Cold, salty liquid filled her open mouth; it stung her eyes. In an instant it destroyed the curls that Furness had spent half an hour creating that morning.

Violet thrashed and clawed. Had Mrs. Crane gone mad? Then the hands were gone, and she came up coughing and sputtering. "Why did you do that?" she demanded when she was able to speak.

"The cure's no good without full immersion," replied Mrs. Crane, seeming to savor the last word. "It's all there in the instructions." She reached for Marianne.

Violet's friend backed away. "No, no. I don't care about the cure. I will not be—" She slipped a little sideways and apparently stepped into a hole. Her head disappeared into the water, replaced by flailing arms and bobbles of flannel.

Violet stepped forward. After two tries, she grasped one of Marianne's wrists and pulled her back to safer footing. Her friend choked and coughed and glared at her from under a mass of dripping blond locks. When she'd finally regained her breath, she said, "Violet, you...you villain. I swear you'll pay for this."

Taking in Marianne's ruined coif and reddened eyes, Violet wondered if she looked as bedraggled. But of course she did. In fact, she undoubtedly looked far worse. Even wet as a drowned rat, Marianne was still beautiful. "Perhaps we should go back now?"

"Perhaps? I don't think there's any question." Marianne pushed her soaking hair off her forehead.

"You haven't had your full hour," said Mrs. Crane. "I can't be answerable for the effects if you don't take your full—"

"We will not blame you," Violet interrupted. "I think the effect is…sufficient."

Marianne gave a snort of laughter. It sounded a bit hysterical this time. She propelled herself over to the stairs, needing a hand from Mrs. Crane to boost herself up onto the lowest one. As Violet followed suit, Marianne moved up one step. Their gray smocks collapsed around them, the wet cloth molding every curve. Water dripped off them onto the boards. The breeze felt icy through the soaking fabric.

"Leave your bathing costumes outside the door," Mrs. Crane instructed. "Else you'll get your own clothes wet."

Marianne met Violet's eyes. Violet suddenly understood why so many gentlemen in Brighton possessed—and used—telescopes.

"No one can see," Mrs. Crane assured them. "We're turned right away from shore, and I always get the proper angle."

Violet looked around. It was true she couldn't see the shore, so presumably people there couldn't see her either. And she did *not* want to soak her gown. The thought of dry clothes was so alluring. She glanced once more at the empty sea, took a deep breath, and reached down for the hem of the smock. She pulled it quickly up and off, dropped the sodden mass of flannel, and ducked past Marianne into the bathing machine. Her friend blinked wide eyes then copied her. The door shut behind them.

They grabbed the same towel. After a brief, accidental tug of war, Violet let go and snatched up the next. Hurriedly, they dried themselves, swaying as the floor bumped into motion again. Violet wrapped a second towel around her sopping hair and began to dress.

"You were always such a quiet, retiring girl," complained Marianne as she confined her dripping tresses. "Of all my friends, the last I would have expected to half-drown me."

"I was what my grandmother made me," Violet replied.

"So, in reality, underneath, you have always been…outrageous?"

"It was always my ambition," replied Violet with a straight face.

A giggle escaped Marianne, then another, and a whole trill of them. It set Violet off, and they leaned together in their petticoats, laughing.

"They might have put a mirror in here," Marianne complained a bit later, when they were in their own gowns again.

"What? You want to see the results of our—"

"Healthful 'immersion'?"

Violet snorted. Her skin felt itchy from the saltwater. She was going to have to order a regular bath when she got home, right after she explained to Furness how she had destroyed her intricate coiffure.

The bathing machine came to a halt. With a brisk knock, Mrs. Crane called, "Back on shore, all safe and sound, my ladies."

"I suppose she expects a handsome tip," Violet whispered.

Marianne, both hands trying to twist her sodden hair into a knot, started to reply, but the door opened a crack, and then wide when their keeper was assured they were clad once more.

Marianne held out a lock of her hair and looked at it. "Oh, how am I to walk along the Marine Parade like this? I won't come out."

"Can't stay in the machine," said Mrs. Crane. "I've got others coming forby."

Violet looked toward town, observing the fashionably garbed strollers with resignation, and simply shoved her bonnet down over her ruined hair. The hat would never be the same, and she'd liked it. On the other hand, it partly hid the results of her sea bath.

Marianne frowned, holding her beribboned and feathered bonnet, but finally did the same. "I see now why people come in carriages even when it is no distance," she commented as they stepped down from the apparatus. "They don't care to be seen afterward."

"I am sorry," said Violet. She gave Mrs. Crane the expected gratuity as they passed. "I had no notion—"

"Don't apologize," Marianne interrupted. "I haven't laughed so much in months. Perhaps years." Marianne held out a hand, and when Violet took it, she pressed her fingers. "Oh, Violet, there is so much I should like to tell you."

It seemed that despite the rigors of sea bathing—or perhaps because of them—the old bond between them had been reestablished. The thought filled Violet with gladness.

"If, that is, I weren't freezing half to death," Marianne added.

Violet laughed as they hurried off toward their lodgings.

Seven

VIOLET WAS SURPRISED TO FIND NATHANIEL STILL IN the parlor when she returned. He was bent over the writing desk and scarcely looked up. "I would have thought you'd be out riding by this time."

"I've been writing letters," he said.

"All this time? To Alan?"

"And Sebastian and Randolph."

"Randolph too?"

Nathaniel turned in his chair, started to speak, and blinked. "There's something wrong with your bonnet."

Violet reached up to see what it might be. At the first touch, her hat came apart in her hands. The brim sagged over one eye, and the crown slid down the back of her neck, coming to rest on the nape. Bits of ribbon and ornament fluttered to the floor around her. "Oh dear." She untangled the mass of unraveling straw and picked it off. "You'd think it would be sturdier," she said, looking for a place to put the ruin. "I suppose it was not constructed to be wetted from the inside."

Nathaniel made a choking sound.

"Oh, go ahead and laugh," Violet told him. "I know I look demented."

He did. After a moment, she joined him.

"I didn't realize one wore bonnets into the sea," he said.

Violet made a face at him. "One does not. It got wet because the bathing attendant ducked me under water and—" She indicated her ravaged hair. "I'll have you know I've been cavorting practically naked in the Channel."

"Indeed?" The idea was curiously intriguing.

"Well, I had on a perfectly hideous flannel…thing. Although when I got out—" She cocked her head at him. "Yes?"

"I had to take it off on the steps of the bathing machine."

Nathaniel had a sudden vision of her standing unclothed above the sea, like Venus emerging on her clamshell. He wished he could have seen it. He gazed at her now. Her sandy hair—its hue darkened by seawater—drooped and dripped onto her shoulders instead of curling about her face in the new style she'd adopted. Her gown was streaked with damp and clung in the most enticing places. The fashionable young matron of recent days had been replaced by a bedraggled tatterdemalion. And yet Violet looked amazingly alluring. The mischievous vitality dancing in her gray eyes drew him far more than the latest modes.

"We were quite turned away from shore," she assured him. "No one could see us."

"Doubtless that is why Brighton's seaside is lined with men holding telescopes." The thought of them tempered his enjoyment. He hadn't realized that sea bathing would leave his wife so exposed.

Violet burst out laughing. "That is exactly what I thought! Why would they have them if they cannot see? But I'm sure we were out of sight. I had no view of land at all."

"Still, perhaps—"

There was a brisk knock at the parlor door. In the next moment, the round face of their landlady appeared around it. "You have a visitor, my lord, my lady."

"Not now," said Violet.

"But, ma'am"—the woman looked both cowed and awed—"it's the Dowager Countess of Moreley."

"What?" said Violet and Nathaniel at the same time. And then, again in unison, "Don't let her—"

But it was too late. Violet's grandmother walked into the parlor, punctuating each step with a solid thump of her stick. She was followed by Renshaw, all in black like an attendant crow. The two of them stalked into the middle of the room and looked Violet up and down, surveying her wet hair and shoulders, her dampened gown, the ruined bonnet. "Whatever have you been doing?" the old woman said. "You look an absolute fright."

Nathaniel rose from the desk and went to stand beside Violet.

The landlady had not shut the door, and Furness chose this moment to look in. At the sight of Violet, her new lady's maid gave vent to a wail. "Oh, my lady, what have you done to yourself?" She rushed into the room and fluttered about, making ineffectual gestures at Violet's head. Renshaw looked daggers at her.

Violet shoved her ruined hat into Furness's hands.

"I have just returned from sea bathing," she told her grandmother. Annoyingly, her voice shook. "Naturally, I got wet. It is thought to be very healthful…"

"If it leaves you looking like that, I cannot imagine—"

"You have to get into the *sea*!" Violet's voice nearly broke on the last word. She gritted her teeth in annoyance.

Her grandmother sniffed. "Undoubtedly. And does it prevent you from going directly to your bedchamber afterward and setting yourself to rights? Or are you required to linger in the parlor, making a spectacle of yours—?"

"We were not expecting anyone," put in Nathaniel.

The dowager turned her gimlet eye on him. "I see that Anabel Dunstaple was correct. It is past time for me to take a hand and get Violet back under control, since her husband seems unable to keep her from acting like a hoyden." She pointed with her cane. "That gown! Disgraceful."

Violet didn't bother to defend her dampened attire. She knew Grandmamma wouldn't listen. She hadn't realized Lady Dunstaple—one of her grandmother's cronies—was in Brighton. She must have been spying on them from afar.

"Who are you?" the dowager said to Furness.

"Her ladyship's dresser," replied the young woman, bobbing a curtsy.

"Dresser," muttered Renshaw, just at the threshold of hearing. "Hoity-toity."

"Indeed? *You* are Renshaw's replacement? Far too young. And quite incompetent, apparently. A pity."

Furness's face wrinkled with distress. "But…I… when her ladyship went out…"

"Thank you, Furness," said Nathaniel. "You may await her ladyship in her bedchamber." He turned to the landlady. "Thank you, Mrs. Jenkins." He offered her a nod that was an unequivocal dismissal. The woman retreated reluctantly, and Nathaniel made sure the parlor door latched behind her.

With the room cleared, he turned back to the dowager. He'd been shaken, briefly, by the old woman's frontal attack, but he'd now reminded himself that the dowager countess had no power over them any longer. She'd been able to keep them apart before marriage, when she ruled Violet's life. That time was over. "We had no notion you planned a visit to Brighton," he said. "Had you told us you were coming, we would have made some arrangements to…receive you." *Or made sure to be out every time you called*, he added silently.

"I told you why I had to come," their unwanted guest snapped. "And a great inconvenience it was too." Uninvited, she marched over to the sofa and sat down, positioning her cane before her with another thump and folding both hands over its head.

With her beaky nose and constant glare and spare, bent figure, the dowager evoked all the old witches in fairy tales, Nathaniel thought. The wicked old witches. Her willingness to say inexcusable things and make a scene remained intimidating. He hated fusses and deplored unkindness. There was no excuse for it. She must be made to understand that he would not tolerate such high-handed tactics in his own household. Nathaniel put all the hauteur he'd acquired as the eldest son of a duke into his voice. "This is not a convenient time for a visit. Nor will there ever be a convenient time for the sort of remarks you have been making."

The dowager reared back in a state of outrage that was almost comical. "You dare to speak to me in that tone?"

Nathaniel held her burning gaze. She was clearly used to staring people down, but the longer it went on, the more confident Nathaniel became. What could she do to them, in fact? Nothing, unless they allowed her to overset them. Without looking away, he said, "I thought it reasonably temperate, under the circumstances."

"What circumstances, you...impertinent...jackanapes?"

Nathaniel almost smiled at the inadequacy of her insult. "Your rudeness to my wife," he replied.

Renshaw gasped audibly. Nathaniel rather thought Violet did the same, more quietly.

"Ru—? I will speak however I like to my... granddaughter."

"She's a Gresham now," Nathaniel responded. "And you will treat her with respect."

Violet's grandmother gaped at him. For once, she seemed to have no response. Her mouth opened and closed several times, like an ancient bird of prey deprived of an expected morsel. Had her eyes actually been capable of shooting fire, she clearly would have incinerated him. She raised a hand from her cane, saw that it trembled slightly, and let it fall. "You...you dare?"

But clearly he did, so she had nothing to add.

Oddly, in this fraught moment, Violet's former maid stepped forward. Renshaw looked down at the dowager, and when she'd received a nod, she grasped the old woman's forearm and helped her stand. With identical outraged glares, they swept out of the room together.

Lord and Lady Hightower listened to their footsteps retreat down the stairs. The front door of the house shut quite loudly.

"Oh, Nathaniel"—Violet looked near tears—"you were…just splendid…heroic."

It seemed an exaggeration, but Nathaniel rather enjoyed the admiration in her eyes.

She swallowed. "I imagine Grandmamma will go and see Lady Dunstaple now, and they will chew over all my bad points and failings. Oh, why did she have to come here?"

"Would you like to leave Brighton for a while?" offered Nathaniel. "I wouldn't mind discovering exactly what is going on with James in Oxford."

Violet's mouth trembled. "I was so enjoying myself. But it is all spoilt, I suppose." She clasped her hands together. "Why must Grandmamma always…?"

Nathaniel watched as she visibly struggled with strong emotions. His sympathy was tinged with confusion. The old woman was unpleasant, but Violet seemed disproportionately affected by the encounter.

She took a deep breath, then another. Her face changed. "If we go, then she has chased us off," she said. Slowly, her shoulders grew straighter. "And she will think she can do it again, or dictate to us in some other way. Here, or elsewhere. Even in London."

Nathaniel saw what she meant. There was a long-standing tyranny here, and it had to be broken.

Running away would not accomplish that. "Very well, we will stay." At some point, however, he needed to understand precisely was going on with James.

Violet threw her arms around him. "You are the best of husbands. When you said there would never be a convenient time for such remarks, I almost… Oh! I'm getting you wet."

"I don't mind," replied Nathaniel, drawing her closer.

"No, no, I mustn't spoil your coat as well as my bonnet. And I have to go and mend fences with Furness and allow her to rescue my hair. We are to attend the assembly at the Ship Inn tonight." She checked in the doorway. "Do you suppose Grandmamma will be there?"

"We must expect that she will be. In order to be prepared."

"Oh. Yes." Violet raised her chin. "I shall wear my new red silk gown. It will drive her mad."

Nathaniel smiled.

"But you will be with me?" she added quickly.

"Right by your side."

The look she gave him over her shoulder made Nathaniel ready to fight any dragon, even her irascible old dragon of a grandmother, for her sake.

❧

Violet certainly felt a degree of tension as they went out that evening. The carefree gaiety of Brighton had acquired a lurking menace with her grandmother's arrival. And indeed when they entered the assembly room, she was there, sitting in a corner with her friend Lady Dunstaple. The dowager leaned a little forward in her chair. Once again, both hands rested on the top of her cane, and she eyed the people passing as if they were miscreants presented for judgment. Violet saw more than one veer off in another direction rather than pass close to the muttering pair.

At least she was confident that her appearance had been totally restored. Her hair was once again in its cloud of curls, and the rose-red silk gown she wore was very flattering, if not in a way Grandmamma would approve. She had refused the touch of color in her cheeks tonight. There was only so far she could dare. Just as she could not ignore her grandmother's presence. That would look very odd, and certainly be remarked upon. Still, she was very grateful for Nathaniel's company as they approached, and she prayed that the dowager wouldn't create a humiliating scene. She made herself smile. "Good evening, Grandmamma."

The old woman gazed at them over the knobby joints of her crossed hands. Her lips bowed downward; her eyes glittered with censure. Violet was reminded of an African idol she had once seen in a book. She seemed to remember that it had been cursed or it cast a curse or...

"So you allow your wife to dress like a lightskirt?" the dowager said.

Violet felt Nathaniel stiffen. She couldn't help glancing around to make sure no one had overheard. Well, no one but the smirking Lady Dunstaple. And she also couldn't help—though she wished otherwise— glancing down at her dress. Its neckline scooped, but not more than those of many other ladies in the room. The lines of it subtly followed her form—to flatter not to flaunt! Part of her longed to point to Lady Jersey and Adeline Lawrence, whose gowns were far more revealing. But she knew her grandmother would not be moved by comparisons.

"You go beyond the line," replied Nathaniel.

"I? Rather, Violet has lost all sense of decorum."

"Nonsense."

Violet looked up at Nathaniel, full of admiration. He had said "nonsense" to her grandmother, just as she had longed to do so many times.

The dowager thumped her cane on the floor. "You are insolent, young man."

"Only when being insulted."

It was actually she who'd been insulted, Violet thought. Though she was terribly grateful for Nathaniel's support. It was becoming irritating, being talked over as if she weren't present. "I am right here, Grandmamma, Nathaniel." Neither of them appeared to hear her.

"The consequences of this laxity will be on your head," said her grandmother to Nathaniel. "I wash my hands—"

"Splendid. There is no need for you to stay in Brighton, then."

The dowager looked astounded. "Do you presume to order me…?"

"I'm merely pointing out that I—and Violet—can manage our affairs perfectly well without you." Nathaniel turned his head. "They're playing a waltz. Shall we join in?"

"I just wish to say that"—under her grandmother's gimlet eye, Violet quailed a little—"that I agree. We can manage." She wished it had sounded as masterful as Nathaniel's pronouncement. Or that it had any perceptible effect.

Nathaniel held out his hand. She took it. They offered her grandmother a small bow and curtsy and turned away.

∽

Holding his wife in the dance, his even temper gradually restored, Nathaniel began to puzzle over the outrageous recent exchange and the dowager's abrupt arrival in town and her visit to their lodgings. This brought up memories of events that had come before. And questions. Something didn't quite make sense. "You have brothers, and cousins," he said to Violet as they turned at the end of the room.

She looked startled. "Yes. Two, and five."

"They are all Deveres," he mused.

She nodded. "My mother had no brothers or sisters."

"Does your grandmother take such an…intense interest in their behavior?"

"Interest?"

"As she does in yours," Nathaniel added dryly.

"Well, the boys—"

"She holds them to a different standard," Nathaniel said. It was the way of the world. "I don't recall. Are all of your cousins male?"

"No, four are, but there's…" Violet paused, as if struck by some thought, then went on more slowly. "There is my cousin Delia."

"Yes?"

"Uncle Frederick's daughter. He is Papa's youngest brother."

"And does the dowager concern herself with every detail of Delia's conduct and dress and...er...associates?"

Violet looked out over his shoulder, her gaze suddenly gone distant. "Grandmamma always lived with us, so she never saw as much of Delia."

It seemed to Nathaniel that his wife was working something out in her mind, so he made no reply.

"But Delia was presented this year," she added.

"Exactly of an age, then, to be overseen and... guided." It was a kind word for the dowager's interference.

"Yes." Violet looked up at him. "I didn't notice that Grandmamma expressed any particular opinions about her dress or conduct. Not as she did with—"

"You."

"Of course, Delia had her mother to watch over her."

"As did you," Nathaniel pointed out. "Is Delia ugly or evil tempered?" He had probably met her. He must have. But he didn't remember. Each year brought a new crop of debs, and each year they seemed more alike somehow.

"No!" replied Violet with an indignant laugh. "She's charming and quite pretty. Prettier than I..." Her voice trailed off. "Why didn't I notice this?"

Nathaniel wondered the same. "Was she always so... harsh with you? Did anything happen to set her off? "

"What could have happened? She began when I was ten years old."

"Ten?" That was young to begin worrying about proprieties.

"I'll never forget it." Violet's mouth trembled. "Grandmamma called me into her parlor and made me sit opposite her, and then she just stared at me until I was ready to sink. I was already a bit afraid of her. But this was…worse."

Feeling sorry for that child, Nathaniel drew her a little closer.

"Just when I thought I couldn't bear it any longer, she started talking about the pitfalls of society and how easy it was to destroy one's good name forever. She described the hordes of people poised to find fault at the first wrong move, like a circle of carrion birds with wicked beaks, waiting to pounce and tear me apart."

"She did not say that!" Nathaniel exclaimed.

"She did. I can still hear her." Violet swallowed. "I felt as if I'd done something very wrong, but I couldn't make out what it was." For a moment, she looked as if she might cry. "And I've felt that way with Grandmamma ever since."

He should not have initiated this discussion in the midst of a ball, Nathaniel thought. Where was his common sense? But he hadn't realized where it would lead. "You had not," he declared. "How could you, at ten?"

"I don't know," she replied, her tone forlorn.

"Violet, you have always been a model of propriety."

"Haven't I, though?"

That sounded sarcastic, which was better than sad. Nathaniel swung her through a final turn as the waltz ended, and he saw her red dress bell out around her. It was a perfectly acceptable gown. A bit dashing, but the dowager's criticism was unreasonable. As he led her back to the chairs along the wall Nathaniel noticed many gentlemen casting admiring looks at Violet. The Prince Regent had arrived, and he was among them, though his expression was more of a leer.

Nathaniel felt just the ghost of a qualm. Violet's grandmother was an unpleasant old harpy, but she had been a fixture of the fashionable world for many years. She had a wide-ranging acquaintance, a circle of powerful friends. Most people would assume that she was a far better judge of what was proper for a noble lady than he.

But…no. There was nothing wrong with the dress. Violet was attracting well-deserved admiration, not censure.

❧

For the rest of the evening, Violet kept well away from the corner where her grandmother lurked. She tried not to be conscious of her disapproving stare. Though the dowager's presence made it far more difficult to enjoy her Brighton success, part of her wanted to flaunt it before her. Did the old woman notice that Violet had many more dance partners than when she was the mousy product of her ferocious dictates? Did she hear any of the compliments Violet received? Her expression said that, if she did, she deplored them. But that was nothing new.

Midway through the ball, Violet saw Marianne standing across the room. She'd been wondering if her friend would attend. She started toward her, noticing that Marianne looked anxious again. Before Violet reached her, Marianne slipped through a doorway and out of the ballroom.

Violet hesitated. Nathaniel would be along in a moment to claim her for the country-dance before supper, which they planned to take together. But she hated to see her friend looking so distressed. So she followed.

Marianne was past the parlor reserved for cards, and then another where those not wishing to dance could retreat. Violet wondered where she could be going. The retiring rooms were in the other direction, as was the front door of the inn.

Marianne moved down a corridor to the inn's back premises. Violet called her name, but her friend didn't hear. She seemed intensely focused on some mission. Marianne paused to peer around a half-open door, then hurried through it.

Violet was only a few steps behind Marianne by then, She heard a low exclamation, a murmur of voices, and then she was at the open threshold, her friend's name again on her lips.

Beyond was a small room, one of the private parlors the inn offered its guests. Marianne stood in the middle of it, crushed in the embrace of a young man Violet had never seen before. Even as she looked, they kissed passionately.

Violet froze. She hadn't expected anything like this. And Marianne was… What was Marianne thinking? Even as Violet gaped, her brain cataloged the scene. The man was very handsome—tall and athletic, with unruly black hair and chiseled features. She couldn't see the color of his eyes, but she imagined they were a deep, melting brown. His clothes were of good quality without being particularly fashionable.

The kiss ended in whispered endearments. Marianne drew back a little. As the man clung to Marianne, Violet heard the word "tomorrow" spoken as if his life depended on it. Marianne nodded, turned, and saw Violet looking on.

Violet jerked back, her cheeks flaming. She hadn't been spying; she hadn't known there was anything to spy on. If she had... She took a step away from the door, then another, and turned to go.

Marianne hurried out of the parlor, closing the door carefully behind her. She stood before Violet, her head held high, arms crossed over her chest, defiant.

"I didn't mean... I saw you leave the ballroom, and I wanted to speak... I never thought..." Violet stammered to a halt.

"I suppose you are shocked," Marianne said, her gaze pure challenge.

"It's not my place... But, Marianne, what are you doing?"

"Snatching a moment—a bare moment—with the man I love!"

"Love?"

"Desperately, totally!"

Violet stared at her.

"Are you going to go all prudish on me?" Here, suddenly, was a different Marianne, a wild, fierce interrogator. "Like your grandmother?"

The comparison silenced Violet. The last thing she wished was to preach proprieties like Grandmamma. But although she had eagerly anticipated the wider freedoms granted married women, Violet found she was not prepared for this. "Anthony?"

"My husband has no interest in what I do." Marianne said the word "husband" with open contempt.

"This, he might," Violet had to point out.

"He has a mistress. He has had one or another since three months after we were married."

"Are you sure?" Violet tried to hide her shock. Their marriage had been sighed over as a great romance. Was this the reality of the tale she'd secretly envied?

"He never made the least effort to hide it from me," replied Marianne bitterly. "None! Or from anyone else. All society is aware. And indifferent. Or…not that. The gossips love it. It is like a game to them—keeping track of his amorous adventures. My aunt wonders why I expected anything else. My parents…" She made an angry gesture.

Which just showed the limitations of her own knowledge, Violet thought. This piece of gossip had never reached her. "Isn't it different for us?" she couldn't help asking. "For women, I mean." This bit of unfairness had been pounded into her by her grandmother. She realized that she felt afraid for her friend.

"I've fulfilled my duty, all Anthony wanted me for," said Marianne harshly. "I've produced the heir and the spare. Now I can do as I please, as long as I'm discreet."

Violet had understood that some of society took this attitude. Now she found there was a goodly distance between theoretical and actual knowledge. Did Nathaniel share this view? The question so shook her that she shoved it out of her consciousness. She looked around. Was it discreet to sneak away from a public ball to meet a…lover? And Marianne hadn't even closed the door properly. Anyone might have found them. She almost said so, but bit off the words when she imagined her friend's angry reaction. Instead, she asked, "Who is he?"

Marianne gave her a sidelong look. "Does that matter?" Her tone was still belligerent.

Violet didn't know. The young man had obviously been a gentleman. Was it any of her business? What was she supposed to do? Perhaps simply walk away. She drew in a deep breath.

"You've been a good friend to me, Violet," Marianne said. "In the past."

"I hope I have."

"I deserve some joy, some happiness," her friend declared.

This echo of a thought that Violet had had about herself unsettled her further. The strains of a country-dance drifted down the corridor. Nathaniel would be wondering where she was. "We should go back."

"You will not betray me."

It wasn't a question. And Violet realized that it wasn't a possibility, either. What would she do? Run tattling to…who? Anthony? Seeing how little he cared about Marianne's doings, she hadn't liked him much. And anyway, that would be…low. To picture herself piously reporting to anyone… She shook her head. The vision was repugnant. But that didn't mean she thought Marianne was right. Violet shook her head again. The new freedom that she'd so anticipated was more complicated than she'd imagined.

Misunderstanding the gesture, Marianne squeezed Violet's hand, making her feel even more like an unwilling conspirator. Together, they slipped back along the corridor toward the dancing.

And just as they passed the archway to the card room, the portly, overdressed figure of the Prince Regent emerged. His round face was set in peevish lines. He looked like a spoiled child who had been deprived of some promised treat. But when his eyes lit on Violet, he smiled. "My Lady Hightower. How delightful to see you again."

Both women sketched curtsies. The Regent came closer, all his attention concentrated on Violet. To her consternation, Marianne edged away.

He came closer, too close for polite company. His bulky figure blocked her escape. Violet pressed back against the wall of the corridor. She couldn't see where Marianne had gotten to. Had she abandoned her? "You are looking particularly…toothsome tonight," said the Regent. He shifted closer still and looked down the front of her dress.

Two men came out of the card room and passed behind him. Their smirks showed Violet that they were not potential rescuers. Did some tinge of Marianne's exploit cling to her? Where had her friend gone? The pungent scent of the Regent's cologne was making her dizzy. It enveloped her in a cloying cloud. He must drench himself in it. He also smelled strongly of drink.

"What say we toddle along to the pavilion?" the Regent suggested. "I could give you a private tour, show you things only my *special* friends get to see." His smile suggested all manner of things that made Violet wince. His substantial stomach pressed against her arm.

You couldn't shove a prince, she thought. Not in public. Or in private, she supposed. Wasn't it illegal? Even treason? Well, probably not treason. But what if she pushed him away and he fell? That would be very bad. The Regent lying at her feet, flailing about, most likely unable to get up again. He didn't look steady on his feet. She had to do something, though, say something clever to get him to move away. "I...I wouldn't presume to call myself a special—"

"Oh, but you could," he interrupted, leaning closer still.

His whiskey-laded breath puffed across Violet's cheek. It felt as if a small building was about to fall upon her. She was going to have to shove him off, Violet decided, whatever the consequences. She simply couldn't think what else to do.

"There you are, Violet," said an urbane voice from somewhere beyond the Regent's plump shoulder. "The country-dance has begun. We were going to join in."

The Regent stepped back, and there was Nathaniel, like the answer to a prayer. His expression looked perfectly pleasant, yet also somehow implacable.

"Yes," she breathed. "Of course." With her back tight against the wall, she edged around the Regent and gladly took her husband's hand.

"Hightower," grumbled the Regent.

Nathaniel gave him a minimal bow. "Your Grace."

"Can't say you're wanted just now," the older man complained. He made a small shooing gesture. "Why not have a hand of cards, eh?"

Violet knew that some men allowed—even encouraged—their mates to form connections with the Regent, for the influence it might bring them. Those whispers had reached even her.

"My *wife* promised me this dance," Nathaniel replied. Though still perfectly polite, his tone was steel.

The Regent glowered at them for a moment. He swayed slightly, and Violet worried that he was so foxed he would stage a scene. But at last, he said, "Humph." With an irritated wave, he moved down the corridor away from the ballroom, sulky and muttering. From what Violet caught, he appeared to think that she would have been glad to go with him if not for the inopportune appearance of her husband. She let out a long sigh of relief and gratitude. "Oh, Nathaniel..."

He offered his arm and steered her in the opposite direction. "You must take some care about the prince," he said. "It is an...unfortunate fact that he will take liberties if encouraged."

"I didn't!"

"Sad to say, it's best not to linger alone in his vicinity." He led her back toward the ballroom.

"I wasn't..." But she couldn't tell him she'd been with Marianne. Who had abandoned her! Because then Nathaniel would wonder where Marianne was and why they'd been standing near the card room and... Memories of her grandmother's exhausting interrogations rose in her.

"His...habits require a degree of finesse," Nathaniel said.

"How is one to finesse a royal prince?" Violet replied. "*Is* it treason to shove him?"

"I beg your pardon?"

"Can one push him off?" Violet imagined it again. "What if he fell? Is that some sort of crime or—"

"Violet!"

He was gazing down at her with grave censure. As far as Violet could recall, he'd never looked at her that way before.

"I realize that you lack the…address that might be expected of a female of your age and position. I suppose your grandmother has that to answer for, as well as… In any case, we must both make allowances…" He sounded as if he was arguing with himself.

"Allowances?" Suddenly, Violet was sorry she'd told him about that childhood incident. "Make allowances?"

"You must learn to take care."

"He pushed himself onto me!"

They had reached the ballroom. One or two heads turned at her vehemence.

Nathaniel stopped walking. The country-dance well under way, Violet saw. They couldn't join in now. He turned toward a corner.

"Not that way," Violet hissed. He was heading straight for her grandmother's perch. She dropped Nathaniel's arm and looked around. There was no one she knew nearby. Marianne had apparently gone.

"Violet," said Nathaniel. He pulled her hand through his arm again. More people were looking at them. Crowds like this could sense upset like a pack of foxhounds on a scent. He'd seen it so often. They were poised, waiting for some tidbit to chew over. He must see that they didn't get it. Which meant they could not simply leave the ball, as he most wished to do. "We will go to the supper room," he declared, turning, pulling Violet with him.

"They won't have opened the doors yet," she objected. "Not until the set is over."

"We'll walk slowly," he answered.

"Nathaniel?"

"Smile," he said. And he followed his own order with an expression that looked stiff and unnatural to her. "We will be a duke and duchess, one day."

Old familiar feelings washed over Violet—a sense of perpetual inadequacy, despair at forever falling short. She did as she was told.

Eight

BREAKFAST IN THE HIGHTOWERS' BRIGHTON PARLOR was generally silent the following morning, with conversation limited to requests to pass the jam or the saltcellar. To Violet, the scene felt both new and terribly familiar; meals in her parents' house could be laden with tension like this, especially when she was in disgrace over some infraction. Her whole body tight with nerves, she watched Nathaniel for signs of temper, braced for the sort of unjust scold that made life with her grandmother such a trial.

They'd stayed until the very end of the ball last night, presenting the image of perfect young nobility, as he had wished. And when they'd returned in the wee hours, Nathaniel hadn't come with her to her room. Violet had tossed and turned through the remainder of the night and risen feeling both worried and resentful, a combination that made her stomach roil.

The longer she watched him, however, the more puzzled she became. He didn't appear angry. She got no sense that he was waiting for the servants to be gone so he could rake her over the coals. He seemed much as usual, in fact—equable, polite, silent only because he was absorbed in the packet of letters that had arrived with the early mail.

Violet looked at the four white squares, neatly lined up on the table. She recognized his brothers' handwriting by now. The missives came from various parts of England where they lived or were staying, some in answer to his own. Nathaniel's family were great letter writers, apparently. She envied the kind of closeness this implied.

For a bit longer, she watched him read. No, he definitely wasn't angry. "It looks to be a fine day," Violet said experimentally.

"Ummm," was the only reply.

Violet's relief came out in a long breath. She really wouldn't have been able to bear it if her new life had begun to resemble her old one, she realized. But it didn't. She mustn't begin imagining that it could. Last night... With the memory, she felt a spark of resentment flicker again. The Regent's bad behavior had *not* been her fault. Any more than she could be blamed for the fact that he was royalty and couldn't be given a good kick when he went beyond the line. "It's unfair," she muttered.

Nathaniel tore his eyes from the page. "What?"

As a final test of her hypothesis, Violet gave him a brilliant smile.

Nathaniel smiled back. "What?" he repeated.

"Nothing. Go back to your letter."

He gestured apologetically with the page. "I've been waiting for news about James and this shooting."

"I know," said Violet. She rose. "I must speak to

Furness about…" She had no ending for the sentence, because it was just an excuse to leave him with his letters, but Nathaniel didn't appear to notice.

Violet left the parlor with a bounce in her step. The Regent didn't matter a whit. She would avoid him in future. All was well.

For Nathaniel's part, he hadn't really noted the lack of conversation, and the arrival of the letters had driven any lingering concern about the previous evening out of his head. The ball had joined a seemingly endless parade of other such occasions, when he'd had to play the duke's estimable heir, leaving no indelible impression behind. The communications from his brothers, on the other hand, were full of novelty and surprise. He returned to the pages.

Over a second cup of tea, he read again that Sebastian had developed an absolute detestation for lapdogs. He wondered if Nathaniel knew of any herb or ointment with a scent that would discourage canine interest in one's trouser legs, without repelling one's human, particularly female, companions, of course. Could he discover such a mixture and have it sent along posthaste?

"How, precisely?" muttered Nathaniel. He took a fortifying sip of his tea.

His dashing cavalry major brother also claimed to be desperately in need of books or games—or anything, really, however costly—that would absorb the attention of girls aged fifteen and thirteen. He begged Nathaniel to provide such distractions without delay. With several underlinings, he emphasized that this was more important than the ointment.

"Why?" murmured Nathaniel. There was, of course, no response.

Sebastian closed by saying that he would be most grateful if his elder brother could spare twenty pounds as soon as might be.

Contemplating this litany of demands without explanation, Nathaniel shook his head. "Sebastian seems to be…" But when he raised his eyes from the page, he remembered that he was alone in the parlor.

With a shrug, he moved over to the writing desk under the front window and took up the next letter in his pile. Randolph was urgently in need of a bishop, or better yet, an archbishop. He seemed to think that Nathaniel could easily scrape acquaintance with a power of the church and fulfill his brother's desire for an appointment much closer to the "center of doctrinal innovation." Whatever that might mean. Surely Randolph knew far more about how livings were granted than he did? Nathaniel was aware that their father had several in his gift, but they were all currently filled by worthy men of middle age. This had been discussed in the family. Steps had been taken to find Randolph a suitable post, though it had turned out to be quite far north. Now, Randolph was for impatient for advancement. Nathaniel tried to imagine a conversation he might have with an archbishop that would aid his brother. He failed.

The landlady's maid came in to clear up the dishes. Against a background of muted clatter, Nathaniel scanned the final paragraph of the letter. Randolph invited him to bring his new bride to Northumberland.

He was sure Violet would enjoy the wild beauty of the landscape and exploring the ruins of Hadrian's Wall.

"What the deuce?" said Nathaniel.

"My lord?" replied the maid, turning from her work.

"Nothing," he told her.

Setting the teapot on a tray with the other breakfast things, she went out.

Violet came through the open door as the maid vacated it. "I am going out to the library," she said.

"*Would* you like seeing the ruins of Hadrian's Wall?" Nathaniel wondered.

"What?" She blinked at him, startled.

"Randolph believes you would." Nathaniel smiled. His wife wore a fetching bonnet and carried a bright paisley shawl.

"I don't know what it is." She frowned.

"Something Roman, I believe."

"In Italy?"

"No, Northumberland. If I remember my history correctly, it was built by the ancient Romans to keep back the barbarian hordes."

"Oh. Well, I…I'm sure it's very…"

"Precisely. A pile of moldy stones. I don't know what Randolph was thinking." He glanced down at the neatly written lines. "You are not, by any chance, acquainted with a bishop or an archbishop, I suppose?"

Violet's mouth fell open. "Roman?"

"No, no, Church of England."

"I don't… Grandmamma knows a bishop. She has him to tea now and then."

"Ah. No help likely there." Nathaniel offered a

wry look and received blank confusion in return. "It's nothing. I don't mean to detain you."

Violet hesitated. He couldn't interpret her expression. Was she worried about something? "Are you well?" he asked.

"Yes. Yes, of course. Just going to the—"

"Library."

"Yes." She hesitated, then gave him a nod and went out.

Nathaniel slit open a third letter and began to read. He hadn't progressed beyond two sentences before it was his turn to gape in astonishment. His brother Robert, Pink of the *ton*, master of airy nothings, and perhaps just a bit scatterbrained, wished to know if he recalled the name of a book on the art of disputation. Robert thought he remembered it from his days at Eton, but he could not bring the title or the author to mind. Could Nathaniel find out and send word—or better yet the book itself—to Robert's London rooms.

"Disputation?" Nathaniel said to the empty room. And what was Robert doing still in London? He was always off on a round of house parties at this season, when it was quite unfashionable to stay in town. He had, apparently, paid a flying visit to Alan in Oxford, but that was not at all the same.

From there Robert's letter descended into a series of snipes at Flora Jennings, who sounded like a disagreeable young lady. Nathaniel vaguely remembered previous mentions of her. A distant cousin…ah, yes, she was the daughter of Aunt Agatha. That was it. No wonder she was prickly. But it didn't explain what she had to do with Robert.

He turned the sheet. Robert's letter ended by inquiring whether Nathaniel realized that the Akkadian language was being used in documents as late as the first century AD?

"What?" He read it again. That was what it said.

Nathaniel sat back in his chair and gazed out the window, not really seeing the building opposite or expanse of blue sky. All manner of odd things seemed to be happening to his brothers, and they appeared to expect minor miracles from him. An ointment to keep dogs off you without repelling human females? He was fairly certain there was no such thing. An amenable archbishop? A nameless book? Did they imagine he had nothing else to do?

For some reason he remembered the wolf skin that had graced the night before his marriage. Though the memory brought a smile, it was followed by a shake of his head. His unruly mob of brothers did not seem to realize that being married made a change. His time was not all his own any longer. He supposed he could make some inquiries about the book, but the bishop was right out.

The final letter in his pile came from Alan in Oxford. Nathaniel had saved it for last because he thought it would be most important. But when he opened and read it, he found no more information about this matter of a shooting. Alan only said that James had left Oxford to visit the naval yards at Portsmouth. And Alan wondered if Nathaniel knew any admirals who might be willing to authorize a search for information about James's former crew?

"Do they think I am some sort of master of

ceremonies?" Nathaniel wondered. "In the business of making introductions?"

Beyond this cryptic request, Alan told him not to worry. Alan! The youngest of them all. Nathaniel had ten more years of experience, yet it seemed to him that James, and others of his brothers, were flocking to Oxford and turning to Alan for guidance. They wanted Nathaniel to do their errands, but told Alan what it was all about. Or perhaps it was Alan's wife. He paused to consider this idea. That might be it. Ariel had been full of suggestions last season in London.

Nathaniel was annoyed to realize that he felt jealous.

And here, at the end of the letter, was a note from Ariel herself. She asked after Violet and invited them to visit later in the summer. Well, he didn't think they would join the parade of Greshams to Alan's abode.

With an unaccustomed irritation, Nathaniel put all the letters aside. He would go out riding, he decided. A good gallop would clear his mind.

Violet sat in a quiet corner of the circulating library, which provided comfortable chairs for reading the latest London newspapers and other periodicals. She was not doing so, however. She held a sheet of paper in her hand. It showed her list of forbidden activities, things she'd been determined to do as soon as she was married. Some were checked off—new clothes, champagne, setting her own schedule and choosing her own friends. She had not yet tried gambling, though she meant to, judiciously. As for flirting… When she'd written that word she hadn't imagined being accosted by the Prince Regent and feeling pawed over by a mere gaze. Her grandmother had never allowed any man to get her alone, still less to stare down her dress and... Violet was chagrined to discover in herself a morsel of gratitude for that protection. Did she have to reconsider her entire list, perhaps remove some items as impossible?

Her chin came up, and her jaw tightened. That was ridiculous...completely unnecessary. She could take care of herself. One must have experiences in order to learn. Wasn't that the whole point of her tally? She would not be put off by a slight misstep. She would simply make certain she never found herself in such a position again. Her desire to expand her life was as strong as ever.

This resolve somehow led her to thoughts of Marianne. Violet let her hand fall to her lap, the list resting on the cloth of her gown. Her thoughts of flirting had never—in her wildest moments—stretched to taking lovers. Or to observing her friends' acquisition of them. Was it a failure of imagination that she hadn't even conceived of such a thing? Had her grandmother made her, in fact, dull and prudish? Going back over the sequence of events that had revealed Marianne's intention, Violet felt confused. She was worried for her old friend, and curiously excited at the possession of a sophisticated secret, and sad too. It was an uncomfortable mixture. Was there something she should do? But Marianne had made it clear that she didn't want advice from a young woman who had far less knowledge of the world.

Violet couldn't argue with that. She wasn't feeling

particularly wise and perceptive this morning. She had misinterpreted signals from Nathaniel. She had failed to convey her complete lack of interest to the Prince Regent. And then there was her cousin Delia.

Violet rested her head on the back of the chair and frowned.

There was a puzzle that Nathaniel had…not uncovered. Because once you looked, it was right there before your eyes. But…brought to her attention? Suddenly unveiled like a magician whipping back a curtain? She and Delia, two young female members of the same family, with the same relationship to Grandmamma, but being treated quite differently.

Thinking back on the previous season from this perspective, Violet could remember seeing Delia at many gatherings where their grandmother wasn't even present. This would have been unthinkable when Violet came out. Grandmamma had been prominent among the chaperones then, brooding from a corner, much as she had last night. Violet had hardly been allowed to take a step outdoors without her along. And she could not recall Grandmamma ever mentioning Delia's appearance or behavior or the necessity of training or "curbing" her. Violet had to conclude that she was not overly interested in Delia—no more than any usual grandmother would be.

Why such a difference?

Violet frowned down at the page in her lap without really seeing it. She didn't know Delia well. Their homes were far apart, and the seven years that separated them in age had meant that they were always at different stages of life. The gap was less now that

Delia was out, but Violet had been busy with wedding preparations during her cousin's first season. Still, their birth and breeding were the same. Violet couldn't see a reason for their grandmother to single her out and leave Delia free.

Violet was the daughter of Grandmamma's eldest son, but girls had nothing to do with the earldom. Delia than prettier than Violet, and thus more vulnerable to male attentions. From what Violet had observed, her cousin was lively and open and mildly flirtatious. It just made no sense! Rack her brain as she might, Violet could find no reason for the difference in their treatment.

But there had to be one. The alternative was just too random and cruel. Violet sat up straight. She was going to find out what it was, the mysterious thing that had so oppressed her life. And then... Well, then they would see.

Violet folded her list and put it in her reticule. As she made her way back to their lodgings, determination built in her, and another list began to fill her head—ways and means of family research.

She found Furness in her bedchamber when she went to remove her bonnet.

"The new green silk gown arrived, my lady," said the dresser. "And a footman brought a note for you." She indicated a heavy cream envelope propped up on the dressing table.

Violet went over and picked it up. At the sight of the royal crest embossed on the flap, her heart sank. A private communication from the Prince Regent was the last thing she wanted. Why couldn't the

Regent see when his attentions were unwelcome? And how did he imagine his communications would remain private when he used this distinctive stationary? She slipped it into her reticule to look at later. The envelope barely fit. Her list crackled against the heavy paper.

If she'd had any hope that the crest hadn't been noticed and discussed, it died when Violet turned and saw Furness's disappointed expression. Clearly, her maid was curious about the note's contents. "You know that you can trust me with *anything*, my lady," said Furness, confirming Violet's apprehensions.

"Thank you, Furness."

Though it was clearly a dismissal, the lady's maid remained. She folded her hands at her waist and looked mournful. "Was there something else?" Violet wondered.

"I fear so, my lady."

Apprehensive now, Violet said, "What is it?"

"I'm sure I'm very sorry to have to mention it to you, my lady. But I believe Mr. Cates has stolen the key to your jewel case."

Violet gaped at the slender, dark-haired young woman. Whatever she might have expected to hear, it was not this. "Stolen?" she repeated. Surely she had not heard correctly.

Furness nodded with downturned lips.

"But…" Nathaniel's valet was the most proper creature on Earth. "Why in the world would he do that?"

"To make me look bad, my lady." Furness's posture remained stiffly correct, but her brown eyes smoldered. "He's saying that I must have lost the key, but

I never would. I'm ever so careful with your ladyship's things. It's only because of the razor."

"The…razor?" Violet's bewilderment increased.

"Mr. Cates has misplaced his lordship's second best razor, and he's claiming I moved it when I was tidying up. But of course I never touch his lordship's things." Furness positively exuded virtue.

This was more than unfortunate, Violet thought. Here in lodgings, the two attendants had to share working space. And she'd thought that Furness and Cates were getting along quite well. "I know we are in rather close quarters here," she said. "We must all make allowances. I'm sure this must be a simple misunderstanding. Cates has been with his lordship for many years."

Furness answered this implied threat with a sniff. "I declare I'm not accustomed to such treatment, my lady. If I'd known when I took the position…"

The counter threat was clear—Furness would look at her other options. Violet didn't want to lose her. "I'll…look into it."

"Thank you, my lady." Furness dropped a curtsy and went out.

Violet tried to imagine asking the eminently decorous Cates about the theft of a key, and could not conjure the scene in her mind. She would…she would think about it later.

❧

Early in the afternoon, Nathaniel came in to find Violet sitting at the writing desk by the parlor window. A blank sheet of paper lay before her, and she held a pen, but the nib looked quite dry to him. "Writing letters?" he asked.

She started as if she hadn't heard him enter. "Oh! Yes, to my mother."

"Ah. No need for that," he said.

"What?"

"I have just seen both your parents. I passed their traveling carriage as I was returning to town after my ride."

Violet blinked. She put down the pen. "Really?" Then she nodded as if she should have thought of this before. "Grandmamma must have sent a messenger to get them here so quickly. I wonder if Lady Dunstaple is prepared for that many guests? Not that Grandmamma will care."

"You think she sent for them?"

"Undoubtedly. They had no plan to visit Brighton. Papa hates the sea."

"Hates?"

"He says that sea air clogs his lungs and stops up his nostrils."

"I'm surprised he came then," said Nathaniel.

"Oh, they would never oppose my grandmother. In anything."

As far as he had observed, this was true. "But why bring them here, if your father...?"

"To harry me back 'into line,'" Violet replied. "She will get Mama to cry and Papa to bluster..."

"You're not joking, are you?" How different this sounded from his own family, he thought. He couldn't imagine anyone persuading his parents to enact such a drama. And his brothers might be irritating, but they wouldn't stoop to tactics like that.

"Not in the least. She has them well trained. They'll be here to visit as soon as they're settled. Or before. I daresay Grandmamma is already chivvying them in our direction."

"Shall we go out?" offered Nathaniel. "For the remainder of the day? And the evening?"

"No, this is perfect."

He didn't understand her attitude. She'd been distraught when her grandmother appeared. And it sounded as if more of the same was coming. Perhaps it was having some warning that bolstered her spirits? "You don't mind?"

"There's something I need to find out, and it will be much easier in person." She looked down at the letter paper before her. "In fact, I suspect it will be possible only in person. One can always ignore a letter." She turned back to him and smiled. "For once, Grandmamma has done me a service."

"And what is this mystery?"

"My cousin Delia," said Violet.

It took Nathaniel a moment. Then he remembered their earlier conversation. "Ah."

"I refuse to believe we are treated so differently because of some whim of Grandmamma's. She doesn't actually indulge in baseless crochets. It must be more, and I am going to find out the true reason."

Her eyes were positively snapping now. It was a pleasure to see. It was also rather enticing. "If I can be of any help…"

"Be sure I will call upon you."

The bell rang below. Violet gave him a mischievous smile. "Didn't I tell you?"

"You think it's your parents?"

"I'd wager ten pounds on it."

Nathaniel shook his head. "I don't believe I'll take that bet."

❧

It was a wise decision. In a moment, the housemaid came up to announce that Violet's parents and grandmother had called. As Violet told her to bring them up, Nathaniel murmured in her ear, "I wonder if she even let them step out of their carriage?"

Thus, when the Earl and Countess of Moreley and the dowager countess entered the parlor, they found the Hightowers laughing. The sight appeared to disconcert them. Which kept Violet smiling as she went to kiss her parents. "Mama, Papa. I had no notion that you were coming to Brighton." Her parents did look as if they'd been hustled over here without an opportunity to refresh themselves. They wore creased traveling dress and looked tired. Violet felt a little sorry for them. But why couldn't they just refuse her grandmother's tyrannical demands? This thought led her to add, "Has Papa overcome his aversion to sea air?"

Her father put a hand to his throat and looked apprehensive.

"No doubt they missed you," said Nathaniel. "And wanted to see how you were getting on."

When her father and grandmother looked surprised, Violet's spirits sank a bit. She'd been enjoying the new game, but this cut a bit close to the bone.

"Indeed we did," said her mother in a tremulous voice. She nearly always spoke that way, Violet thought.

The present Countess of Moreley was a creature of tentative opinions and disregarded wishes, easily crushed by her formidable mother-in-law. *I suppose I learned submission from her*, Violet thought. She felt a bit disoriented. She'd longed for her life to change with marriage. Now that it had, she found the sudden shift in perspective unsettling.

"Of course," declared the dowager. "Precisely. That is why we are here, to discuss how Violet is getting on."

Pleasantries over, Violet thought, battle joined. "Come and sit down," she said.

Her parents sat side by side on a sofa, rather like errant schoolchildren awaiting punishment, Violet thought. Her grandmother took the large, comfortable armchair by the hearth, punctuating her choice with a rap of her cane on the wooden floor. The smaller side chairs were left for the Hightowers.

"I have told your parents how you treated Renshaw," the dowager intoned. "And about your lapses in conduct. Of course they can see perfectly well for themselves." She condemned Violet's dashing gown and hair with a sweeping gesture.

Her mother looked distressed, her father very uncomfortable. As they always did on these occasions, Violet realized. Watching their faces, she felt as if she'd fallen into a frenzy of observation, seeing her childhood world from the outside. She scarcely knew her father. She'd been told he was an exceedingly busy man. But the truth was, he took himself out of the house at every opportunity. A picture rose in her mind: the earl talking with a group of his male cronies in a card room in London. She'd been hurrying by, occupied with some drama of her own, but the image had remained with her somehow. He'd looked like a different man—at ease, jovial.

Here and now, however, he was the familiar peevish presence of her youth. "Must listen to your grandmother," he blustered. He glanced at the old woman, then away.

Violet's mother was near tears. She was so often near tears. That creased, desperate expression and mournful trail of liquid down her cheek had so often brought Violet to heel. She'd hated to see her mother so unhappy. She still did, but today she also wondered why Mama didn't object to her mother-in-law's presence in her household. She was a married woman, and a countess. And then a simple fact struck Violet like a thunderbolt. The Moreley estate had an empty dower house, at the far end of the park, about a mile from the main residence. She'd ridden past it countless times without thinking. The building was attractive and commodious. It was run down, but could easily be refurbished. Why didn't her grandmother live there? Many older noblewomen removed to such a place when their eldest sons married. Why hadn't her mother, her parents, insisted upon it? She gazed at them with incomprehension.

"Are you listening?" her grandmother demanded.

She wasn't. She was lost in the past. What had made her so blind? She looked over at her family, noting that all three seemed surprised at her silence. Grandmamma had just been there, she thought, since she was born. And a small child didn't question... reality. She'd simply followed her parents' lead and submitted to it, year after year. Grandmamma was the center of attention and the arbiter; all activities revolved around her. There was no other choice. She was unstoppable. Violet felt the old drag into hopelessness threaten.

"Have you nothing to say for yourself? " her grandmother said now, clearly frustrated.

But as she started to slump in her chair, Violet remembered. Cousin Delia. This fatalistic view didn't explain Delia.

"Answer your grandmother," said her father gruffly.

Violet turned to him, meeting his pale eyes, holding the gaze. He blinked and looked away. Not him, Violet thought. And it was obviously no good trying to talk to her grandmother, or in her presence. She needed to get her mother alone...

With the thought, Violet suddenly realized how little time they had actually spent alone, just the two of them. Almost none, really, since she'd been quite small. That was odd. Wasn't it?

"This is ridiculous," said Nathaniel. The words seemed to burst from him, as if he couldn't hold them back another instant.

Violet had almost forgotten he was there.

"There have been no 'lapses in conduct,'" he went on. "And if you've been summoned here upon that pretext, then you've made a long journey for nothing."

Violet's heart warmed at the indignation in his face, his voice. Her grandmother looked dumbfounded, which was gratifying. She couldn't seem to learn that

Nathaniel wasn't the least bit afraid of her. Violet's parents gaped like beached fish.

"You're welcome to call…" Nathaniel continued.

She couldn't let him take on the whole burden, or give them the impression that she required his defense. "Of course," said Violet, putting as much warmth as she could muster into her tone. "We are glad to see you, if we can agree that there is no need for…criticisms. Perhaps we could go together to—"

The dowager cut her off with another hard thump of her cane. "Do you refuse to listen to sense?"

"Well"—Violet drew in a breath—"yes."

Her grandmother rose, glaring. She gathered Violet's parents with an imperious gesture. "You have not heard the end of this!" she promised.

Violet stood and moved to intercept her mother on her way to the door. "We could do a bit of shopping tomorrow, Mama."

Her mother checked. She seemed to search for a reply.

"Harriet!" snapped Violet's grandmother. "Come along!"

With a start, like a rabbit flushed from cover, she obeyed.

She'd been overeager, Violet thought. Of course she shouldn't have spoken in front of her grandmother. But she would find an opportunity to reach her mother. She would not be denied. And then they would see. The prospect filled Violet with nervous excitement.

"Are you all right?" asked Nathaniel.

She nodded.

"What are you thinking? It's fascinating to watch you think."

"It is?" Violet was startled by the idea.

Nathaniel nodded. "It seems to me that you think more intensely than anyone else I know."

"I?" It was an entirely novel concept to her. "How can you tell?" she asked.

"Something in your expression. And then, of course, the things you come out with."

This statement in itself made Violet thoughtful. "I didn't used to think very much at all," she replied. "In fact, I don't understand how I could have done so little thinking. But now I am…making up for that, I suppose."

"How?" he asked.

"I'm making plans."

He moved closer. "Do they involve me?"

"No. At least, I don't think so."

"Alas. I'm disappointed."

At his pretense of woe, Violet laughed and threw her arms around his neck. "I have other…different plans involving you. You came to my rescue so valiantly again today."

He pulled her close. "It was my pleasure, my lady." Bending nearer, he murmured, "Shall we…discuss those other plans of yours in the bedroom?"

She smiled up at him. "Now? In the middle of the day? What will the servants think?"

"It is of no interest to me what they think. In fact, here is a plan of mine. Let us lock the door and forget all about them."

Violet was only too happy to agree.

Nine

As he walked along the Steine the following morning, wishing he was at Fairleigh and could take out a fishing rod or hack across country, Nathaniel noticed a shop that sold playing cards, silver loo counters, and other games, mementos of Brighton, and a general welter of small items. The cluttered display called to mind one of Sebastian's requests, and he turned to go in. He was met by a tall, thin shopkeeper in a blue coat with brass buttons, perhaps designed to give him a nautical air. The man's receding hairline further lengthened a long, dour face that seemed quite at odds with the frivolous nature of his merchandise. "Good day, sir," he said. "How may I serve you?"

Nathaniel was scanning the crowded shelves. "Can you recommend any…uh…games, playthings that would fascinate a fifteen-year-old girl?"

"Fascinate?" the man repeated.

"Yes. Oh, and a thirteen-year-old girl as well."

"Thirteen?" the shopkeeper asked. His eyebrows moved up, the corners of his lips down.

Nathaniel nodded. "Or, both together, I suppose. Yes, both together."

"Fascinate them, both together," the man repeated woodenly.

"That is what I said," replied Nathaniel, wondering if the fellow was slow-witted, or perhaps a bit deaf.

The shopkeeper stared at him as if memorizing his features. "Perhaps if you told me a bit more about your…daughters…sir."

Nathaniel frowned. Did the man imagine he was old enough to have a fifteen-year-old daughter? Technically, yes, he supposed…if he'd been markedly precocious. But what had that to do with his request? The query was impertinent. "They are not my daughters."

"Nieces, then?"

"They are no relation to me, and I do not see what that…" Nathaniel broke off, noting that the skinny shopkeeper was positively radiating disapproval. How did he sell anything if he treated customers in this manner? And then something in the fellow's pale blue eyes struck him. "Oh my God, man. It's nothing like that."

"'That,' sir?"

"I don't want to 'fascinate' them. I don't even know their names."

"Indeed?"

Nathaniel would not have thought it possible, but the man's face grew even more censorious. "It isn't even for me," he added. "It's my brother."

"Your brother?" The shopkeeper's tone dripped with disbelief.

"Yes. Oh, not in that way!"

"What way would that be…sir?"

Torn between embarrassment, indignation, and laughter, Nathaniel threw up a hand. "Never mind." He left the shop and walked off down the street, certain that the dismal shopkeeper's gaze was fixed on his back. What sort of man was *he*, if his thoughts jumped to such conclusions from a simple request?

After several minutes, well out of the man's sight, Nathaniel began to chuckle. How much less…varied his life would be without his brothers. He would not know what it was like to wake up under a moth-eaten wolf skin. Or how to juggle three irate debutantes, each convinced that he had engaged to take them in to supper, and ready to defend their rights with metaphorical tooth and claw. Or the best ways to navigate when you were hip deep in a pile of manure—granted that was a long time ago. Nor would he have had the pleasure of being considered a degenerate by a Brighton shopkeeper. The lengths he went to for his family!

Well, he would not attempt this particular errand again, that was certain. Perhaps Violet could suggest something. That was it. She had, after all, been a fifteen-year-old girl, and a thirteen-year-old, come to that. He would ask her for advice and get her to purchase the—whatever it was—herself.

❧

The object of his thoughts was sitting at the writing desk in their parlor, plotting. She'd begun a note to her mother, inviting her to go walking and visit the circulating library. But she'd scarcely written the salutation when she realized that her grandmother would surely intercept it and force Mama to share the contents. And there was no sense in trying to arrange a secret delivery as long as her mother was staying in Lady Dunstaple's house. Violet didn't know any of her servants, or wish to confide in them. Besides, Renshaw was there. Her former lady's maid would have established connections in the household, forming alliances so she knew everything that transpired within its doors. That was Renshaw's invariable habit. So she would expose any message, and gladly do Violet a bad turn if she could.

No, Violet needed a more subtle way of getting her mother out of the house on her own, or encountering her as if by chance. As she tried to list the likely times and places for that to happen, Violet realized that her mother rarely ventured out alone. Grandmamma was always part of her outings in London, whether shopping in Bond Street or attending an evening party. Even in the country, her grandmother joined in visits to needy tenants or sociable neighbors. Could this be right? Memories crowded in, but none of them featured her mother alone, apart from an occasional walk in the garden, under the scrutiny of rows of windows.

Violet leaned her chin on her hand. Here was another thing that she hadn't really noticed about her early life. Or, rather, had simply taken for granted, a truism that one didn't examine. The insights were accumulating at an uncomfortable rate. She wondered if this was how a horse felt when they removed a set of blinders and its perspective suddenly widened to include new vistas. The comparison made her smile.

"My lady?"

Violet turned to find that Furness had come in without her hearing the door open.

"I was just tidying your things, my lady, and I found you'd left something in your reticule." She held out the bag. It crackled. "Of course I did not look inside," she added virtuously.

She forgotten about the Prince Regent's note, Violet realized. And of course Furness knew perfectly well it was in the reticule. She'd seen her put it there. Hiding her chagrin, Violet held out a hand. "Thank you, Furness."

She waited until her maid left the room, then took out the crested envelope. There was no choice but to see what it said and answer immediately. She might wish to ignore the letter. Actually, she longed to throw it away. But one could not be openly rude to a royal prince. *He* could be as rude as he liked, but…

The parlor door opened again, and the housemaid appeared. "Lady Granchester," she said, bobbing a curtsy. Marianne came in on her heels, so Violet could not refuse the visit—not that she necessarily wished to. But she had to keep reminding the landlady's maid that she was to inquire whether Violet was at home before bringing up guests.

"I came to lure you out for a walk," Marianne said. "It's a fine day, for once." She gestured at the windows. "Quite warm."

The sun was shining, Violet saw. The sky was a flawless blue. She'd been too preoccupied to notice the beautiful July day. Turning back to her friend, she observed that Marianne looked eager and lovely in a morning dress of rose pink under a gauzy shawl, with two matching feathers curled in her bonnet. There was no sign of self-consciousness in her expression, still less remorse. "You abandoned me at the ball," Violet said. "You left me there in the…the clutches of the Regent."

"Clutches?" Marianne laughed as if it was a joke. "We were right outside the card room. There were people all around."

"Yes, to watch him…loom over me like a…a…"

"Hot air balloon?" suggested Marianne.

The picture this called up in Violet's mind—a small figure crouched under one of the giant gas bags that lifted intrepid voyagers into the sky—made her laugh. "It was too bad of you," she insisted. "Surely you could see that he was—"

"Soused." Marianne shrugged. "I'm sorry. I had to get home before… I had to get home." She drew her shawl closer. "You will come for a walk, won't you? You can stay in when it rains."

"Is it going to rain?" Violet looked out at the clear sky again. Marianne gave her a quizzical glance, and Violet laughed. Of course it was going to rain, probably sooner than later. The weather at the seaside was notoriously changeable. And she couldn't stay angry with her friend. "Very well. I'll just get my hat."

They set off together a few minutes later. Marianne unfurled a rose-pink parasol that she'd retrieved from the front hall. It threw a flattering ruddy light over her pretty face. Violet carried no sunshade. She'd found that a touch of sun warmed her pale complexion and made Furness's rouge pot less necessary. "Shall we walk along the Marine Parade?" she asked. "Or down the Steine?"

"I'm tired of crowds," replied Marianne, dismissing Brighton's fashionable haunts. "Let's look about the town."

Violet had no objection, and so they strolled along one street and into another, glancing in shop windows and chatting. "William and Colin are not with you?" Violet asked when they had paused before a display of children's toys.

"Anthony prefers that they stay in the country," said Marianne, the vivacity gone from her voice. "The air is better. And little boys would be bored in Brighton."

"Ah." It appeared that Violet had hit upon another awkward topic. Her friend's life seemed rife with them.

"I would have stayed with them, of course," Marianne continued. "I would have preferred that over… But Anthony feels it is unhealthy for mothers to hover over their sons."

"I'm sure you don't…"

"It's nonsense, of course," said Marianne, walking faster so that Violet had to hurry to keep up. "An excuse to prevent me from doing what I want. Not that the boys care. My sons look just like their father and have the same temperament. It's as if I had no part in their existence except to bear them."

"I'm sure they adore their beautiful mother." Sons did, didn't they? Violet thought. "And wish you were with them."

"They idolize their father," Marianne replied. "Shall we look at the church?"

Surprised by the change of topic, Violet looked up at the large gray edifice ahead. There didn't seem to be anything noteworthy about it.

"I understand it is quite…historical." Not waiting for Violet's agreement, Marianne closed her parasol and led the way inside. The vaulted interior space was dim and nearly empty. In the far corner, a couple with an open guidebook bent over some monument, and a lone gentleman stood not far from the entry, his eyes on the door. With a sinking feeling, Violet recognized him as the man she'd seen kissing Marianne at the ball. His eyes were brown, she noted, but not melting. They practically simmered. He was even handsomer than she'd remembered.

Her face gone radiant, and without a word to Violet, Marianne hurried over to him. Their meeting was rapturous. And obviously prearranged, Violet thought. She stood stock-still on the stone floor, trying to take in the fact that she'd been used as a cover for Marianne's tryst. Her friend had known all about this meeting when she called, with her talk of enjoying the fine day. She'd been anticipating it as they walked together. Perhaps she'd purposely invoked Violet's sympathy, with her complaints about her sons. Was she that devious? Violet didn't think so. She didn't want to believe so. But Marianne had forced her into subterfuge, with no chance to object. This was not like the old friend she thought she knew.

Violet watched her enfolded into the stranger's arms. It would serve her right if she marched over and pulled them apart, Violet thought. Or asked them what in the world they thought they were doing. Marianne was trusting that she wouldn't. And, deuce take it, she was right. She didn't quite have the nerve.

And so they stood there, leaning together, not

kissing, though they might as well be, conscious of nothing but each other. Violet looked around the church. The couple with the guidebook was paying no attention, not yet at least. They were engrossed in their explorations, and nobody she recognized. That didn't mean anything, however. They were clearly curious individuals, and they might know Marianne. And why was she worrying about Marianne's exposure when she'd been manipulated?

She couldn't stand here staring. Violet moved farther down the nave. She found a placard explaining that St. Nicholas Church dated from the mid-fourteenth century, although the tower contained stones of Norman origin. There was a font carved around 1170 in Caen stone. Dutifully, Violet trudged over to examine it, discovering that it was the object the couple had been poring over when they came in. She rubbed her arms as she took in the scenes carved into the large stone cylinder six hundred and fifty years ago. It was chilly in the church. So much for the fine day they had come out to enjoy.

There was an intricate carved screen, the oak black with age. Pews radiated outwards from the font, and there were galleries with more seating around the roof of the church. Violet tried not to overhear Marianne's murmurs to her lover, and yet some part of her also strained to discover what they said. She had become— willy-nilly—a part of their plots. Was some disaster looming? Was there something she must do?

The couple with the guidebook left the church, scarcely glancing at their fellow visitors. Violet heard a clock chime the quarter hour outside. She moved restlessly about the space, then finally sat in a pew, fuming.

The clock had rung twice more before Marianne returned to her. The man walked quickly out of the church. There was to be no introduction then. "Marianne," she said.

"You're angry with me."

"How would you feel if I…tricked you into such a position?"

"I believe I would be glad to help," her friend murmured, head down.

"Marianne! This man… I don't even know his name."

"Daniel Whalen," Marianne replied.

It meant nothing to Violet. She'd never encountered a family with that name. "Who is he? Where did you meet him?"

"He is the younger son of a nearby landowner. I lost my way walking in the upper town one day. He found me, rescued me." She sighed at the memory.

"That's all you know about him?" Deciding the man must be well away by now, Violet headed for the church door.

"I know he loves me," replied Marianne, following her out of the church.

"After an acquaintance of…?"

"Three weeks." Marianne sighed again. "It is so hard to believe that it was just three weeks ago that he—"

"Three weeks? Marianne." Violet started back the way they'd come.

Marianne hurried after her. "Don't be this way," she said, raising her parasol. "You don't understand. You can't understand what my life is like now."

"I don't suppose I can," replied Violet. "I can only see how you treat me."

Marianne winced. But she said, "I had to see him. If I'd told you, you might have refused, and I needed—"

"A story to tell, to explain your absence. 'I went walking with Violet.'"

"Yes," Marianne admitted baldly.

"But you said Anthony cares nothing for what you do."

"As long as I am unhappy."

"What?"

Marianne stared straight ahead, her expression gone stony. "He is perfectly indifferent to me as long as I'm miserable. But if I find any little crumb of happiness, he makes sure it's taken away."

Violet stopped before the windows of a butcher shop. "That makes no sense, Marianne."

"You think I don't know that?" It was an anguished cry, and it attracted curious glances from several passersby.

Violet started walking again. "Why would he…? What did you do?"

"Of course that is everyone's first question," responded Marianne bitterly. "Even mine. You cannot imagine how long I puzzled over it. Examined every word I'd said, every action I'd taken. For years, Violet. Years!"

The heartbreak vibrating in her voice made Violet uneasy—partly because they were in a public street, but more because it was so sad. Seeing her old friend's misery, Violet found sympathy overcoming her embarrassment. "Marianne…"

"I finally concluded that he would be the same

no matter what I did," she continued. Her tone had flattened, emotion stripped out of it. "The cause was not my flaws and shortcomings, though I freely admit I have them. He simply enjoys my suffering."

Violet couldn't conceive of such a thing. But she could see her friend's pain.

"He's teaching my sons to despise me," Marianne added, eyes on the cobbles beneath their feet. "And they're soaking it up like little sponges. He treats them like miniature kings. And every treat comes from his hands. Every servant looks to him."

"I don't understand." Violet knew the words were feeble, but she had no others.

Marianne straightened and gave her a raw, direct look. "It is not a logical proposition; you can't work it out in your mind. It is simply a fact. Anthony is a wicked, perverse man. He hides it from most of the world. But I am his…personal plaything. His possession."

"Oh, Marianne, what can I—?"

"Nothing. There is nothing you can do." Her friend looked away. "And it doesn't matter. I don't care anymore. I've found a man who cherishes me, and I'm going to become his lover." She said the last word with a kind of triumph.

"You haven't yet?"

"There has been no opportunity. For all his professed indifference, Anthony keeps close track of me. All the servants spy for him." She looked around. "I wouldn't be surprised to see one of his grooms lurking in a doorway."

Violet knew what that felt like. Still, she wasn't reconciled to being used as a shield. "You should have told me you were meeting him," she said again.

"And you would have come with me?" Marianne challenged.

"I would like to help you," Violet replied instead of answering. "There must be something. Could you not appeal to—?"

"Anthony does not strike me," Marianne interrupted. "He provides for me quite lavishly. Indeed, he insists I order fine new gowns and…and everything. Violet! No one cares what he says to me, or about me to my children."

"I do," she protested.

"Then you will help me bring some happiness into my bleak existence."

Violet couldn't hold her demanding gaze. "What are you going to do? Run away?"

"I will not lose my children," was the fierce reply. "Despite everything…in a few years they will both be at school. I can see them there, without him. I will do so! Then I can show them that I'm…worthy."

Violet found the word unbearably poignant. "So you are only going to…?"

"Enjoy myself! Grasp some pleasure in an arid life."

Violet again heard an echo of her own resolutions. "I just don't know—"

"Of course you don't," Marianne interrupted again. "You're married to a man who cares for you."

"We are good friends," Violet acknowledged.

"Friends!" Marianne gave her an incredulous stare. "Haven't you noticed the way he looks at you?"

"What way?" Violet was suddenly riveted, and desperate for her friend to elaborate.

But before she could, they came out onto the

Steine, and Violet saw the Prince Regent strolling along the fashionable promenade with a group of his cronies. She stopped abruptly, then retreated a few steps into the street they had just left. She became acutely conscious of the Regent's note, still in her reticule. She'd forgotten it again. Her brain seemed bent on erasing it from consciousness. She couldn't see him until she'd replied. And her lodgings were on the other side of the Steine.

"What's wrong?" wondered Marianne.

Violet discovered that she didn't want to tell her—partly because her problem was trivial compared to Marianne's, and partly because her trust in her friend had been shaken. If Marianne would use her as she had today, what other indiscretions might she commit?

The Regent turned to walk the other way. Violet seized the opportunity to rush across the open space and into a street opposite. She felt ridiculous.

"Violet?"

"I must get back. I have to write a letter." She hurried along.

Marianne kept pace. "You're not going to tell?"

"Oh, Marianne, of course I'm not going to tattle on you."

"But you aren't going to help me."

"I need to think."

"Very well." Marianne stopped and let her go ahead.

After a moment, Violet realized she was gone and turned.

"Let me know when you have finished thinking," said her friend, and walked away.

Violet hesitated. But she really didn't know what else to say to Marianne right now. It had been the simple truth; she wanted to think. Marianne disappeared around a corner with a flurry of rose-pink skirts.

Violet sighed. Moving more slowly, she returned to their lodgings and took off her hat. Then she sat in the parlor once more, the Regent's envelope in front of her on the writing desk. An acute desire rose in her to ask Nathaniel's advice. He always seemed to know exactly what to do.

But he'd been so abrupt when he found her with the Regent at the ball. He'd said she should be able to take care of herself, which she ardently wished to do. As to how he might view Marianne's situation… Years of her grandmother's strictures shuddered through her. Violet didn't want to inquire.

He'd said she was thoughtful. And Marianne claimed that he looked at her in some marked way. Violet found she wanted him to continue to…look at her. She wanted him to admire her. Admire, respect, esteem…perhaps more? Violet was shaken by a shiver of…what? Hope? Excitement? She couldn't risk upsetting the delicate balance of…whatever was developing between them. She'd have to figure things out for herself.

But there was so much to consider. Freedom was far more complicated than she'd imagined when she'd chafed under her grandmother's thumb. She'd thought it was…free. But it seemed to entail an ever-increasing burden of knotty issues and onerous obligations. Of course she wouldn't want to retreat to her old life, but…

Violet picked up the envelope and used a letter opener to slit the flap.

"There you are," said Nathaniel from the doorway.

Violet jumped and shoved the note under her reticule.

Coming farther into the room, Nathaniel noticed the convulsive movement of her hand and wondered what she was hiding. But he didn't quite want to ask. "Can you suggest any fascinating games for girls?" he said instead. "Ages fifteen and thirteen," he elucidated.

"Games? Why would you want—?"

"Don't begin with me. A shopkeeper down the street already suspects me of dastardly deeds."

"What?" She looked completely befuddled.

"Sebastian wants them." Nathaniel found his brother's letter and quoted, "'books or games—or anything, really, however costly—that would absorb the attention of girls aged fifteen and thirteen.'" He folded the page again. "And before you ask, I'm certain Sebastian is not trying to seduce schoolgirls."

Violet looked shocked. "Of course I would never think… Who would do such a thing?"

Nathaniel realized that he had outpaced his wife's level of sophistication. And thank God for it. "Never mind. I can only conclude that Sebastian is referring to someone at Georgina Stane's home."

"Perhaps she has younger sisters," Violet said.

"Of course. That must be it. I suppose they hang about and disrupt Sebastian's…courtship."

"As they do," she replied, smiling.

Catching her meaning, Nathaniel smiled back. Violet's young brothers had often been assigned to accompany them on walks or strolls in the garden, and they'd proved an active hindrance to any expression of affection.

"We must help him," Nathaniel declared. "What games did you like best when you were that age? At school perhaps?"

"I was sent to a very strict school. We didn't play games."

"Favorite books then?"

"Well, we weren't allowed to read novels. We did find one collection of old sermons in the library that was so outlandish we laughed ourselves into stitches."

"We?"

"Jane and Marianne and I. We first met at school." Indeed, they had been her only allies within the dismal halls her grandmother had chosen.

"Marianne, who is now Lady Granchester?" Nathaniel asked. "Perhaps she would have some ideas?"

"No!" The word came out too loud, propelled by the image of Nathaniel and Marianne engaged in conversation, after what had occurred with her friend today. "Her...her children are boys. And still very young."

Nathaniel gave her a quizzical look, then shrugged. He sat on the sofa and crossed one pantaloon-clad leg over the other. "The games we played at Eton were all some form of sport. Not likely to interest Sebastian's pursuers. And they require teams, in any case."

"Did you like Eton?" Violet asked. She'd found school a trial, shut up in a place where discipline and morality had been considered far more important than learning.

"I did. I was accustomed to a crowd of lively boys."

"And being the ringleader?" Violet continued. She wanted to learn everything about him. She longed to understand what he thought, how his mind worked.

Nathaniel laughed. "No, no. Much more the…the sentry, who sees trouble rumbling down the pike and steers out of the way," he replied.

She liked the picture this conjured. "Did you play pranks like your brothers?"

"Certainly not."

For a moment Violet worried she'd offended him.

"My…exploits were far more ingenious."

Relieved, Violet laughed. "For example?"

Her husband shook his head. "Sworn to secrecy, I fear. Until we reach decrepitude—at the advanced age of fifty—when all can be revealed."

"We?"

"Swore a solemn oath," Nathaniel assured her, blue eyes dancing.

Violet could easily imagine him as a handsome youth, plotting and promising with his fellow students. "Well, then…what was your favorite area of study?"

"Mathematics," replied Nathaniel promptly.

"Really?"

"Is that so surprising? It was by far the most useful thing I learned."

"For keeping account books?" Violet asked. It didn't seem like the sort of task a duke's heir would do.

He shook his head. "One needs to be able to check the tallies, of course, but I calculate other things. Like… last year, we planned the sequence of oak plantings."

"Sequence? What is that?"

Nathaniel leaned forward, elbows resting on his

knees. "Oak beams need replacing every century or so. Do what you will, damp and insects damage one here and there. And there are many beams on the Langford estates. So I must see to it that when my great-grandson requires a sixteen-foot span, twenty-four inches on a side, he will have a suitable tree to harvest." He gave a nod and then met Violet's admiring gaze.

And as they looked at each other, the atmosphere in the room shifted. Barring some unforeseen accident, his great-grandson would also be hers, Violet thought. The years spooled out before them—rearing children, seeing the next generation do the same, passing out of this life having left a legacy to the future. The connection stretched between them, a different bond from the soft intimacies of the bedroom, differently intense. She felt it like an invisible strand, braiding their destinies together.

"And so we plant new stands of oaks at intervals," Nathaniel finished, his voice a little thickened.

Violet nodded. "I…I should like to see them," she said.

"We'll ride out the next time we're at Langford, and I'll show you."

She nodded again. And then she didn't know what to say. She was linked with Nathaniel for life, yet there were so many details she didn't know about him. "So…you liked Eton but did not go on to Oxford?" She did know that, at least.

He sat back, took an easy breath. "I saw no need. The things I needed to learn came with working on the estates. Randolph went up to be ordained as a clergyman, Alan to become a scientist. The rest of us had had enough schooling." He paused as if struck by a thought. "Robert did consider university for quite a time. Perhaps he should have gone, with all this stuff he's spouting about Akkadian."

"About what?" Violet had never heard the word.

"Precisely." He smiled at her confusion. "It is of no importance. And we have wandered from our original task. Distractions for young girls. To further Sebastian's wooing."

"I'll think of something," Violet told him.

"And buy it too," he said. "You are a...more appropriate purchaser, apparently."

"Buy it too," she agreed.

Nathaniel eyed the corners of the crisp envelope showing beneath her reticule on the desk. Its hidden presence nagged at him. "Are you occupied just now? We might go out walking."

"I must...write a letter."

She didn't seem very happy about it. Nathaniel wondered if her grandmother had fired off another salvo. But she said nothing further. And he would not stoop to press. "I won't keep you then," he said, rising to leave.

When her husband's footsteps had died away, Violet at last opened the letter from the Regent. It turned out to be a thick card rather than a folded page. Her hands trembled slightly as she read, and discovered that the much dreaded billet-doux was in fact a summons to a tea in support of a charity for indigent gentlewomen. As it was to be held by special permission at the Prince Regent's pavilion, his household had issued the invitation. The ornate handwriting looked like that of a secretary. Various noble ladies were named as sponsors.

Violet started to laugh. She'd worried herself into a state over nothing. Had she really imagined that the Prince Regent would pursue her? In writing, when he wasn't thoroughly foxed? Hadn't she noted the many far prettier, and more accessible, women around him? Really, the whole idea had been ludicrous. The quarry was her contribution, not her person.

She reached for a pen to draft an acceptance. She would go to the tea and give generously to the cause, and that would be that. If only all her dilemmas could be resolved so easily.

Ten

AT THE NEXT OF BRIGHTON'S TWICE-WEEKLY BALLS, Violet kept an eye on the entry, even when she was dancing. For the first time in her life, she hoped to see her grandmother arrive, because her parents would no doubt be with her.

Midway through the second set, all three came in. As soon as the music ended, Violet went over to greet them. She'd even worn a gown with a higher neck and demure sleeves to placate her family. But when she suggested that her mother might enjoy a turn about the room with her, her grandmother replied, "Nonsense." And when, later, she asked her mother to go with her to get a glass of something in the refreshment room, her grandmother judged it, "A ridiculous idea." Her mother might have protested or insisted, of course. But she didn't. She never had, Violet thought, with a mixture of pity and frustration. Couldn't Mama make a tiny effort? But she would not be angry with her. No one knew better than Violet how futile it was to battle her grandmother.

She gave up and accepted a solicitation to dance,

plotting other ways to separate out her mother. As she moved down the line with her partner, she noticed Marianne standing at the side of the ballroom, following her with questioning eyes. Violet began to feel hunted. Her grandmother stared at her from one side, her friend from the other—crossed gazes drawing a bead on her, practically palpable in their intense desire to influence her conduct. When the dance ended, she turned away, eager to escape, and saw Nathaniel. He'd been dancing as well. She walked over to him. "Can we go outside? It is so hot."

"Of course." He offered his arm.

They strolled out into the night air, laden with the scent of the sea. It was a bit damp, but Violet didn't care. There was a glorious absence of pressure.

"Is something wrong?" Nathaniel asked.

She wouldn't mention Marianne, but… "I'm still puzzling over my cousin Delia, and the different ways we are treated. I thought if I could talk to my mother, alone…"

He nodded. "Good strategy. Attack the weakest link."

A giggle escaped Violet, even through her frustration. "I tried to detach her, just for a brief conversation, but Grandmamma doesn't allow it. And Mama gives me no help at all." She heard the touch of bitterness in her voice.

"A ball is perhaps not the ideal—"

"I know." Violet walked faster in her vexation. "But otherwise they're all at home together. Mama never goes out on her own."

"Never?" Nathaniel sounded incredulous.

She stopped and looked up at him. "That is strange,

isn't it? She can't wish to have Grandmamma always with her. Well, I know she does not. I can tell that much. But why didn't I ever notice that she is always accompanied?" Violet made a dismissive gesture. "Because it's difficult to see what's right in front of your nose from childhood."

After a short silence, Nathaniel said, "Perhaps I could help."

She turned to him. "How?"

"I could get your grandmother out of the way, so you have a clear field."

"We can't kill her," Violet pointed out.

Nathaniel laughed. "No. I could take her on an outing, though."

"An outing." For some reason, Violet's mind conjured an image of her husband trying to tow a huge naval frigate with a rope over his shoulder. "You would do that for me?"

"Yes."

Violet swallowed to ease a suddenly tight throat. He said it as if it was simple. Could it be? "Papa might still…" But her father rarely took any initiative at home. "I can probably handle Papa."

"I'm sure you can vanquish the lesser foe."

"It's not funny," replied Violet, responding to his tone.

"I know it's not. Or, rather, I try to understand. The thing is…" He hesitated as if seeking the right words. "My brothers do some outrageous things. Well, only think of the wolf skin."

They exchanged a reminiscent smile.

"They sometimes go too far, but they're never

mean-spirited," Nathaniel continued. "I suppose I can't quite…comprehend, in the end, a family that would hurt each other."

Violet thought of her contentious girlhood, and Marianne's marriage. "I love that about your family."

The word "love" seemed to hang in the air between them. To Violet, it felt almost tangible. She wanted to say it again, to explore all its ramifications. And she felt terribly shy of that single syllable. It seemed, at one and the same time, full of promise and peril. She swallowed again and said, "Where would you take Grandmamma?"

"That is the question. What would tempt her? What sorts of activities does she particularly like?"

Did her grandmother like anything? Liking was not an emotion Violet associated with her. "Tyrannizing," she said finally.

"It's too bad that Grand Duke Nicholas has gone home then. We could call on him and discuss Russian autocracy."

Violet burst out laughing—a spontaneous, full-throated laugh that seemed to lift a weight from her chest. "Oh, you are beyond anything!"

Nathaniel gazed down at her, a smile slowly blooming on his face. "Why?"

"You take Grandmamma lightly."

"Well, it is easier for me."

"Perhaps so. But it makes everything seem less… portentous."

"Portentous?" he repeated with open amusement.

"Yes. And…possible."

They stood close together in the street, eyes locked.

Nathaniel's head bent, and Violet waited breathlessly for his kiss. But a rowdy group of young men came out of a tavern farther down the street, joking and shoving one another, and the spell was broken. As the jostling crew approached them, Nathaniel turned and guided her back toward the ball. "We haven't established what outing might tempt your grandmother," he said after a moment.

"No." Violet hadn't quite regained her equilibrium. "She... I don't know, Nathaniel. All she likes is stating her opinions."

He considered, then stopped walking as if struck by an idea. "I have it. I'll ask *her* about books and games for girls. We must be right—that Sebastian wants them for his fiancée's sisters. I'm sure she'll find it a perfectly natural question. And then I shall beg her to come with me to buy them. The proprieties, you know."

Violet was aghast. "She'll choose dreadful, edifying things."

"Which will serve Sebastian right for pushing the task off on me."

"Nathaniel..."

"We'll find other things later," he assured her. "But I don't think your grandmother will be able to resist the temptation to 'advise.'"

"And waste your money," protested Violet. But it was half-hearted.

"We'll donate her choices to poor orphans."

Violet snorted. "I see no need to further oppress girls who are already orphans." She paused just outside the door of the inn. "It could work. But what if she refuses?"

"I shall exercise all my charm to convince her."

"Ah. It's settled then."

"You doubt my capacity to charm her?"

"On the contrary, I was quite sincere. You are… exceedingly charming."

Their eyes met again as they moved together into the doorway, unconscious of anything but each other. The portal opened, and two other couples came out. They stepped aside to let them pass. And Violet wished that they were headed in the opposite direction, toward their lodgings and a chance for some delicious privacy.

⁓

When they returned to the ballroom, it seemed as if Marianne had been lying in wait. She approached them at once and said to Violet, "May I speak to you?"

With a polite bow, Nathaniel walked away.

Marianne pulled her into a quiet corner. "You haven't told him?" she whispered.

"I said I wouldn't tell anyone," Violet replied, a little offended.

"It's just that you looked so cozy," her friend said wistfully. "As if there could be no secrets between you."

Violet was briefly gratified—except that all her recent transactions with Marianne were such a secret.

"I need to see Daniel tomorrow. Will you go with me? Please?"

"Marianne…"

"There is no one else I can ask," she insisted. "You are my only friend."

"What about your family?"

Marianne grimaced. "They're so proud of my brilliant match they won't hear a word against Anthony."

"Not even your mother or your sisters?"

"Mama is excessively relieved to have all her children married off and her social duties done," was the acid reply. "She never leaves Shropshire now. She told me straight out that she is finished exerting herself for her 'offspring.'"

Could mothers…abdicate? Violet wondered. Yet hers had done even less.

"And my sisters are busy with their own concerns. I…" Marianne looked away. "They were made to feel that I had outdone them in the…the Marriage Mart. I'm afraid they might be glad, in a way."

"Surely not!"

"It doesn't matter," muttered Marianne, reacting to the sympathy in Violet's face. "I am finished worrying about Anthony and why he is the way he is and…oh, all of it. I am going to enjoy myself! Why would you deny me that?"

"It isn't me. I don't deny you anything."

"If you refuse to help me, you do," she declared.

"That's not fair, Marianne!"

"Ah, ladies telling secrets," insinuated a deep, caressing voice.

Violet turned to find that the Prince Regent had descended upon them unawares. His large figure was resplendent in a scarlet brocade waistcoat; a cloud of scent wafted over them as they curtsied, again with overtones of fine brandy. "There is nothing more charming." He gazed at Violet like a jeweler valuing a precious piece. "I'm so pleased you're coming to the countess's little tea, Lady Hightower. I was glad to offer the pavilion when she asked, of course. Worthy cause, you know, and I'm never averse to hosting the lovely ladies of Brighton. I shall come by to greet you all"—he fixed Violet with a knowing smile, as if he was about to hand over a treat she had requested— "and make good on my promise of a private tour," he finished. With a complacent nod, he moved on.

Violet struggled to hide her dismay. It seemed her relief over the invitation had been premature.

"Violet? Will you come tomorrow?" Marianne said.

"What?"

"It's just another walk, like before. Nothing more than that."

"Oh, Marianne."

"Do you want me to beg? I will if I must."

"No, of course not. I don't want…" She didn't wish to be involved at all, Violet thought. And then wondered if this was just cowardice. What did she owe her friend? And what did helping her really mean?

"If you come, I'll help you with the Regent," Marianne murmured.

Violet stared at her.

"I'll go to that tea with you and stick by your side every moment, so there is no opportunity for a 'private tour.' And I'll tell you all the ways I've used to discourage unwanted male attentions."

"I don't know what you…"

"Oh, come, you aren't going to go all missish about this?"

Violet slumped in defeat. "I didn't mean to attract the Regent's interest."

"Well, of course you didn't. Who would? But he never waits for encouragement."

"How does one fend off a royal prince?"

"Will you walk with me?"

"Marianne!"

But her old friend merely waited for an answer.

The thought of an ally at the tea was so tempting. "Oh, very well."

"Splendid. I'll call for you at ten tomorrow." She started to turn away.

"Wait! You have an invitation to the tea?"

"There will be no problem with that."

Marianne hurried off before Violet could say more, and the deed was done. Violet might have gone after her. Or perhaps she wouldn't have. But just then she noticed that Nathaniel was speaking to her grandmother, and she had to rush over to make sure he wasn't setting up their expedition for the same time as the walk.

Eleven

"YOUR GRANDMOTHER HAS AGREED," NATHANIEL told Violet the following morning, holding up a folded note. "After a bit of cajoling. Our appointment is set for tomorrow morning." She showed no reaction. "And Lady Dunstaple never receives visitors before noon; she said so when I was talking with them last night. She does not leave her bedchamber until then." He waited once more. "I thought you would be glad," he added.

"Oh! I am. I was just thinking about this tea at the pavilion. I mean…"

He waited, but she didn't finish the sentence. He wasn't certain why this particular event was occupying her mind. "If you're interested in charities, my mother will be eager to recruit you," he said.

"Does the duchess solicit donations for indigent gentlewomen?"

"I'm sure she would gladly contribute," he replied with a smile. "But her chief cause is education for women—or girls, actually. She says that it is all very well to help people when they're poor. And one should, of course. But if they had been educated when young, perhaps they wouldn't be. Poor, that is."

"An interesting view," Violet said.

"She has established several boarding schools for girls without means. From all walks of life."

"I'll have to talk to her about them."

"Be prepared to spend a good deal of time if you do." Nathaniel softened what might have seemed like a criticism with another warm smile. He was pleased to see that he gained her full attention.

"Do you and your brothers help with them, too?" she asked.

He shook his head. "Mama feels that women should be in charge. As a model to the pupils, you see. Females hold all the positions of authority. She even found a woman blacksmith—"

"What?" Violet looked across the breakfast table in astonishment.

"To demonstrate that a woman can do any task, if necessary."

"But…blacksmiths are always such big men."

"I don't believe any of the pupils has actually set up a forge," Nathaniel said. "But Mama did say that some of the girls seemed to relish pounding the anvil with the hammer." Seeing that Violet was trying not to smile, he continued, "It's all right. She laughs about it herself."

"I wonder why Sebastian didn't ask her for ways to amuse his pesky girls," Violet said then, taking a sip of her tea, then frowning at it as if it had gone cold. "It seems she must be an expert."

"Indeed." It would have made sense. Nathaniel

shrugged. Sebastian hadn't because Nathaniel's brothers always asked him. That was why. And their mother would have posed a host of shrewd questions, and seen far more than Sebastian wished her to, and then more than likely told Sebastian to do it himself.

But Sebastian was far from any shops, and... Nathaniel enjoyed helping out. He acknowledged it. It was a pleasure to tick tasks off a list, to...bring order. He'd found a dealer who recognized the book Robert wanted, and arranged to have it sent. He'd ascertained from an experienced apothecary that there was no ointment to repel dogs. The man had thought the request... Eccentric was a kind word for it, he recalled with a smile.

He'd even discovered an admiral. He was rather proud of that, though it had been purely coincidental. Stopping on the beach to chat with a friend, he'd discovered that the man's companion was high up in the navy. It came out as they discussed the merits of telescopes and their uses. Nathaniel had mentioned James's naval career even before he knew the man's occupation. And in the end, the fellow had agreed to write a letter on James's behalf. It had been pure serendipity.

He was just as glad to go on this outing with Violet's grandmother, even though before their wedding, the old woman had frankly scared him. The scheme they had formed together, the help he could give, made Violet feel even more like a family member.

He looked over at her. She seemed unusually pensive today, quite far away, in fact. She was gazing at the empty hearth as if it held mysteries. Her shawl trailed off the back of the chair to brush the floor, and her face was appealingly lovely.

The physical side of his marriage had turned out to be so much more satisfying than he'd anticipated, Nathaniel thought, appreciating the way Violet's gown skimmed the lines of her body. Not that he'd expected problems. But…he supposed, looking back, that he'd imagined it would be…ordinary. Or…he didn't even know what he meant by that. He did know, however, that he'd been wrong.

Indeed, the whole marriage was more than he'd expected. Each day seemed to reveal new facets of this woman who'd once seemed so quiet and prim. A year ago he might not have described Violet as interesting. Now, he knew that she was fascinating.

"What is it?" she said.

"What is what?"

"You were looking at me strangely."

"Admiringly," he corrected. "Appreciatively. Is that strange?"

"Well…" She smiled at him. "Of course I must say no."

"I was only thinking how much more captivating you are than you used to be."

She cocked her head. "Is it a compliment when a gentleman praises one's current self at the expense of one's past personality?"

"I am going to assert that it is."

"You scarcely have a choice." Violet looked gratified nonetheless. "I wanted to…escape my bonds." She extended her arms as if she wished she could spin in the chair. "Expand."

"I always knew you'd be an exemplary duchess," Nathaniel said, drawn toward her like iron to a lodestone. "Now I understand that you will be a splendid one." He stood and went to pull her up as well.

"Oh, a duchess. That is what matters to you?"

He caught her in his arms and whirled her around as if they were waltzing. "I think we agree on the importance of our families. Their respect, our legacy. Yet I've also been granted the extraordinary gift of a duchess who is also a delectable woman."

Violet's eyes gleamed with tears.

"What have I said to make you cry?"

"Nothing, I just… I didn't expect it either…to…"

Nathaniel found he was holding his breath, waiting for her next word.

But he never heard it. The parlor door opened at that moment to reveal Cates and Furness jostling for entry. Eschewing his customary correctness, Nathaniel's valet won the contest by pushing Violet's personal maid so sharply she nearly lost her balance. He marched ahead of her into the room. "I cannot have my arrangements…usurped," he declared. "It is intolerable. Any proper abigail would be ashamed…"

Nathaniel and Violet stepped apart.

Furness hurried forward and stepped directly in front of the valet. "Mister Cates left the flatirons heating by the fire for more than an hour. He never came near them! I couldn't wait any longer to press out your ladyship's…"

Cates's face had reddened further. "I set them out for my own purposes! You had no right to touch…"

"You can't hoard the only set of flatirons in the

house. Other people have work to do, and can't wait on your worship's *convenience*."

The maid hadn't quite mastered sarcasm, Nathaniel thought. It needed a lighter hand.

"*Some* people possess a modicum of consideration," answered Cates in freezing accents, "and ask before they snatch up someone else's things."

Cates was better at it. It was ice versus fire.

"They aren't yours," began Furness.

"Enough," said Nathaniel.

Both servants fell silent and looked abashed at their outburst.

"Must I set up a…schedule for use of the, er, flat-irons?" he continued. He punctuated the query with raised brows and mild astonishment. As he'd hoped, the mere question, from him, made them see the error of their ways.

"Of course not, my lord," said Cates, though he spoke through clenched teeth.

"No, my lord," agreed Furness, dropping a curtsy.

"You can manage that yourselves?" he asked.

Cates actually blushed. It was the most emotion Nathaniel had ever seen from the man. Furness gazed at the floor. Both servants nodded without meeting his eyes.

"Good."

The word was a dismissal, and the two went quickly out, hardly elbowing each other in the doorway at all.

"I don't understand why they cannot get along," said Violet when the door had shut behind them. She looked guilty. "Cates never quarreled with Renshaw."

"He never had to work with her in cramped lodgings," Nathaniel pointed out.

"That's true." She sighed. "Does Cates complain to you about her?"

"He has mentioned one or two things."

"Furness, too. About Cates. I'm not sure what to do…"

"Leave them to work it out between themselves, as I hope I made clear."

Violet looked thoughtful. "I suppose."

"What else?"

"Nothing."

"Why do I doubt that?"

"It's only an idea about an idea," Violet replied.

"A…what?"

She smiled at him. "I'm not plotting, but I'm wondering if perhaps I should. And if I did, what would I plot?"

"What would you—?"

"I told you, I don't know yet."

"Would you like to go riding?" asked Nathaniel, abandoning the subject.

She started to nod, then her face fell. "Oh, I can't. I promised Marianne I would…go out walking with her."

"Put her off," Nathaniel cajoled.

Violet shook her head, looking quite sorry, at least. "I promised."

"Another time then."

"Oh, yes." She held out an impulsive hand, and Nathaniel took it. "I *wish* I could go," she assured him.

He didn't quite understand the fervor of her tone, but he appreciated it. He dropped a kiss on her fingers. "We will have many other opportunities to ride together." She clung to his hand. "Is something wrong?" he asked. Her mood had been a bit strange all morning.

"No." Violet let go and stepped away. She glanced at the mantel clock. "I should fetch my hat. Marianne will be here in a few minutes."

"You can always come to me if there is," Nathaniel said. "Anything wrong."

"Of course," she said.

He thought her smile as she went out not as sprightly as usual. Something seemed to be depressing her spirits—ah, most likely the looming confrontation with her mother. The Devere family was enough to make anyone turn somber. Satisfied with his conclusions, he headed for the stables.

❧

The following morning Violet woke full of anxiety. At first she couldn't imagine why, then she remembered that this was the day she was to corner her mother. On the one hand, it felt ridiculous to worry about such a simple thing. Children and parents had serious conversations every day of the year. But some young part of her seemed to believe that her scheme challenged the very nature of the universe, that all would collapse if she persisted. Which was idiotic. Mama might be reluctant—well, all Violet's past history suggested she would be. She might be distressed, and of course Violet didn't want to make her mother angry or unhappy. But it was hardly earth-shattering. A few simple questions, a natural desire to understand some puzzling elements of her childhood. There was no reason to feel as if doom hovered over her head. And she could always apologize afterward. Mama never held a grudge.

As he left their lodgings to call for her grandmother, Nathaniel squeezed Violet's hand. It should have been reassuring. It was. But it also reminded her, somehow, that she was keeping secrets from him.

Her expedition with Marianne the previous day had gone just like the last one. They'd walked to the church, and Violet had sat in a pew while Marianne murmured in her admirer's arms. After a time, he left, again without any introduction. Then, all the way home, Marianne had enthused about his good looks and charm. In her eyes, he was astonishingly thoughtful and gentle and kind—in short, the perfect man. This was, of course, impossible for Violet to judge, but she thought it unlikely. Particularly when she asked for some details about the gentleman and found that Marianne knew little about his activities, tastes, habits and...everything really, except that he professed to love her to the edge of distraction. And that was all that mattered to Marianne.

The situation made Violet uneasy, even though it remained innocent in the strictest physical sense. She knew that Marianne's family would be appalled. She knew that her own would condemn her involvement. If Grandmamma found out...! She suspected... no, she knew that Nathaniel wouldn't care for it either. That weighed on her the most. She wished she hadn't gone. But it was so hard to resist the pleas of her old friend.

The mantel clock chimed ten. She couldn't think

of Marianne any longer. Half an hour had passed since Nathaniel's departure. It was time to go.

Violet fetched her bonnet and shawl and walked the short distance to Lady Dunstaple's house. As expected, the servant at the door told her that her ladyship was not available. To be perfectly certain, Violet asked for her grandmother. When told she was out, Violet breathed a sigh of relief. She asked for her mother, and had just time to wonder if Grandmamma had perhaps left orders that she couldn't see her when she was admitted and taken upstairs.

Her mother was alone in a parlor at the back of the house. Entering on the servant's heels, Violet saw her parent's face change when her visit was announced, shifting from contentment to anxiety. Mama always looked that way when caught unawares, she realized. She was happiest when left alone. Her mother put aside her embroidery frame and rose, clasping her hands together. "Violet. Is something wrong?"

It was doleful to feel so awkward with one's own mother. Sad to see her glancing at the door as if waiting for a headmistress to surge in and scold her. "Not at all," Violet said. "I've come to take you out walking."

"Me? Oh no." She looked startled, and even more frightened.

Facing her mother's small, plump figure, really noticing her hunched shoulders and the lines constant anxiety had etched into her round face, Violet nearly burst into tears. Mama looked so unhappy; she always looked unhappy. In the background, in the shadows, mournful. Had Violet somehow trained herself—or been strongly encouraged—not to notice this?

She almost abandoned the whole enterprise there and then. How could she add to her mother's burdens? But…what if she could help? She was a married woman now, with her own household and resources. Grandmamma no longer ruled her. If there was anything she could do… And what in the world could be so bad? Still, she had to swallow twice before she could say, "A pleasant outing, just the two of us."

"But I can't…"

If she hesitated now, all was lost, Violet thought. She just had to push through. "I'll come with you to get your bonnet." She couldn't give her mother a chance to argue or delay.

"Your grandmother may be back at any—"

"Not for two hours," Violet assured her.

Her mother gazed at her as if she'd run mad. "How can you know that?"

"Because I made sure of it."

"You?" She could not have looked more amazed if the Earth had stopped turning.

Feeling uncomfortably like another tyrant in her mother's confined life, Violet took her arm and led her out into the hall. "Let's get your things," she insisted. "It's quite warm out."

There were more protests and foot-dragging, but at last they were on the stairs and then outdoors. And in that moment, Violet realized that she hadn't thought where they would go. She couldn't believe she'd been so heedless. She'd spent hours worrying about her feelings and the oddities of her childhood, but she'd made no proper plan. What was wrong with her?

Her mother was casting furtive glances up and

down the street. When a cart driver at the intersection shouted, she jumped as if she'd been shot. They couldn't risk encountering her grandmother, not even a passing glimpse. Where could they go?

And then Violet thought of the church. It had been as sparsely populated on her second visit with Marianne as on the first. Nathaniel and her grandmother would never think to go there. It would serve for a private meeting with Mama.

Feeling almost as anxious as her mother, Violet hurried her along the streets. Only when they entered the church and found it empty did she relax. She examined the space, found a shielded spot at the end of one pew, and urged her mother over to sit there. A sigh of relief escaped her as she sank down beside her.

"A…a fine church," said her mother in a quavering voice.

"Yes, Mama. I wanted to—"

"The font looks very old."

"It is Norman."

"Really. As old as that? Fancy how—"

"Mama, I need to speak to you about something."

Her mother looked at her like a rabbit facing a fox.

Violet had to force herself to continue in the face of this pathetic fear. "I must understand why Grandmamma treats me as she does."

"Wh…what do you…?"

"So harshly," Violet continued. "And so completely unlike the way she treats Cousin Delia, for example."

Her mother looked startled.

"We are both, equally, her granddaughters. Why has she criticized and…and oppressed me all my life when she does no such thing with Delia? Or her grandsons, of course. There must be some reason."

Her mother looked frightened.

"There is a reason, isn't there?"

She hunched in the pew and looked away.

"I can see that you know what it is."

Her mother started to cry—slow, hopeless tears. Hands limp in her lap, she didn't bother to wipe them away. They dripped off her chin onto the bodice of her gown.

"Mama, please don't…" Violet was deeply shaken, but she was also more curious than ever. What could cause such a reaction? "Please don't cry. I'm not going to do anything to you."

The silent tears simply continued. Her mother said nothing, offered no protest or argument. She merely hunched on the wooden seat, seemingly unable to lift a finger to alter the situation. As she always did, always had. "It's not fair that I shouldn't know!"

"It's far better than you don't," said her mother.

At least she was speaking. "No, Mama, it is not."

"It is! Won't you trust me on that?"

"What cause have you given me to trust you?" It came out bitter. Her mother flinched, and Violet felt cruel. But her curiosity and sense of justice were on fire. "We are not leaving here until you tell me," she declared. "Grandmamma can institute a search of the whole town. She can call out the troops—"

"I swore never to mention it again as long as I lived," her mother cried.

"What?"

"I can't tell you—"

"Did you murder someone? Or commit high treason?"

Her mother jerked as if she'd been struck. "Violet! How could you even imagine…?"

"I have a very good imagination. And if you will not say, I can imagine all sorts of dreadful things."

"I can't, I can't," she moaned.

"Mama!" Violet could see that she was winning. Her mother didn't have the fortitude to resist a determined assault. Hadn't she shown as much all Violet's life? "Just tell me," she commanded.

Her mother hunched even lower, as if she might hide her whole person in the pew. "Please don't make me—"

"I have to know!"

"I don't want you to think badly of me," her mother murmured, almost too low to hear.

Violet did not say, and would never say, that she already viewed her mother as weak. Whatever had happened, whatever secret she was about to reveal, she should have stood up to Grandmamma, and for Violet. "I won't," she said.

"How do you know?"

"Shall I promise you?"

Her mother took her hands in a painful grip. "Will you?"

Violet nodded. "I promise."

A long silence followed, but Violet was wise enough not to interrupt it. She could see her mother gathering the courage to speak.

"There was a murder," the older woman whispered finally.

"What?"

"It wasn't me!" She shook her head, eyes on the stone floor. "It had nothing to do with me, in the end. Except that it wrecked everything."

Although she was shocked to the core, Violet controlled her voice. "Everything?" she prompted softly.

Her mother nodded, swallowing. Then she sat a little straighter. She took a deep breath. When she spoke again, it was in a stronger voice. "My family arranged the match with your father. He was heir to an earldom. That was all that mattered to them. I had a large dowry. The Deveres cared only for that."

She gazed out over the church, or perhaps into the past. Violet wondered if she should acknowledge these facts, which she had always somehow known.

"But I was in love with someone else."

Violet was silenced.

"This was soon after the troubles in France, you know, and London was full of émigrés." Her mother's tone had gone dreamy. "Rene was the son of a marquis, though they had lost everything, of course. They'd had huge estates and a fortune." Briefly, it sounded as if she was arguing. But with the next sentence, her hopeless tone was back. "The revolution took all that away. But, oh, Violet, if you could have seen him in his blue satin coat, with the lace falling over his wrists. He was the handsomest man I'd ever met. And such an air about him! Like a fairy-tale prince among the English clods. And he made me feel like a princess. A beautiful princess."

Violet gazed at her mother in amazement. She'd never heard her speak at such length in her life.

"When they announced my engagement to your

father, Rene threatened to put a bullet through his
head. He said losing me had already killed him. He
railed and ranted. I was so frightened that he would
really do it. And so unhappy. And in love. So...I said
I would run away with him. To Gretna Green. So we
could be married and be together forever."

Violet nearly exclaimed aloud. Her timid, anxious
mother had eloped? Seeing the worried looks being
cast her way, Violet nodded, and smiled. The tale
mustn't stop here.

"I...I gave him what money I had, and Rene
found the rest to hire a chaise. We slipped away early
from a ball and raced out of town. It was terrifying.
Every minute I thought my father would find us.
And exciting. The most exciting thing that has ever
happened to me."

She stopped and began to twist her hands in her lap.
Violet was afraid she wouldn't go on. But finally she
did, in a whisper almost too low to catch.

"We stayed at inns along the way. Together. It
was...he was...glorious."

Violet felt her cheeks heat with embarrassment. It
was...odd to hear such words from her mother.

"We nearly made it to the border," she went on, a
little louder. "We came so close. A few miles... But
someone caught up to us."

"Your family?" Violet asked.

"No. It was another Frenchman." Her mother
hunched in the pew once again, looking as if she
wanted to disappear entirely. "No one I knew," she
murmured. "Though I will never forget his face. A
hard, vulgar man. He had some quarrel with Rene

about a debt. They spoke in French, and I couldn't catch it all. I believe he thought Rene was running away to escape paying him. He pushed into the inn parlor where we were, shouting. They fought."

She shivered. Violet put an arm around her.

"They struggled back and forth, knocking over the table with our dinner and the other chairs. And then..." She panted as if she'd been running. "He had a knife. I didn't see where it came from. But he...that terrible man...he got hold of Rene's chin and...and slashed his throat. The blood...it...it fountained out. In a great scarlet stream. It hit me in the face, splashed down my gown..." She choked. "It was everywhere. Horrible!"

Violet held her closer. "Oh, Mama."

Her mother gazed at her, wild-eyed.

"I'm so...sorry." The words were utterly inadequate, but they seemed to have an effect nonetheless. Slowly, the terror in her eyes subsided.

"I told you there was a murder," she continued mechanically. "He ran out. I don't know what became of him. No one does. I suppose he went back to France." She stirred under Violet's arm—not as if to get away, but as if she wasn't accustomed to gestures of comfort. After another pause, she went on. "So...I was left all alone at the inn. With...the blood and hardly any money. People kept questioning me. All these men. The...the coroner and the justice of the peace. Staring at me and asking the same things over and over. I couldn't think. I didn't know what to do except to send word to my father. There was no one else, any longer."

Violet tried to imagine it. Her mother would have been—seventeen? A sheltered young lady suddenly in a perfectly dreadful situation.

"Papa came for me," her mother continued in a toneless voice. "He was terribly angry. Of course. He brought me back to London. And then there were days and days of shouting." She shivered under Violet's arm. "People said such horrid things. Mama was particularly…" She shook her head. "In the end, the Deveres agreed to take me even though I was ruined."

"You still had a fortune," Violet said.

"Yes," her mother agreed. "As long as I did what Papa ordered. Not if I'd refused to marry. Then, nothing. Mama said they'd turn me out on the street."

She didn't acknowledge Violet's gasp.

"They all said the money was what Rene wanted too. I suppose it was. I was never pretty. Never even striking, as you are now. Have I told you how well you are looking, Violet?"

Tears flooded Violet's eyes. "Th-thank you, Mama," she replied.

Her mother nodded. "So, the dowry saved me. Your…the dowager made certain no one knew of my…slip. She told everyone I'd been visiting her to cover up my absence, and made sure none of her servants said differently."

Violet struggled to absorb the horror and pathos of this story. It was heartrending, and outrageous. Her mother had been treated shamefully. Still, it had all happened almost thirty years ago. "But… Mama. I don't see what this has to do with the way Grandmamma treats me."

For the first time, her mother turned to gaze at Violet. "Haven't you understood? You are Rene's daughter," she whispered.

"What?" Violet froze, her brain struggling to process these words.

"We went to Ireland when it…became obvious that I was…that you were on the way. To the most out-of-the-way place you can imagine. In case, you see. And indeed you arrived at a time when it could not have been your…the earl who fathered you. Your birthday is really in March, not May."

"March." Oddly, this small fact transfixed Violet.

"The dowager said it was so lucky you weren't a boy."

And heir to the earldom, supplied Violet's reeling thoughts. "What would they have done?"

"I don't know." She shivered slightly again.

Violet sat there, frozen, barely noticing her mother's anxious looks. "So, Grandmamma…but she isn't my grandmother, is she?"

Her mother shook her head. "You are no relation."

"And so I deserve no consideration from her."

"She has always feared that you inherited my wanton tendencies, along with…foreign blood."

A harsh, startled laugh escaped Violet. "And Delia's mother is above suspicion?"

"She has always been very respectable," said her mother. "The dowager says these things run in families."

"And you let her take this position all these years? You made no argument?" Violet was still trying to accept the total alteration in her view of her life.

"They saved me…and you. Moreley—"

"Who is not my father." The world was falling to pieces around her head.

"He treated you as his own."

Violet thought back. Had…the earl treated her just as he did her brothers? Her half brothers! But they were boys. She'd expected her—the earl to be more interested in them. So when he hadn't paid much heed to her… Violet swallowed. She couldn't get her mind around the fact that half of her family had been eliminated at a stroke.

"It was kind," her mother said.

"Except that they weren't, certainly not Grand— the dowager. Not at all kind. And you let her… oppress me. All my life."

"I owed them everything!" Her mother slumped again, gaze back on the flagstones. "After that night…all that blood. I wasn't…I couldn't…I just couldn't manage."

"Then. Yes, I understand. Of course you were shocked and deeply upset. You had to put yourself in their hands. But it's been…"

"Something in me died with Rene," her mother declared. She put her face in her hands.

For one wild, anguished moment, Violet wanted to hit her, an impulse she quickly suppressed. She swayed under the onslaught of confused emotion. She was stunned and resentful and anxious and…ashamed. Despite the arguments of common sense, a thread of mortification ran through her. She'd done nothing wrong, she insisted silently. She had nothing to be ashamed of. But she was.

With a terrible sinking feeling, she remembered Nathaniel's proud statement—that she'd make such a splendid duchess. Her husband thought—knew—that she was the daughter of an earl. Their match had been agreed—she'd been married—on that basis. Lineage was important to people like the Greshams. The nobility. She'd been taught to value it herself. The next Duke of Langford was supposed to be the grandson of an earl, on his mother's side. But he wouldn't be. He'd be the grandson of a murdered Frenchman, who might or might not have been the scion of a marquis. It was well known that many émigrés had wildly exaggerated their heritage. Even if he hadn't… What was she thinking? She couldn't tell anyone even if he'd been the King of France himself.

"We must go back before your grand—before she returns," her mother said, raising her head.

"You go on," Violet said. "I need to think."

"About what?" She looked alarmed. "You won't tell anyone…"

"That I am not who they think I am? That I am not even a Devere? No, Mama, I won't."

She winced at the tone, but said, "I don't want to leave you here by yourself."

"I'll be all right."

"I know it is a great shock. I begged you not to ask me…"

"You should go. You don't want her to find you out." Violet felt a twinge of guilt at her mother's hunted look, but she really didn't think she could talk anymore just now.

"If you're sure…"

"Go ahead, Mama." She put all the kindness she could muster into her voice. "It will be all right."

With a final anxious glance, her mother departed. Violet sat alone, grappling with a life turned upside down.

The silence of the church fell around her. And just as she was managing to calm down a little, she thought of Marianne. If her grand—if the dowager countess ever found out that Violet had helped forward her friend's clandestine meetings, she would conclude that all her worst fears had been proven right.

Twelve

"YOUR GRANDMOTHER ACTUALLY HAD SOME GOOD ideas about amusements for girls," Nathaniel said to his wife that afternoon. "Not too dreary at all." He'd been eager to tell her this, and more, to hear what had occurred with her mother. Violet had been out far longer than he expected. He'd finally found her in her bedchamber, sitting at the dressing table, gazing into the mirror. When she said nothing, he added, "I succumbed to the temptation to ask her about her friend the bishop."

Violet sat curiously still.

"Are you listening?" he said. She certainly gave no sign of it.

"What? Yes."

"For Randolph," Nathaniel added.

"Randolph?"

"The bishop. Your grandmother actually said that he might take an interest."

"My grandmother!" An odd sort of laugh escaped her, like a hiccup.

"What's wrong?" Nathaniel felt awkward standing

behind her, seeing her face in the mirror rather than directly. The room was not large. There was no place else to sit except the bed, and that didn't feel right somehow. "Come out to the parlor," he said. "Tell me what happened with your mother."

He held out a hand. She took it and rose and went with him, but it felt as if she was hardly there. Nathaniel led her over to the sofa and sat beside her, keeping her hand folded in his. "Shall I ring for some tea?"

"If you want some," she replied absently.

"Did it go badly with your mother?" He squeezed her fingers.

She turned to him, and finally seemed to return from a great distance. Her gray eyes focused on his face. Emotion flickered in them, but he couldn't interpret it.

"No," said Violet. Her chin came up. She sat straighter, cleared her throat. "No, not at all."

"What did she tell you?"

"About?"

Nathaniel supposed it was quite unsettling to force a conversation on one's mother after years of avoidance. It was nothing he'd experienced, of course, but he could imagine the difficulty. So he suppressed his impatience. "About your grandmother's conduct. Everything we discussed."

Violet blinked. She looked down at their linked hands. Gently, she pulled hers free. "She…she…"

It was as if his wife had lost her knowledge of words. Nathaniel frowned.

"She simply doesn't like me," Violet said. "She never has. It is one of those…inexplicable aversions.

You know. Occasionally you meet someone and dislike them at once, for no apparent reason. You…just do."

Something in her voice sounded false. Bewildered, Nathaniel said, "You're telling me that your grandmother took a dislike to you at birth? Like an annoying stranger encountered at a club?"

"Stranger," murmured Violet. "Yes."

Nathaniel gazed at her. It was obvious that she was shaken, and impossible for him to accept this explanation. "This is all you have to say?"

"Why…yes." Sitting very still, she suddenly looked apprehensive, like a child braced for a thundering scold.

For the first time in their long acquaintance, she was lying to him. It was plain in her tone and her posture and…in the whole feel of the connection between them. Nathaniel couldn't comprehend it. "Whatever she said, it is quite safe with me," he tried. "You must know that."

"I…I have told you." Her voice trembled a little.

Nathaniel waited, thinking that this quaver might herald true confidences, but she said nothing more. "You actually are not going to tell me?"

"I did."

He was startled by the degree of hurt flooding through him. "Of course you have no obligation to speak. I only wished to help you."

"Help," she muttered. Her hands opened and closed in her lap.

"Yes." He didn't want to be angry with her, or say the reproachful things that crowded to his lips. It was true; she wasn't required to share what she'd learned. If she didn't wish to. He waited a minute more, hoping. "As we discussed, diverting your grandmother…"

A small sound escaped Violet. "Helping. You're always helping. Sending your letters and speculating about your brothers' lives. Must you poke into everyone else's business?"

Nathaniel felt as if something had struck him square in the chest. "What?"

"How much is help, and how much sheer interference? Can't some things just be left alone?"

Nathaniel found himself on his feet. He couldn't stay still. Distress and bewilderment surged through him. His thoughts tumbled and clashed. "Are you calling me a…a meddler? You asked for my assistance!"

"Couldn't you see that I need some time to think?" Violet cried.

"Think! Splendid. Think all you like." He strode out, down the stairs, and into the street, seeing nothing of his surroundings, wholly engaged in an inner debate with his utterly mistaken wife.

Yes, he liked helping people—his family. Why should he not? What could be wrong with that? Of course he didn't do it out of a desire to pry into their private affairs. No one thought so. No hint of such a… despicable motive had ever been suggested.

Nathaniel walked faster, passing one person after another, noticing none. His chest felt tight and hot— with outrage, not fatigue.

He didn't help out of obligation, either, or for the thanks that his brothers…mostly…didn't bother to offer. It wasn't an exchange. And absolutely it was *not* a case of—I do this for you and you tell me all your secrets. None of his brothers had told him the specifics of what was going on in their lives. When someone… one of his brothers…made a request, he…simply enjoyed fulfilling it. Didn't he?

It was a sort of…pleasure to think of small services he could perform without being asked. And if no one noticed these things had been done…well… Gratitude wasn't the point.

Nathaniel turned a corner, moving so fast now that he nearly bowled over a gaggle of chattering young ladies. They shrieked and scrambled out of the way in a flurry of ruffles and dropped parasols. He had to pause and apologize and restore their scattered property while every fiber of him longed to move.

What was *the point?* he wondered when he could stride onward.

In truth, he didn't understand how someone…his brothers…could walk right by a task that needed to be done and, seemingly, not realize it existed. Such things practically shouted out to him. And they were usually easy to accomplish. A moment's thought, a word to a servant. His brothers were perfectly admirable men, but they…left it to him.

Nathaniel stopped so abruptly that a man plowed into him from behind.

"What the devil? Take some care, will you?" The fellow pushed around him and hurried off.

Care. He did take care. He was the eldest, the brother who kept his head, who rallied round, who stood fast and fulfilled the request and tidied up without tallying what credit was owed. That was who he'd always been. And his brothers had been glad of it. So why, this time, with Violet, should it be so different?

Because it was, Nathaniel thought, stock still in the middle of the narrow street. This time he'd wanted some acknowledgment. He'd wanted, yes, admiration. Not that she owed it to him for helping her. Not that. But he'd wanted her to gaze at him with…appreciation, with that beguiling light in her eyes, with…more than he could frame to himself in this moment. He'd wanted the feeling—which he'd experienced with her before—that they were in harmony, working together, understanding each other. Instead, inexplicably, she'd shut him out.

An odd sort of flutter moved through Nathaniel. He felt…what? Forlorn, some part of his mind supplied. Immediately, another voice rejected the idea as nonsense.

He ran a hand over his face and looked about him. He was in an unfamiliar part of Brighton, and tired of walking. He didn't want to return to their lodgings. In London, there were clubs in which to seek refuge. At Langford, he had the whole countryside, or the choice of many empty rooms where he could retreat. Brighton offered none of that. Except…he had joined Raggett's Club when they arrived, though he almost never visited it. He wasn't fond enough of gaming. Still, today it might serve.

Nathaniel moved on until he got his bearings, then turned toward the sea. Entering Raggett's a little later, he realized he'd come out without a hat, a solecism that disconcerted the servant at the door. He was admitted, however, and he paused before a mirror in the entry to correct any other fault in his attire. Adjusting the folds of his neckcloth, he examined the figure in the glass. He'd been told often enough that he was a handsome man. He didn't set much store by it. His face and form were gifts of his lineage, not personal achievements.

Did he look pompous, though? Like a man who would interfere in others' business? He tried a different expression. He smiled and felt like an utter fool. Soon after their wedding, Violet had said that what she wanted was to have fun. There had certainly been no fun in their recent conversation. Again, Nathaniel remembered Robert's claim that he had no idea how to have fun. What if he was right, after all?

An acquaintance came in the front door and nodded as he passed by. "Hightower."

Nathaniel abandoned the mirror and followed the man into the largest clubroom. It was sparsely populated at this hour. Two tables boasted desultory card games. In one corner a solitary young man diced right hand against left. He looked up hopefully when Nathaniel entered, then subsided when Nathaniel showed no interest in joining him.

One of the games was breaking up. Two of the players departed. Another accepted the dicer's invitation of a few goes. The fourth paused to observe the play at the other table, and then turned toward the entry.

It was Thomas Rochford, Nathaniel saw, an old acquaintance. They'd known each other fairly well at Eton, but then their lives had gone in different directions. Nathaniel had devoted himself to estate business, while Rochford employed his considerable wit and charm to become one of the chief ornaments of society. His large fortune had helped, of course, but money alone hadn't made him one of the most sought after gentlemen in London. His presence was said to make any hostess's party memorable. And fun? Nathaniel wondered. He was aware that all manner of females swooned over Rochford—misses fresh from the schoolroom, their mothers, the high flyers of the demimonde. And Rochford made the most of it. "Where are you off to?" Nathaniel asked him after they'd greeted each other.

Rochford raised one blond brow. "The cards are cold. I'm giving them a rest."

"May I walk with you?" Nathaniel endured the other man's surprise.

"Of course," Rochford said politely.

They were of a height. Rochford was rangier and moved with a careless grace that Nathaniel knew he didn't match. They paused at the door for Rochford's hat, and a slight quirk of his lips when Nathaniel was found to have none, then moved out into the street.

"What is it, Hightower?" At Nathaniel's quick look, he added, "We haven't had an extended conversation since Eton."

"I suppose we haven't," Nathaniel replied. "Why is that, I wonder?"

"You are the worthy and serious heir of a duke, with important matters on your mind. And I fritter away my time in pursuit of pleasure."

"I am not 'worthy,'" said Nathaniel, disgusted at this description.

Rochford made an airy gesture. "A joke."

Had it come to this, that he was unable to see a joke? But he didn't think it really had been.

"Is there something I can do for you?" asked the other man.

One did not ask another fellow about fun. It was too ridiculous. As Nathaniel tried to frame what he wished to say, they strolled down toward the sea.

"I should warn you that I am known to be odiously selfish."

"You say that as if you were quite proud of it." Nathaniel would have been offended had anyone used the word about him. He would have argued against the accusation.

"Oh, I am one of the chief proponents of creative selfishness," replied Rochford.

"Creative…?"

"The art of making one's self-interest so compelling that others delight in indulging it."

Nathaniel laughed. "You can do that?"

"It is my constant study, at least." Rochford smiled. A pair of young ladies walking arm in arm simpered and preened encouragingly.

There was no doubt about the man's charm, Nathaniel thought. But he also seemed to possess an intriguing attitude toward life—and not a shred of pomposity. "I wanted only…to renew an old acquaintance," Nathaniel said.

This earned him a speculative look. "My dear fellow. Delighted, of course."

❧

Violet hadn't known before that a tea party could be pure misery. The large, ornate room roared with the conversations of a hundred women. It was hot, and the tables were crowded elbow to elbow. Even if she hadn't been falling to pieces inside, it would have been a trial. With her mind and heart in turmoil, it was unbearable.

The conversation that she had—foolishly, idiotically—insisted upon having with her mother, played over and over in her head. She couldn't stop thinking about it. She felt as if everything she'd known and counted upon about her life had been thrust into a box, violently shaken, and then dumped out before her in a tangled mess. Since then, her heart pounded for no reason; her stomach roiled so she could hardly swallow a crumb of the lavish spread set out before them.

And she'd made Nathaniel angry. She couldn't quite remember what she'd said to him on that dreadful day after she'd seen her mother. It must have been bad, from the way he was acting. Violet's hand closed tight on her teacup, fingers trembling. Her memories of their conversation were overwhelmed by the emotional strain she'd been under. With every word he spoke, her brain had screamed that he mustn't learn the secret of her birth, that it would wreck her marriage. Maybe even end it. That fear had left no room for anything else.

She had apologized, but since she didn't know precisely what she'd done, it was ineffective. After her first few words, Nathaniel had hardly seemed to listen. Perhaps he'd thought her insincere, rather than insensible. And now they were scarcely speaking. Oh, they spoke, of course. But they said nothing important. He'd gone off to London, claiming business. She suspected, worried, that he just wanted to get away from her.

So here she sat, her world falling apart, and she had to pretend to enjoy the buzz of empty chitchat.

"Oh, remarkably calm," said the woman on her right.

Violet became aware that she had missed at least one remark addressed to her.

"If *my* husband had gone off to London with Thomas Rochford, I'd be frantic with worry," agreed another farther on.

Marianne, on Violet's other side, gave a start and turned to look at her. Violet was bewildered. Were they speaking to her? Nathaniel hadn't mentioned a traveling companion.

"Alvanley saw Hightower in Rochford's curricle, driving off," said the first woman.

Nearly everyone at the table was looking at Violet now.

"Lud *knows* what sorts of mischief they'll get up to," tittered another.

"Did you know…?" began her overly informative neighbor. All the others leaned forward to catch her whisper. "I overheard my husband say that the 'two most beautiful lightskirts in London' came to blows over Rochford. Screaming and hair-pulling, right in the street."

Gasps of delicious horror went round the table.

"They say he fought a duel when he was only nineteen," piped up a younger woman across the teacups. "With swords, not pistols. Like the old days. To first blood."

Women around the table paused, bright-eyed, to imagine the scene.

"I heard that Cecily Saunders went into a decline when Rochford didn't offer for her," said someone else.

Polite snorts met this assertion. "She was the only person on Earth who expected him to," was the reply. "What a ninnyhammer!"

"Yes, but… When he fixes you with those blazing blue eyes…"

This time, it was sighs all around. "He has the face of a fallen angel," murmured someone.

To Violet's dismay, the group's attention turned back to her.

"Of course, Hightower is handsome as well," said her neighbor.

"The two of them together…! Oh, my."

"I daresay they'll…make quite an impression in town." Women exchanged speculative looks.

"But no one's there at this time of year," said one of the youngest at the table.

"My dear, there's plenty of a…certain type of female available."

Violet knew she had to say something. She just couldn't think what. Marianne nudged her surreptitiously. Exerting stern control over her voice, Violet said, "Nathaniel had business in London, and he wanted to leave me the carriage." He had said this, without revealing that he had a fellow traveler. Violet had gotten the impression that he was hiring a chaise. Or made an unwarranted assumption, apparently. "He'll be back tomorrow." The moment she said it, she wished she hadn't. It was like a promise she couldn't keep, because she couldn't remember if he had said that.

"You must hope so," murmured one of her table-mates. Violet didn't see who it was.

She couldn't reply. To assure them that he would indeed be back could only sound defensive. To ask what she meant would sound concerned. Violet sipped her tea instead, and had difficulty swallowing past the lump in her throat.

"Gossiping, ladies?"

Violet started and almost spilled her tea. The Prince Regent had come up behind her. For such a large man, he moved remarkably silently. But what was she thinking? The noise in this room would cover the sounds of a stampede. She felt a hand heavy on her shoulder, and then she was enveloped in the heavy scent of his cologne, and his breath ruffled the curls falling past her ear. "I promised a tour…"

On her left, Marianne stood, smiling brilliantly. "Oh, how kind of you, Your Grace! The pavilion is the most splendid place I've ever seen."

The Regent did not hide his chagrin, but he was too gracious to actually reject her. And Marianne's beauty and enthusiasm for his architectural creation clearly softened the blow. When Violet, perforce, rose as well, he offered them each an arm.

Recent events had driven the Regent right out of Violet's mind. Now, she tried to remember what Marianne had told her about discouraging unwanted suitors. Her lovely friend had had much more experience in that area than Violet. What had she said about the Regent? "Avoidance and evasion. That's what a wise old dowager told me. From personal experience, I believe. He has no patience. And he's easily diverted. Like a cranky child." It might have been funny, except that avoidance was currently impossible. The Regent had pulled her hand through his arm and was clutching it with damp, pudgy, and startlingly strong fingers.

What else had Marianne said? "Laugh at inappropriate times. Quite heartily. It worries men very much not to know what you find so amusing. If they ask, simply laugh again. They'll soon take themselves off."

Violet summoned all her skills of dissimulation and laughed, right in the middle of the Regent's lecture on Chinese nodding figures.

It came out a bit feeble, so when he turned and stared at her, she tried again. This laugh was much louder.

Marianne caught her eyes and joined in.

"Is there some joke?" The Regent did look uneasy. He also looked petulant. Violet wondered if her friend had ever tried this technique with royalty?

Still, she had no other stratagems, so she proceeded to laugh unpredictably as their host conducted them around his beloved dwelling. And quite soon it was apparent that the scheme was working. The Regent asked twice more what was so funny, and received only dazzling smiles from Marianne in reply. He progressed from disgruntled to bewildered to annoyed, and finally to muted anger. Violet grew certain that only the Regent's legendary graciousness kept him from ordering them out of his house. By the time the tour ended, cut short she thought, she was no longer worried about fending off his advances. She didn't think he would wish to see her again any time soon.

༺ঌ

They returned to their table, and the seemingly eternal tea wound to a conclusion. Walking home with Marianne, Violet could at last give vent to the question that had been occupying her for more than an hour. "What can Nathaniel be doing with Thomas Rochford?"

Marianne indicated ignorance.

"I didn't know he knew him. I mean…everyone knows him." Rochford was a fixture in society, one of its leading lights. Violet had heard anecdotes about him, though before her marriage, she'd been excluded from stories like those repeated today. Rochford was one of the people who provided the *haut ton* with titillating stories and bon mots, the currency of social exchange. She'd never paid much heed. She'd hardly ever spoken to the man. Her grand—the dowager countess hadn't allowed it. And anyway, she hadn't been pretty enough for Thomas Rochford. Or, more likely, dashing enough. Rochford's acknowledged flirtations skirted near the line. And from what had been said at the tea, his less public liaisons were far more racy.

Marianne said nothing.

Violet found her silence more unsettling than speech. "Nathaniel has *not* gone off with Thomas Rochford to indulge in some sort of debauchery."

Marianne looked away.

"We are speaking of *Nathaniel*," Violet pointed out. "His interests and habits are well known."

"That's true," her friend admitted. She shook her head as if to clear it. "Of course they are. I was just… Living with Anthony has made me cynical."

"He needed to go to London, and Rochford was driving there. He took advantage of an opportunity."

"Of course."

Marianne did not say that such an impulsive action wasn't like the Nathaniel who was so well known. Who was prudent and straightforward and reliable. She didn't have to. Violet was well aware. And although she didn't for a moment believe that he was up to something disreputable, had he done this because he was angry with her? Was it a punishment?

Violet jerked her shawl closer about her shoulders. Why must people make a great to-do out of nothing?

Marianne stopped, and Violet looked up to find that they stood at the door of her lodgings. They must have passed right by Marianne's rented house. She hadn't been paying attention. She was about to thank her friend for her kindness in walking the extra distance, when Marianne said, "If anyone should ask, I was with you till eight o'clock."

"What? No."

"No one will ask."

"The servants will know that you were not—"

"No one is going to submit them to question," said Marianne impatiently.

"How do you…?"

"I helped you, as promised."

"That was a different case!" Violet cried.

"I've made up my mind." Marianne turned and walked quickly away.

Should she run after her? Violet nearly did, but then she saw all too clearly the argument in the open street. Impossible. And Marianne hadn't listened to her before. Then it was too late. She was gone.

Violet stood a bit longer, until an old man passing by asked if she was unwell. Her expression must reflect her worries all too clearly, she realized. With a polite denial, she went inside. Leaving her bonnet and shawl with Furness, she sat down in the parlor. Alone.

And contemplated what a pleasure this might have been just days ago. She had time to herself, and the ability to decide just how to spend it. There would be no one looking over her shoulder to criticize. How she would have reveled in this unprecedented freedom, if only…

Why had she meddled? She'd been happy. For the first time in her life, everything had been going splendidly. Why hadn't she simply settled down to enjoy it? But no. She'd had to poke and pry, and now all was ruined. Nathaniel had left her…

At that point, Violet's common sense took her sternly to task. He had not left her. He would be back tomorrow. And she would not sink into maudlin unreason. She'd always despised that sort of person. One made mistakes—even very large mistakes—and one found a way to make amends or leave them behind. And so she would. She *would*, she told herself fiercely.

Yet an insidious part of her mind insisted upon wondering if any of the older generation knew about her mother's misfortune. Had there been any whispered questions about her early birth, about her parentage? Rumors arose about the most ridiculous things. Look at the talk today about Nathaniel…which she was not going to rehearse yet again.

She'd never seen any sign of it, but then she'd never been looking, never imagined… And her grand—the dowager had kept her well away from gossips.

Was the Regent pursuing her because he thought she was like her mother?

Stupid, absurd. She would not have been married into a great ducal house if there had been such talk. Which was true, but far—very, very far—from comforting. If the Greshams learned the truth…

They wouldn't. Why should they? How could they? This was a secret that had been kept for years and years. All her life, in fact. It was not going to get out now. She needed to forget it, push it from her mind, and let her life return to its pleasant new routine.

She would, Violet vowed. She would do exactly that. As soon as Nathaniel came home to her.

Thirteen

THERE WAS NO SIGN OF NATHANIEL THE FOLLOWING day, and no word. Violet pretended to the servants that she hadn't expected any, while she wondered what she would do if he stayed away. But of course he was not going to do that. He was not the sort of man who would do that. She was being ridiculous.

Violet sat down in the parlor and gathered her faculties. All right, it was natural that she'd been shaken, after her mother's revelations. Perfectly understandable that she'd gotten…off balance. But that must end. Not least because one did not keep a perilous secret by moping about and acting quite unlike one's familiar self. People—Nathaniel—would ask what was wrong, and she would have no explanation.

Violet sat straighter on the sofa, as if her old deportment teacher from school had walked into the room. Nathaniel undoubtedly did have matters to occupy him in London. He had many responsibilities—which would often take him away from her. It wasn't as if they would spend every day of their marriage together. Far from it. Perhaps their disagreement caused him to think of his obligations as he wished to get away. She would mend matters there.

As for making the journey with Thomas Rochford… He'd ridden along with an acquaintance who was going up to town. No more than that.

She went to the ball that evening with friends and danced as if she hadn't a care in the world. When women from the tea party asked after Nathaniel, she said his business had taken a bit longer than he'd planned. If she gave the impression that he'd written, and met knowing looks with bland incomprehension, well, what else did the gossips deserve? They certainly didn't have her best interests at heart. But when another day dawned with no communication from her husband, she found that her chest was knotted with worry.

Then, in the afternoon, as she was once again sitting in the parlor alone, Violet heard Nathaniel calling her. His voice rang distinctly in the empty room. Was she was going mad with worry?

"Violet!"

This time she realized that the sound came from outside. But Nathaniel wouldn't shout her name in the street. That was quite improper.

"Violet!"

She rose and went to the open front window. There below her—but not nearly as far below as would be expected—was her husband. He held the reins of a shiny new high-perch phaeton. Its great wheels and tall springs brought his head almost to the level of the sill.

Seeing her, he grinned like a boy. "How do you like it?"

She didn't know what to say. It was one of the

sportiest carriages she'd ever seen—buffed and lacquered and glinting with embellishments.

"I bought it in London, along with the new team," Nathaniel added when she didn't speak. He waved one hand at the horses. "They're a pair of sweet goers. I drove here in under five hours, faster than the stage."

She'd never heard him speak so, or express such enthusiasm about a vehicle. "I didn't know you were thinking of buying—"

"I did it on a lark," he interrupted. "On the advice of an old friend."

"Thomas Rochford?" It came out accusing. She pressed her lips together.

Nathaniel nodded. His horses sidled and backed. He controlled them with easy competence.

"He is an old friend?" She couldn't stop herself.

"We were at Eton together." He didn't seem to be paying attention. His eyes were on the phaeton. "It's quite a beauty, isn't it?"

Violet looked from his beaming face to the carriage. She wasn't used to seeing Nathaniel drive this sort of vehicle. This phaeton was created for wild races and reckless bets, slipping through gates with inches to spare and feathered corners. Her young brothers exclaimed over and coveted equipages like this. Half brothers, offered an unwelcome inner voice.

"It can easily take four horses, but I only bought a team for now. Get your hat and come down. I'll take you for a spin."

"I'm not dressed for—"

"Just a few minutes. No need to fuss. Come, I can't keep the horses standing too long."

Their disagreement seemed forgotten, and this was reason enough for Violet to throw the proprieties of dress to the four winds. She rushed to her bedchamber and grabbed a bonnet at random. The August day was warm. She wouldn't need a wrap for a brief spin. A nagging preceptor in her mind insisted that she should don a carriage dress and a proper hat with a veil. She dismissed it and tied the strings of her bonnet as she hurried out. She did pull on gloves as she went down the stairs.

Nathaniel was walking the pair of glossy chestnuts. He turned them neatly in a wider space down the street and came tooling back to her, stopping precisely at the doorway.

Violet looked up. The phaeton's back wheel was nearly as high as her head. Its seat was higher still, seeming to float in the air. Nathaniel smiled down at her from that summit, and her heart skipped a beat at the welcome in his face.

The step at the front of the carriage was above her knee. How did a lady climb up without showing her stocking to the whole street? Nathaniel held out a hand, easily managing the reins with the other. Violet grasped his warm fingers, lifted her skirts, and stepped up. He pulled her smoothly onward and into the seat beside him. A breathless laugh escaped her. Then he gave the team its head, and they moved off.

As the phaeton picked up speed, the ground seemed very far away, racing by at an alarming rate. Violet held on to the seat below her with both hands. She'd never ridden in a carriage like this. Along with wild races, it was ideal for a tête-à-tête, since there was no space for a groom to perch behind and overhear a young man's wooing. She'd never been allowed such an outing—not that any rakish young blades had ever asked. As far as she knew. "How did you get a new carriage so quickly?" she wondered. It took time to build even a small one.

"Some fellow ordered it and then couldn't pay," Nathaniel replied. "Or wouldn't. The coach maker was discreet, of course, but Rochford suspected it was Darrinforth. Said his trustees have applied the brake on his spending. How he knows such things…" He shook his head. "Whatever the case, there she was, just waiting for me."

"She?" They took a corner at a speed that made Violet squeak.

Nathaniel grinned at her as he patted the side of the phaeton. "No opportunity to add my own touches, of course. But I don't know what else I could have asked for."

"Shouldn't you use both hands?" Violet ventured as they sped past a row of shops. Her voice was a few tones higher than usual.

"Are you questioning my skill with the ribbons?"

"No, just… Look out!"

A cart was backing out of an opening between two buildings ahead. It seemed that the driver had found the alley too constricted to pass. Someone shouted at him, but he was oblivious. The gap between the back of the cart and the opposite pavement slowly, inexorably, shrank.

"Stop!" cried Violet.

Nathaniel ignored her. He checked the horses

only slightly, gauged speeds and distances, then neatly threaded the narrowing opening. His left rear wheel might have just kissed the back corner of the cart, but he didn't think so. "I'll have you know, I'm a notable whip," he said.

Violet put a hand to her chest, then quickly gripped the seat again as they knocked against a stone and the phaeton rocked on its springs. "I'm going to have a nervous spasm."

"Nonsense." Nathaniel didn't mention that his driving skills had been gained in more stable carriages. He'd made sure to take several trial drives with the coach maker's expert, and he was confident he could manage the phaeton. Indeed, he'd just demonstrated as much. But perhaps he'd cut it a bit close just then, showing off. An equipage like this was very likely to tip over if you cornered too fast; he knew of two men who'd been badly injured in such spills. He directed the horses toward the Marine Parade, a wider avenue, without turns.

"Or fall into a fit of the vapors," Violet said.

He gave her a sidelong glance and saw the teasing glint in her gray eyes. "I'm sure the town would find that most entertaining. Wait until we reach the largest group of saunterers."

She laughed. Nathaniel's heart lifted at the musical sound, and he laughed too. From the corner of his eye, he watched Violet begin to enjoy the rush of air across her cheeks, the rhythmic sway of their speeding perch. As he had, she was discovering the exhilaration of flying along in this marvel of a vehicle. At last, she released her death grip on the side of the seat, both hands free as she tightened the whipping strings of her bonnet.

They turned onto the broader avenue by the water, and he risked a bit more speed, rushing past the strollers enjoying a breath of sea air. Heads turned. Without doubt, tongues began to wag. And he didn't even care.

"Everyone is staring at the dashing Hightowers," Violet said. "You can see that some of them long to point at us, but they don't dare be so rude. Ah, there's Mrs. Elton from the charity tea." She waved with aggressive gaiety.

They swept along the seaside, bathing machines in the surf on their left, the town running along on their right. Rather like flying, Nathaniel thought. Or how he imagined that freedom from Earth's bonds would feel. Then Violet said, "Oh dear."

Her tone had changed radically. "What?"

"Mama," she replied dully. "Walking with…my grandmother. What a glare she gave me. I daresay she'll be at our lodgings when we return, to tell me that I am dressed quite improperly. And that my bonnet is wrong and my hair a windblown disgrace."

"Then we shan't go back," declared Nathaniel. He steered smartly past a curricle, giving the other driver a regal nod from his greater height above the road. "Not for hours yet. We'll head out the London road. Not too far, because the horses need a rest. But we'll find an inn and buy our dinner—"

"Like a pair of heedless gypsies," said Violet, imitating the dowager countess's censorious voice.

"Care for nobodies," Nathaniel agreed, smiling.

"I am shocked, profoundly shocked, at your ramshackle suggestion," she said in the same tones.

"So you refuse?" he asked, cocking his head.

"On the contrary." Violet made an expansive gesture. "Drive on, as fast as…as is…wise."

Nathaniel laughed again as he steered off the Marine Parade and headed for the north route out of Brighton.

"I didn't know you were interested in sporting vehicles," said Violet as he negotiated some of the narrower streets. "You never said."

Nathaniel hadn't known himself before his impulsive trip to London with Rochford. Riding along in his old acquaintance's phaeton, some combination of his mood and situation, and Rochford's daring style of driving, had sparked a wild desire. Without his company, it might have blazed up and died, Nathaniel admitted, but Rochford had fed the flame. And taken him straight to the coach maker, to discover the invigorating vehicle he now possessed.

He could have resisted. It was not a case of succumbing to another's urging. Nathaniel was perfectly clear on that. Rochford's languid enjoyment of his enthusiasm could not have been mistaken for influence. But he hadn't wanted to. The thrill of hurtling along so far above the road had gripped him. And then, the exhilaration of handling a high-perch phaeton himself dissipated the frustration that had been dogging him, like a stiff breeze breaking up a fog bank. It seemed to promise a more lighthearted, bracing reality.

"Nathaniel?" said Violet.

She'd asked him a question. "I'd never had a proper ride in an equipage like this," he replied. "Not over any distance." Recognizing the truth of it as he spoke, he wondered why? None of his close friends drove a high-perch phaeton, he realized. They'd turned to more practical conveyances as their familial responsibilities increased. But in the past...in his youth...hadn't there been opportunities? Did he have stodgy friends?

"I'd never been in one at all," Violet said. "It's... rather exciting."

He grinned at her as he spotted one of the largest coaching inns ahead. Pulling up, he turned into its yard. His team could do no more until they had a real rest.

A hostler came to the horses' heads. Nathaniel jumped down and handed over the reins, then turned to help Violet descend. On the long step from the phaeton's seat, she wavered. He put his hands on either side of her waist and lifted her down, breathing in the sweet scent she always wore. For a moment, they faced each other, very close. It would be so easy to bend and kiss her.

Another carriage clattered in. They drew apart.

It was a busy afternoon, with a steady stream of travelers, and the innkeeper had no private parlor available. He did have a dining area set aside for "genteel folk" however, so they weren't forced to sit in the taproom. When Nathaniel would have apologized for the bustle and noise, Violet said, "It's an adventure." Her expression was bright as she watched the servitors maneuvering loaded trays, the three children in the corner driving their mother to distraction, the man nearby shoveling food into his mouth as if he hadn't eaten in days.

Another woman might have complained, Nathaniel thought. Even his mother probably would have. The din was prodigious. Violet's grandmamma...it didn't bear thinking of. But Violet had such a…zest for new experiences. It gave the most mundane surroundings a kind of boost. "Are you hungry?"

She turned to him, eyes alight with interest. "Desperately. I've eaten nothing since…" She faltered for some reason, then recovered. "What shall we have?"

Nathaniel caught the attention of one of the hurrying servants and ascertained their choices. They settled on roast beef and potatoes with some late-season peas and a bit of apple pie to finish. Upon recommendation, he sampled a mug of the inn's own ale; Violet settled on a glass of red wine. Nathaniel suspected it would not be the finest vintage, but he didn't think she would care.

The crowded room made serious conversation impossible. But Nathaniel found that he didn't mind this in the least. With the small size of their lodgings, they were always in each other's pockets. He sometimes missed the sort of large house he was used to, with plenty of private space. And just lately… But why think of that? The…misunderstanding seemed to have passed off. He sat back, sipped his ale, and enjoyed Violet's fascination with the surrounding scene.

They drove back in the evening, timing it to arrive at the livery stable Nathaniel patronized just before darkness fell. No one was likely to be lurking in their lodgings at this hour. They walked the short distance home arm in arm, and entered the place more in harmony with each other than they'd been in days.

As soon as he walked into the parlor, Nathaniel noticed the pile of letters on the table by the window.

He could recognize Sebastian's and Robert's hand-writing from across the room, and others were hidden beneath these visible missives. The envelopes called to him to be opened. They'd already been sitting for…a day? Longer? It was his invariable habit to read his family's communications immediately, to respond to the questions and commissions inside.

"You have letters," Violet said, following his gaze. Which was a foolish remark; obviously, he saw them. With a sinking heart, she waited for him to go to the desk and bury himself in whatever messages they contained. He would…not forget her existence. That wasn't fair. But he would become too distracted by the doings of his family to pay her much heed. And so their pleasant time together was ended.

But he turned away from the desk, put his hat and driving gloves on a table. "I'll look at them later."

For a moment she didn't take it in. She could see that the letters pulled at his attention. "You aren't going to read them?"

"Tomorrow is time enough."

She saw that he meant it, and was filled with ela-tion. Of course, she didn't want Nathaniel to neglect his family duties. But just this once to be put first! Before he could change his mind, or recall the awk-wardness that had plagued them recently, Violet went over and threw her arms around his neck. "Thank you for the adventure," she said, and kissed him.

He caught her in his arms and pulled her tight against him, taking the kiss and deepening it to dizzy-ing intensity. "To many more," he murmured when they at last drew apart.

"I want to ride in your phaeton every day," she declared, breathless. "It was wonderful."

"You may ride whenever you like, for as long as you like," he replied.

The heat in his voice, his look, gave the words heady layers of meaning. Violet felt as if she'd been suddenly dipped in sweet flame. "May I?" she whispered close to his ear.

Still holding her close, Nathaniel began to move toward the bedchambers. Violet held on, her cheek on his shoulder, half walking backward, half-letting him bear her along. Their legs interlaced and parted—again, again—fabric shifting and rustling with tantalizing effect.

A single shielded candle burned in her room. Nathaniel released her to kindle more. Violet admired the grace of his broad-shouldered figure as golden light grew. She was trembling with yearning, a need that was almost painful. Finding the strings of her bonnet tangled and knotted, she fumbled with them.

Nathaniel turned to look at her. His blue eyes burned, the way they did when he was aroused. Violet could feel them on her, like feather brushes of fire. She ripped the ties off her hat and tossed it aside. "Whoever is naked first wins," she declared.

Nathaniel's smile flashed in the soft illumination. "Wins what?" he asked, voice rough with desire.

Violet slipped out of her shoes and began unbuttoning her gown. "Whatever she wants."

"She?" He sat on the bed, but he appeared to pay more attention to the slither of her dress to the floor than to pulling off his boots.

"Well, I am not sure *he* is trying very hard," Violet said.

"Oh, he is…hard." Nathaniel stood and shrugged out of his greatcoat.

Violet could see what he meant. A feverish hunger drove her; any lingering shyness shriveled to ash before it. She had to be rid of her clothes. She stepped out of her petticoat and pushed her stockings down, kicking them off. Her breath came faster. "Are you letting me win?" she asked as he dropped his shirt beside them.

"I don't think there will be any losers here tonight."

She laughed, turning. "Will you untie my stays? I cannot reach…"

"You wish me to help you win the wager?" he queried, even as he did as she asked.

"I do what I must to have you at my mercy." The stays dropped.

"A prospect that fills me with…"

Violet skimmed out of her shift.

"…anticipation." Nathaniel shed his pantaloons.

They stood revealed to each other, skin washed with candlelight, flushed with desire. Violet's pulse pounded at the glorious sight of him. She wondered if she would be able to speak. She had to clear her throat. "Lie on the bed."

Smiling, he obeyed, reclining on his back, arms crossed beneath his head.

Violet took a step, another. Inches from the bed, she put her hands on his calves and moved them slowly upward. The hitch in his breath delighted her, as did his murmur of disappointment when she let her palms slide to the coverlet on either side of his hips.

She climbed onto the bed and set a knee on each

side of his. When he reached for her, she said, "You mustn't move."

His hands stopped inches from her thighs. "Am I not to...touch you?"

She was already so aroused she could scarcely bear it. Holding his hot blue gaze, Violet slowly shook her head. He drew his hands away. Bending a little forward, she let her fingers roam over his chest and strong upper arms, the ridged muscle of his torso. When he groaned out her name, she could wait no longer. She scooted a little forward and took him inside her.

The pleasure of it made her back arch. Her breath escaped in a long sigh. And then she moved—just as she wished to, just as felt most glorious.

Nathaniel ran his hands up her ribs and cupped her breasts, teasing and caressing. But she'd forgotten her orders by this time. She was lost in sensation, in the power of evoking the pleasure she saw in his face.

It rose at her command, as she moved. And rose. Rose. She never wanted it to end, and she was desperate to reach that exquisite peak. And then she was there, shattering. She rode the waves of it while Nathaniel cried out his own release.

Panting, Violet collapsed onto her husband's chest. He wrapped her in his arms. Their hearts pounded together—a frantic drumbeat, gradually slowing with the calming of their breath.

Violet started to pull away, but Nathaniel held on. He kissed her neck, her shoulder. She raised her head and offered her lips, which he gladly took.

Their kisses were soft and tender, the sweet aftermath of desire. They were so beautiful that tears thickened Violet's throat—inexplicable until she realized that she had come to love her husband most desperately, and all she wanted from the world was for him to love her as well. Drugged with pleasure, she almost said so. And then the events of the last few days came crashing back over her. If he ever found out that she was a fraud...

"What?" said Nathaniel.

Unconsciously, she'd stiffened, Violet realized. She relaxed, but slipped over to lie beside him, safe in the circle of his arm.

Once again, she told herself that there was no reason for a secret kept so long to come out. She needed to fix this truth in her mind, to believe it. She would drop the whole matter. She must forget that she'd ever heard the truth. "Nothing," she murmured.

Nathaniel's breathing had slowed. No doubt tired from his long drive, he'd fallen asleep.

Violet watched his chest gently rise and fall. Fierce determination filled her. She had made mistakes. She might face difficulties she'd brought on herself. But nothing, no one, would take this away from her. No matter what she had to do.

Fourteen

BRIMMING WITH A SENSE OF WELL-BEING, NATHANIEL read his letters over breakfast. They held no surprises, being the usual combination of little news and many requests. He felt the pull to begin a list, consider how he might fulfill his brothers' appeals, but he resisted it. He wasn't going to run about on their errands—not today, or tomorrow—not while he could spend the time as he had yesterday. Having fun.

And really, his brothers expected a great deal. Some of their pleas he meant to refuse outright, or turn off with a joke. For example, Randolph's admonition that the churchman he'd found was not the sort of bishop he was looking for at all. Nathaniel meant to ask him if there were ways to tell one bishop from another. Did they have markings, like waterfowl? And then he would let his brother know that he intended to leave such identification to an expert—that is, Randolph himself.

At least his admiral seemed to have turned the trick; James even thanked him. Clearly, in James's years away at sea, he'd forgotten that his eldest brother was designed to be at his service and did not require polite acknowledgments. Nathaniel chuckled at his own silent jest. "James says that the young ladies Ariel is presenting to him as attractive matches are 'colorless,'" he said to Violet.

"What does that mean?"

"I have no idea. He told her he was ready to wed a wellborn English girl. And I'm certain Ariel chose charming candidates."

"Wellborn," she repeated, her tone a bit odd. "That's all he asked for?"

"Oh, I'm certain he wants beauty and a sunny temper and a tidy fortune as well." Nathaniel smiled to show he was joking.

Her laugh sounded half-hearted.

"Ariel will see that he shows proper respect," he assured her. "She is quite the stern matchmaker."

"She helped Sebastian with Lady Georgina Stane," Violet said. "She comes from a…a fine old family."

"A somewhat eccentric one, if his letters are any indication," Nathaniel replied. Rising, he stored the envelopes in a cubbyhole of the writing desk. "But very ancient, yes." When he returned to his cup of coffee, he was puzzled by Violet's expression. He put a hand over hers on the table. "Are you well?"

"Perfectly well." She sat a bit straighter and smiled.

He squeezed her fingers. "You certainly look well—delectable, in fact."

Her smile warmed, and her eyes lit with soft reminders of last night.

The physical side of marriage had turned out so remarkably well for them, Nathaniel thought. Tremendously, really. He was a lucky man. He must remember just how lucky when they disagreed. Why had he thought he needed to hear every detail of her conversation with her mother? It was her business, her family. He certainly had private communications with his own, things his brothers did not wish shared, even with a wife. Perhaps Lady Moreley's confidences had been embarrassing, or troublesome. But whatever the case, he had no need to hear them. Violet's grandmother had much to answer for—and was irrelevant to their future life. He would never mention the matter again, proving that he was not an interfering sort.

A smile crossed his face. Her mother—all the Deveres in England—had nothing to do with the connection between them, as last night had so vividly demonstrated. Females were a marvelous mystery, but he knew when a woman was truly transported, and last night…Violet had been. How he looked forward to going on more adventures together.

Her hand stirred under his.

"You…you aren't going to answer your letters? You always do so right away."

"I am not. They contain nothing pressing." He thought of repeating the joke about bishops. But why talk of his brothers at all? "Rochford invited me to see a race this morning. All high-perch phaetons, a winding course with tight turns, and some of the finest whipsters in the Four Horse Club."

"Rochford," Violet said. "You are…renewing your old acquaintance with him?"

"I'm riding along with him. I would invite you to come, but it is to be all men."

"Not driving your new equipage then?"

"No. But I assure you, you will have many other opportunities to…ride."

The gaze they exchanged then seemed to heat the air between them. Violet turned her hand over and interlaced her fingers with his. "Good," she said.

A brisk knock on the parlor heralded the entry of Furness. "I do not mean to disturb you, my lady…"

These days, any exchange with her lady's maid that began with those words meant precisely the opposite, Violet thought. "Yes, Furness?"

"Mr. Cates has stolen my set of curling irons," she complained.

Violet saw Nathaniel glance at the mantel clock, obviously plotting escape. As who wouldn't upon hearing such a ridiculous accusation? And indeed, he said, "I must leave this in your capable hands."

"Must you?"

He gave her the smile that melted more than her heart. "You are so much better with such matters than I. Designed by birth and training to rule the household."

Wherever the conversation turned, it seemed to come down to lineage, Violet thought despairingly. "I'll do my duty, then," she answered with a valiant attempt at lightness.

Nathaniel offered her a small, ironic bow and departed.

Violet turned to her irate attendant. "What would Cates want with curling irons?" she asked. "He has no use for them."

"Only to spite me, my lady, and make it seem I can't do my job properly. Like he hid the key to your jewel box, so I'd have to hunt high and low through the place. As if I'd ever put it in with your stockings! Plaguing me. That's all he thinks of, day and night."

Violet hid a sigh. "Well, let us go and see."

Cates naturally denied all knowledge of the curling irons. Contempt for Furness dripped from his voice when he suggested, "No doubt she put them down someplace and forgot, my lady. She's that flighty and scatterbrained."

"I did not!" snapped Furness. "I left them by the hearth to cool. I remember perfectly well. I'm not an old man with a failing memory."

Cates sputtered with outrage. He was, Violet knew, not yet five and thirty, despite his staidly correct demeanor. Only nine years older than Furness.

But despite a thorough search, joined by the landlady's servants, the curling irons could not be found.

Violet sent Furness out to purchase new ones. Once the dresser was out of the way, she tried to smooth Cates's ruffled feathers. But despite his polite expression, she could tell that he wasn't mollified. "That young lady exists to sow discord and make herself important," he said when she'd finished. His bow as he left her was stiff.

Something had to be done about the continual friction between these two, Violet thought. When Furness had first come, it had seemed all right. But now they seized upon any excuse to fling accusations at each other. She didn't understand what had gone wrong. She was going to have to figure it out though. This couldn't go on.

An odiously familiar voice boomed up the front stairs. "There is no need to tell her I'm here, my girl. I'm...family."

Violet sprang up to flee, perhaps hide herself in the bedroom wardrobe, but the dowager countess came stalking in before she'd taken more than two steps. The old woman marched over to the sofa and sat down in her customary pose, leaning forward, both hands folded over the top of her ebony cane. Her eyes pinned Violet as if she was a specimen butterfly. "Harriett told me about your bullying, of course," she said. "She's never been able to keep the least thing from me. Had no spine even when she was a reckless girl."

Violet felt as if her insides had frozen. A forlorn inner voice wailed, "Oh, Mama!"

"Did you imagine the servants wouldn't notice you'd gone out together?" The dowager's voice was contemptuous. "Renshaw let me know of it at once."

"Still doing her old job then," Violet said bitterly. "Spying on me."

Her visitor looked her up and down. "That gown is entirely too low cut."

"You have nothing to say about what I wear. Any longer."

"Indeed."

It didn't sound like agreement. Violet waited uneasily for more, but the woman she'd known all her life as her grandmother merely stared at her. Finally she could bear it no longer. "Why must you be this way?"

The dowager's thin brows rose.

"So cold and…unfeeling."

"I don't know what you mean, my girl."

It was the same thing she'd called the servant, Violet noticed. She started to object to the way the old woman treated her, then changed her mind. "Why do you persecute Mama so?"

"Persecute? I saved her life. We took her in after she had ruined herself over a worthless foreigner. Even when we discovered her…condition, I did not repudiate her."

"You wanted her fortune," accused Violet.

But her attempt to embarrass the dowager failed. "Of course we did. It was all anyone ever wanted from Harriett."

"Cruel!"

"Perhaps," the old woman admitted. "But cruelly true. Would you rather we had ended the engagement? George wished to."

"Papa…" But he wasn't. "He did?"

"He's a man. He didn't like losing out to a…rival. But if we had, Harriett's parents would have disowned her, you know. And the money would have gone to some charity or other. It wouldn't have done anyone any good."

"You made him marry her?" Violet hadn't seen many signs of affection between her parents, but she'd never imagined it was as bad as this.

"Of course I did. I forced him to see—at last—that an earldom doesn't survive without some sacrifices. I must say it was more difficult than I'd expected to finally get him into her bed to get an heir." She gave Violet a beady-eyed look, perhaps hoping she was embarrassed by this intimate information.

She was. And distressed by the history of anger and humiliation it revealed. So this was why her two brothers were so much younger.

"Unlike Harriett, he had spirit," the old woman went on, obviously relishing her discomfort. "If no brains. He's just like his father in that. Any mental acuity your half brothers possess comes from my side of the family. Fortunately, it was ample."

Violet was engulfed by a sadness so deep she could scarcely speak. The impatience and distance, even heartlessness, she'd explained away as reticence or tradition were revealed as simple truth. The people she'd been taught to call Father and Grandmother were not only unrelated to her, which would have been troublesome enough. They would have been happy had she never existed.

"So, now it is time for all this nonsense to stop," declared the dowager.

For a moment, Violet thought she meant her girlhood illusions.

"I will not see the work of nearly thirty years wasted," the old woman continued. "You will not be allowed to run wild and create a scandal."

"I have no—"

"Like your friend Lady Granchester." She sniffed. "I never cared for that girl. Far too flighty."

Violet stiffened. As a child, she'd seen her grandmother as omniscient. No deviation from the rules escaped her eye. But she'd dismissed that belief as fantasy some time ago. "What about Marianne? I don't understand you."

The dowager's lips turned down even farther. "If you wish the world to see you as virtuous, you should choose better friends. Lady Granchester is indiscreet, though she seems to imagine otherwise. Her husband will not tolerate it, you know. She is a fool if she thinks so. He will crush her." She shook her head. "Rakes can be so very scrupulous about their wives. I suppose they have more reason than most to suspect their fellow man."

"She is not—"

"Please." The dowager waved her to silence. "Lady Granchester has been *seen*—more than once—in a clearly compromising position. And you've shown your true colors by condoning her lechery."

Violet wanted to protest the word, to argue that her participation had been accidental and unwilling. But she knew the dowager wouldn't believe her, even if she sacrificed Marianne in her own defense. Which she would not. Yet she couldn't help saying, "How do you even know—?"

"Servants chatter, Violet. Good God, you know that. You aren't *stupid*." The old woman flicked this off with a contemptuous gesture. "Or at least, I never thought so. But on top of everything, you begin a flirtation with the Regent."

"I did not—" But as usual, she was not given an opportunity to speak. She'd been judged and sentenced without recourse.

"So, this is how it will be. You will cease making a spectacle of yourself. You will wear proper clothing and behave properly as well."

"Properly," she echoed.

"As you were taught," the old woman replied.

"By you."

This earned her a glare.

"To make sure no one notices me," Violet added, her voice strengthening.

"A true lady does not attract undue notice."

"Or finds me interesting or compelling."

"You cannot afford to compel interest."

"I must be mousy and silent—"

"You always had a tendency to overdramatize, Violet. I put it down to your foreign ancestry. You will simply retire to the country and produce some heirs for Langford. That is your job, after all."

"And all I'm good for?"

The dowager looked pained.

"Perhaps a bit of gardening or charity work?" Violet added.

"Hightower's mother does have an abnormal interest in the indigent," the old woman agreed. "As if it weren't their own fault that they're poor."

"How their fault?" Violet wondered, momentarily diverted.

"Because it is God's plan, or they are lazy or shiftless or immoral. How would I know?"

"How indeed?"

The dowager's cane rapped sharply on the floor. "Do not attempt impertinence with me, girl! You are in no position to do so."

"You don't care about me at all, do you?" Violet said, the full reality of it finally hitting her. Even when she was most frustrated or angry, she'd assumed that her grandmother acted out of concern for her, even affection, of a sort. She'd taken the bonds of family for granted.

The old woman sighed.

"You see me…always saw me as a…a cuckoo in the nest. An intruder."

"Must you enact a Cheltenham tragedy over the matter?" was the exasperated reply.

"But after all these years, all my life, how can you still regard me as a stranger?"

"How else should I regard you?"

"I was an innocent baby put in your care!" Violet heard the hurt in her tone and wished it away, but she couldn't help it.

"You were not born in innocence," said the dowager, unmoved. "You had bad blood from your father's side and inherent weakness from your mother. It was my duty to make certain that this heritage did not infect the Devere line."

"Infect?" Violet's rising anger helped dispel the hurt. "I am amazed you allowed me to marry into a duke's family in that case. What of my bad blood in the Langford strain?"

The dowager shrugged. "I did my best to discourage the match, but…"

"What?"

"Hightower would not be put off. He is quite a determined young man."

"That's why you were so rude to him?" Violet had never understood why a member of her family would risk offending Nathaniel during their courtship.

"I am never rude." The old woman glared. "I was trying to do him a service. But he would not be moved. In the end I decided that my course of training had prevailed over your innate weaknesses. Apparently, I was mistaken. If you retire from society, however—"

"I haven't the slightest intention of doing so,"

interrupted Violet coldly. She rose, annoyed to find she was trembling. "I believe this conversation is finished."

The older woman didn't move. "If you do not, I will have no choice but to act."

"Act?" For one bewildered moment, Violet envisioned the bent old woman on the stage.

The dowager nodded. "I shall be forced to"—she paused, as if running various ideas through her mind—"to tell your husband the whole, and instruct him to control you."

Violet's knees gave way. She half fell back into the chair. "You…you wouldn't."

The dowager nodded as if pleased with her reaction. "Why would you think me incapable? I always do what needs to be done."

"The scandal…"

"Oh, there will be no scandal. Hightower is a sensible young man—despite that ridiculous carriage he has bought. He won't wish to embarrass his family. He will want it hushed up, and I'm sure he will be only too eager to see that you conduct yourself with decorum."

Violet had heard of people dying from fear, and always thought the idea ridiculous. But now her heart pounded so hard she feared it would burst. There was such a roaring in her ears that she could scarcely hear. Her hands shook as she imagined Nathaniel hearing the story of her birth from the dowager. She would put everyone involved in the worst possible light. She might even make it appear that Violet had purposefully deceived him by hiding her true ancestry. She clenched her fists to stop the trembling.

Nathaniel knew her grandmother. He wouldn't

credit all her venom. Would he? Violet remembered the way he always spoke of her as the perfect duchess. Though he made no great fuss over it, he was proud of his family name, its long history. He'd married her because she was the daughter of an equally illustrious line. Partly, mostly. She couldn't think.

"I see that you understand me," the dowager said, her tone and expression smug. Pressing down on her cane with both hands, she stood. "I expect to see the results without delay."

Violet couldn't find words, but that seemed to gratify rather than annoy her visitor. "Well, get up and see me out, girl," she said.

Driven by a lifetime's engrained reflexes, Violet obeyed, despite the old woman's infuriating, triumphant smile. She wanted her gone more than she wanted to argue. Indeed, at this moment, she didn't have the faculties to object. She only wanted to be alone and regain her composure.

She managed the solitude, but her other goal was more elusive. Violet sat, shaking, struggling with the understanding that there was little in her history that she could call love. Her mother had been, remained, too weak to stand up for her. Her—the man she'd called her father had been furious at her intrusion into his life. Her putative grandmother saw her as an alien and a threat. Her young brothers…well, they cared for her, she supposed. Separated by ten years and more, they had little experience in common. She had no real family. The one she'd grown up in was an illusion. She had no one.

Except Nathaniel. Violet shivered with joy and

terror as the days and nights of their marriage lit her memory. Those confidences and delights were real. Her husband hadn't been dissembling while he concealed a whole different story. He cared for her; she knew he did. And she…she'd fallen in love with him. In just a few short weeks, he'd gone from being a pleasant companion and suitable partner to becoming vital to her life and happiness.

Could the dowager take him away from her with this poisonous story? Violet felt as if she'd kill the old woman first. Only…she couldn't really do that. How was she to stop her?

Violet rested her head on the chair back, trying to slow her pulse with deep breaths. She could obey the dowager's orders, as she had all her life. She could return to her drab dresses and banal manner. Her heart sank as she contemplated a life with no more pretty gowns, no adventures. But she would have her marriage. And she liked the country. They'd been destined to settle there eventually. Perhaps it would be all right. Nathaniel would wonder at the change, but…

The trouble was, Violet didn't believe the dowager would be satisfied with that, whatever she'd said. She knew her too well. When the old woman had the upper hand, she couldn't resist using it. There would be further demands, perhaps harsher ones. And some of them might…would involve those heirs that it was her duty to "produce." She would want to influence them, override Violet's authority. The idea made her shudder. And how would she explain to Nathaniel when she complied? They had agreed that her… grandmother was unreasonable.

No, giving in wouldn't work. Even if she could really manage it.

Violet pounded her fist on the arm of the chair. She wanted to shriek. She wanted to run. She wanted to erase the last two days from her life. She'd waited so long for freedom, and now she wondered if any such thing existed. And if it did, did it mean that she had to be completely alone?

Fifteen

It was nearly dinnertime before Nathaniel made it back from the race. The course had run quite a distance, and it had turned out to be fascinating to watch each driver negotiate its twists and turns. Indeed, even the fellow who came last had demonstrated a few tricks that Nathaniel hadn't seen before. He'd found it far more exciting than a horse race. There had been one spill, resulting in a broken arm, and another near overturning, which he decided he wouldn't mention to Violet.

And then afterward, a group had gathered at a roadside inn to review the race over pints of ale. Nathaniel had been inducted into the comradeship of those deep into the arcana of driving a four-in-hand. Men more familiar with the sport had noticed nuances that he'd missed, had suggestions that intrigued. He'd enjoyed their expertise and enthusiasm, and gradually come to see that there was an art to driving that was almost mathematical.

And on the way back, Rochford had allowed him to take the reins of his phaeton, a mark of confidence that Nathaniel appreciated. For some reason, he'd never driven a four-horse team before, and he'd found it a thrill to tool along, right on the edge of his skills, using his physical strength to handle the horses, his judgment to gauge the tolerances, and his fortitude to "thread the needle" of two narrow gates. It had set his heart thumping.

"I've determined to try a race myself as soon as I'm more accustomed to the phaeton," he told Violet as they sat together in the parlor after their meal.

"It isn't dangerous?" she said.

"Not if you know what you're doing." And he did; he would. Several men who'd seen him drive said he showed a natural talent for racing. And there was another thing. Nathaniel had been struck by Rochford's response when an observer wondered about the purpose of the race. Why should gentlemen risk their expensive vehicles and their persons in such a way, he'd asked. Rochford had replied, with that amused languid air he always had, that there was no reason on Earth. Nathaniel had rather liked the idea of doing a useless thing, though the challenge of the sport wasn't quite that. "I shall make sure I'm well prepared," he added. "It's often more a matter of tactics than speed."

As he told her more about the race, it gradually struck Nathaniel that Violet wasn't listening, which was unusual. But then, racing was not a matter of great interest to ladies. "I don't mean to bore you with all the details," he said, expecting a polite denial.

"Do you think," she said in an abstracted voice, "that we should go home now? We have had a fine holiday. Perhaps it is time to take up our duties and... begin life in earnest."

"I thought you were enjoying Brighton," replied Nathaniel, surprised. Her tone was odd. He couldn't quite put his finger on how. Perhaps as if she was testing out an abstract hypothesis?

"Yes, of course. But...I suppose there is a great deal to do back at Langford."

He felt a brief spark of resentment. But surely she hadn't meant to echo one of his nagging inner voices. "The estate is getting along quite well without me." Perhaps there were things he should be attending to. Well, there were. But none that couldn't wait a bit longer.

"I expect your father misses your help, though."

The resentment flared. He couldn't believe she would twit him where he was most vulnerable, particularly when the visit to Brighton had been all her idea. "I thought you wanted to 'have fun.'" Why should she change her tune now, when he'd just discovered a new pleasure?

"Yes."

This one word sounded so forlorn that Nathaniel was pulled up short. "Is something wrong?"

Violet hesitated just too long before saying, "No."

He examined her face. This morning she'd been obviously happy; now, she was abstracted and... Pensive? Melancholy? "It seems to me that there is." He reached over and took her hand. "Are you angry that I left you alone all day?"

"Of course not."

She sounded sincere. But was that a glint of tears in her eyes? "What then?"

"Nothing," she insisted.

Nathaniel had witnessed countless evasions and confessions from five younger brothers. He could recognize an untruth when he heard one. "Have I not earned your trust?" he asked.

"That and more," she exclaimed, her voice vibrating with emotion.

Nathaniel waited. "And so?" he said finally, when she didn't speak.

"Gr… Grandmamma came by."

He nearly cursed aloud. "I wish she would leave Brighton. Surely it is clear to her by now that we don't want her and won't listen to her. I suppose I must go over there and tell her so."

"No!"

The volume and vehemence of her refusal startled him. "You mustn't let her upset you, Violet. I won't allow her to. She must be told—"

"It wasn't her. I'm not… I wasn't…"

Again, he waited. He'd found silence very effective in extracting information from his brothers.

"I am very worried about Marianne," she blurted out.

Nathaniel frowned. "Your friend Lady Granchester?"

"Yes."

"What's amiss with her?"

"She is…she means to… I'm afraid she is about to get into terrible trouble."

"What sort of trouble?" It must be serious, he thought. She seemed so distressed.

"I shouldn't say… I swore not to tell." Her hands twisted in her lap.

Nathaniel suppressed a sigh. "You promised to

keep her secrets," he said, "but now you are afraid that was a mistake. You would like to ask for help. But honor forbids." How often had he heard a tale like this from one of his brothers?

She looked amazed. "Y-yes."

He nodded and said what he customarily did in such situations. "You must make your own decision, of course. Keeping your word is important. But there may be other considerations. You could seek Lady Granchester's permission to ask for help. Be assured that I will support you, whatever you decide."

Violet burst into tears.

This unprecedented response to his set speech threw Nathaniel for a moment. He'd never had a brother do that! Fortunately, in this case, he could take her into his arms and comfort her. "It can't be as bad as all that," he said into her hair, gently stroking her back. "And Lady Granchester has her family to turn to, and other friends."

For some reason, this made her cry harder. Nathaniel hated the sound. What could her friend possibly have done to elicit such desolate weeping? He was ready to consign her and her difficulties to perdition for making Violet so unhappy. Lady Granchester hadn't even been one of Violet's set last season in London. He would have remembered her more clearly if she had. He didn't think they'd seen much of each other for several years. So was this fit of weeping really sensible, necessary? But he knew that such a question would not be well received. He had to content himself with holding her, murmuring vague reassurances.

Violet clung to her husband. She never wanted to

let go. She struggled to control her tears. He must be astonished at this excessive display over Marianne. Because she'd been a coward and sacrificed her friend to hide her own troubles. She was despicable. Perhaps she had inherited low tendencies from her rogue of a father. Stupid, ridiculous! Discovering her true parentage hadn't made her a different person.

Violet caught her breath on a sob and commanded herself to stop crying. At least she hadn't betrayed Marianne's confidences. Though the dowager had said that people knew. Nathaniel hadn't seemed to, however. She was dithering like a ninny. She had to stop weeping! With another deep breath and a heroic effort, she controlled her tears. Sniffing, she raised her head. "Oh dear, I've soaked the shoulder of your coat."

"My shirt too, I believe."

She couldn't yet appreciate his rallying tone. "And I'm sure I look a perfect fright." Violet was well aware that she was not one of those women who could cry beautifully. Her eyes grew red and puffy, while the rest of her face paled. Her nose ran.

"Perfect," he agreed with a smile. He offered her his handkerchief.

"I know men hate weeping women," Violet said as she made use of the square of linen.

"It depends on the woman," her husband replied.

She nearly started crying again. "You don't have to say that." She almost wished he wouldn't be kind just now. It made her feel even more venal.

"Would you rather I declare my coat utterly ruined? And bluster and swear that if you weep on my garments again I shall take to wearing a waterproof cloak indoors?"

A laugh escaped Violet. He'd actually managed to raise her spirits. Looking up at his handsome face, deep into concerned blue eyes, she was moved beyond measure. This match had been so much more than she'd dared hope. She had to find a way to hold onto this happiness. She *had to*! "No cloaks," she replied. She laced her arms around his neck, twining her fingers in the slight curl of hair at the nape. A feather of desire stirred in her at the touch, and Violet marveled at it. She'd been—was—so distressed, and still she wanted him.

It was odd. The physical aspects of her marriage had turned out to be the easier part. She hadn't foreseen that. She'd expected to suffer embarrassment, a period of awkwardness, perhaps mere acceptance in the end. But the difficulties had turned out to lie in other realms. The body had had its own plan and—with her husband's guidance to be sure—she had embraced pleasure like a parched creature given drink. Touch was a revelation, a delight.

It was also a guaranteed diversion from uncomfortable discussions, but she didn't think about that. She kissed him.

His response was all a wife could wish for. All a woman could wish for, Violet thought. Her worries receded with the caress of his lips, his hands on her. She could think of nothing else. She pressed closer, let his kisses sweep her away.

After a time, Nathaniel murmured into her hair, "We should go to the bedroom. I don't intend to be caught by that housemaid again."

Their landlady's maid had gasped with outrage when she found them twined together on the parlor sofa. Rather as they were now. "She finds us shockingly loose," Violet agreed.

"And I really should remove my wet garments," he added, indicating his sodden shoulder. "Don't you think?"

"Yes, indeed. We wouldn't want you to catch cold."

Arms about each other's waists, they moved to Violet's bedchamber. With hands now more practiced, and more tender, they undid buttons and slid cloth aside to expose eager flesh. Every caress, every gasp, intensified Violet's resolve. She wanted to be with him like this for years on end, through all the trials and joys of life. She wanted love to bloom and deepen between them. She wanted to hear him say that he loved her desperately. She would have this. The dowager would not take it from her. She would find a way.

"I'll go and see Marianne tomorrow," Violet muttered as she drifted off to sleep. She had to, in any case, to tell her what the dowager had said.

She hadn't realized that she'd spoken aloud until Nathaniel replied, "That seems wise."

Violet's heavy eyes opened, to find him up on one elbow gazing down at her. Her pulse accelerated at the warmth she saw in his face. "I wish I was wise," she blurted out. Then she might see a clear way forward.

"You are."

"How can you say…?"

"I have observed it. You are as astute and gracious and assured as a duchess already."

His smile seemed expectant. He was pleased with

his compliment and wanted appreciation. "Thank you," Violet managed. But how she wished he was not so prone to praise her in terms of titles and suitability.

❧

The next morning Violet went to call on Marianne as soon as it was decent to do so. She found her rising from the breakfast table and hurried her friend into her own front parlor to repeat the dowager's warnings. "She said that Granchester will crush you," she finished.

"He wouldn't bother. He doesn't care a whit for me," Marianne insisted.

"Perhaps you are mistak—"

"No, I am not, Violet. Didn't I tell you he said as much? Besides, how could he do any more than he has already?"

Violet didn't want to speculate about that. "I suppose he will not like it if people know of your affair."

"If he is humiliated, I'm glad!" cried Marianne.

From what Violet knew of Lord Granchester, this was a dangerous sentiment.

"Oh, I wish I could run away with Daniel. He keeps asking me." She seemed proud of this. "He swears over and over that he would do anything for me." For a moment, her expression softened. Then she bent her head again. "But of course I cannot leave my children." Marianne stiffened and turned to Violet with wide, angry eyes. "That is what Anthony would do. He would make sure I could never see them."

"He couldn't—"

"They belong to him," her friend interrupted. "We all do, under the law."

"But he would not care to deprive his children of their mother."

"Care?" Marianne laughed wildly. "The very word is foreign to him."

"But you told me that he treated his sons like little kings."

Marianne nodded. "He does not see a weak and pathetic mother as necessary to their happiness, however."

"I cannot believe—"

"No one does, or will! Even you, my friend, won't take my word. You think it can't be so bad. But you have no idea what he is capable of!"

Violet supposed that was true. And in any case, her friend did not want to hear argument. "If you were to break it off now…"

"Am I to have nothing?" Marianne cried. "No tenderness, no passion, for the rest of my life?"

Her friend's misery was so palpable that Violet was silenced. She couldn't argue propriety or risks in the face of such wretchedness.

Marianne gritted her teeth as if biting back tears. "How could you know anything about it? You were fortunate in your match. So much wiser than I! You have no need to hide and regret and"—she clenched her fists—"and despise!"

Her friend had no idea, Violet thought. And she didn't dare tell her what she had to hide. She couldn't risk anyone knowing.

"I imagine that your grandmother forbade you to help me?"

Violet shrugged. No answer was necessary.

Marianne examined her face and didn't seem to like what she saw there. "I thought you were finished living under her thumb," she said bitterly.

"I am. But…"

"You do not approve of my…actions. Despite everything I have told you."

Violet couldn't deny it. She also had to acknowledge the dowager's threats, though she was ashamed to admit that she feared them.

"It doesn't matter." Marianne rose, indicating that their visit was over. "I got along on my own before. I can do so again. I understand that I am alone."

"Marianne."

Her friend waited, gazing at her.

"I wish there was something I could…"

"Wishes." Marianne's tone was acid. "We all have wishes. But they so seldom actually come true. Or, if they do, we find that they were foolish beyond measure."

Sixteen

"You're going out with Rochford again?" Violet asked her husband two days later, watching him pull on his driving gloves.

"Yes, we're set to try a lane he knows with a particularly tricky gate." He smiled at her. "I am to learn what 'driving to an inch' really means."

"Must he always accompany you?" Violet couldn't forget the malice of the ladies at the charity tea. Not that she distrusted Nathaniel. It was Rochford she doubted, and his known penchant for mischief.

"Well, he is lending me his team, Violet. Which no man does lightly. It is a great mark of confidence. You can't blame him for wanting to make sure I can handle them." Nathaniel donned his high-crowned beaver hat. "And his advice is invaluable. How often can one get driving tips from a leading member of the Four Horse Club?"

Violet fidgeted with a figurine on the mantelpiece. She couldn't seem to sit still these days. Some part of her was always braced for doom, ready to fight it. "But wouldn't you prefer to drive your own horses?"

"Of course. But I have only pairs for carriage work. And you can't simply harness two pairs in line and expect them to work together without training. I haven't the time for that before the race, and I'm not certain yet whether I wish to buy a four-horse team." He paused in the doorway, a trace of impatience in his face, then came back. "Was there something you wanted me to do today?"

"No." She didn't want to keep him from a pastime he clearly enjoyed. She simply didn't trust Rochford's motives in this game. The man wasn't known for kindly impulses. Quite the opposite. "Perhaps Rochford expects to win a lot of money betting on you?"

Nathaniel laughed. "Training me up as a dark horse and springing me on the competition? He's hardly in need of money." He shook his head. "No, I think I am a project to demonstrate his mastery." When Violet cocked her head, he added, "To show the world that he can sculpt a mere tyro into a winner of races."

"Sculpt." She didn't like the idea of Nathaniel being shaped by Rochford. Her husband was so much the better man. "You don't mind that?"

He started to speak, shrugged a bit sheepishly, then said, "When we were at Eton together, Rochford was quite the figure, you know. I did well enough. I had plenty of friends and even won a few prizes, but he was the…the beau ideal of our school years. Superb at anything he tried. Positively idolized." He shrugged again. His eyes twinkled with self-mockery. "I suppose something of that lingers, even after all this time."

His words and manner called up a twelve-year-old Nathaniel, so clearly Violet could almost see him before her. A handsome boy, charming in his way, but perhaps a little serious for schoolboy tastes. Respected more than adored. Trusted, counted upon, but not elevated to the status of youthful hero. And secretly just a little envious of the careless, daring Rochford. The picture was so touching that she couldn't protest further, though she still wished his companion was anyone but Rochford. "Go and tool through your narrow gate," she said. "Mind you don't scrape the paint on your shiny new carriage."

He grinned like a boy indeed. With a small salute, he went out.

At least his preoccupation with this race kept him away from the dowager, Violet thought. The old woman wouldn't go near the jostle and raillery of the crowd of men preparing for the event. She would expect to see Violet obeying her commands, however. How long would she give her before carrying out her threats?

"I forgot to inquire about your friend Lady Granchester."

Violet jumped like a startled hare. Nathaniel had reappeared in the doorway. "Inquire?" she said in a high voice. Had he heard something about Marianne?

"You were going to ask if you might share the nature of her difficulties."

Violet was touched that he'd remembered, when she'd forgotten that part of it herself. Eager to go, he'd bothered to come back and inquire. Was there any other man so generous? She felt like a worm for having misled him. "She…she did not wish to, no." Which was perfectly true. "There are some troubles in her marriage…"

"Ah." Nathaniel took a step back. "Indeed. Well, then…"

Men didn't care to know such things. Violet had noticed it before. He was happy to be waved off to his driving and forget all about the Granchesters' marital woes. She didn't blame him.

Left alone, Violet couldn't settle. No book held her attention. Needlework was out of the question. Yet she was reluctant to go out and perhaps encounter the dowager in the streets of Brighton. Her hands closed into fists at the idea. She had never been so angry at anyone in her life, or felt so trapped.

Finally, she walked downstairs to tell their landlady that Nathaniel would not be in for dinner. Movement was more satisfying than ringing for the maid and giving her the message. It felt more like doing something. At the foot of the staircase, though, she heard a familiar voice from the parlor where Mrs. Jenkins customarily sat, a voice that had no place in this setting. "Oh, Mr. Cates always has to be sniping at someone," it said. "He's that sort of man. Takes real pleasure in it, he does. He tattles to his master, too. Points out every little lapse in the other servants. I suppose he thinks it makes him look superior. Which just shows you what a fool he is."

Violet stepped forward and looked through the open doorway. There, indeed, was Renshaw, sitting at the round table by the front window with the landlady and Furness. Her former maid wore black, as always, and perched in her chair as grim and angular as a crow at a feast. Violet marched into the room. "What are you doing here?"

Mrs. Jenkins started, and Furness quickly stood, but

Renshaw merely gave her an insolent stare. "Visiting with a friend," she said, nodding at Mrs. Jenkins.

"Who just happens to have let rooms to me?"

Renshaw shrugged. Furness took a step away from the table as if wishing to disassociate herself from the conversation.

"You have nothing to say about where I go," Renshaw added. "I take my orders from Lady Moreley. She is my mistress now."

"And always has been!" declared Violet. "You never had any loyalty to me."

"I'm loyal to those as deserve it," her former maid said, obviously relishing the opportunity to be impudent.

"And does Cates deserve the things you said about him just now?"

Renshaw frowned and looked away.

Here was the root of the strife between Furness and Cates, Violet realized. Renshaw had stirred up the trouble, out of sheer spite. "Get out," she said.

"I believe this room belongs to Mrs. Jenkins," Renshaw replied. "It's her right to say who sits here. I'm sure she can choose her own friends."

The landlady shifted uneasily. Clearly she was torn between agreeing with this statement and alienating a profitable lodger. Her expression showed acute discomfort with the conversation.

Violet didn't bother to argue. "Certainly she can," she said. "Furness, I need you." She turned and walked out, confident that her dresser would follow.

She did. In fact, she was right on her heels as Violet entered the upper parlor. "Find Cates and ask him to join us here," Violet commanded. When it looked as if Furness might speak, she added, "Now, please, Furness."

The maid went out. In the minutes she was gone, Violet marshaled her seething thoughts. Blame should stay squarely on the true culprit in this tangle. She must set aside her feelings about Renshaw and see to the harmony of her own household.

Furness and Cates appeared in the doorway. There was a subtle tussle over who would enter first. Then her husband's valet stepped back and waved Furness in, as if giving her permission. Furness bridled at the implication. For a moment, they stood there, frozen by issues of precedence. Finally, Furness raised her chin and sailed through.

Cates followed. He gave Violet a sketch of a bow. "You wished to see me, my lady?" He acted as if Furness was not there.

"To talk to you both," she answered. "Because I have just discovered something of importance to all of us."

This got their attention. The sidelong glares ceased.

"We have spoken before about various…incidents that have caused friction between you. And found no satisfactory explanation. I now believe that Miss Renshaw was behind them."

Both servants looked surprised.

"For example, I daresay she was here on the day the curling irons disappeared."

Furness frowned, thinking it over. "I'm not sure, my lady."

"She was," said Cates. "She was in the kitchen when I went down after the…altercation. I remember she said…" He broke off with a frown.

"What did she say, Cates?"

"That Miss Furness was scatterbrained and… other things."

"I am no such th—!"

Violet held up a hand for silence. "So the… criticisms you have heard about Furness came chiefly from Renshaw," she said. When Cates slowly nodded, even more thoughtful, she went on, "And, Furness, I just now heard her telling you that Cates is a spiteful sneak."

The valet gasped with outrage as Furness nodded. Her face showed calculation now as well.

"It seems to me that the two of you got on well enough when Furness first joined the household," Violet went on. "Things did not really begin to go wrong until we'd been in Brighton for a while." She gave them a moment to consider this, then added, "After Renshaw had time to sow discord—malign each of you to the other."

Furness had begun to nod. "She did. That bit you heard wasn't the first time she bad-mouthed Mr. Cates. She made me think he was a right…" She trailed off, further understanding dawning in her face.

"She made several remarks to me about Miss Furness," Cates admitted. "Very disparaging of her work and skills. I took it that she knew her business."

"I'm sure that she took the curling irons," Violet said. "And spilled the laundry. And hid the key to my jewel case. She knew very well what it looks like."

"She's here visiting Mrs. Jenkins all the time," Furness said. "As if she had nothing else to do."

"I don't expect she does," said Violet.

Cates cleared his throat. "I suppose Miss Renshaw resents being let go, my lady."

"Undoubtedly. But she brought it on herself by spying on me for my grandmother." It wasn't really appropriate to mention this to the servants, but Violet was too angry to hold back.

"Spying?" asked Furness. She looked intrigued.

"Renshaw was hired to see that I dressed only as my grandmother dictated."

"I was aware that she…admired Lady Moreley," Cates said.

This was enough, Violet thought. There was no need to say more about her unfortunate family history. "So, I ask both of you to consider that the…difficulties between you were created by Renshaw. That they do not, in fact, exist."

There was a short silence. Violet waited. There was nothing more to say. They would either adjust to the truth or they wouldn't.

"Your new way of dressing my lady's hair was much admired," Cates said at last. "Quite a deft touch."

Furness stood straighter and preened a little. "Well, I only wish I could pack a trunk as neatly as you, Mr. Cates," she conceded.

They looked at each other. The accord of Violet's household hung in the balance. Then Furness dropped a small curtsy. Cates responded with a courteous bow. It was enough mutual apology for Violet. She let out a relieved breath. "I would…suggest that you avoid Renshaw from now on. And keep your…tools out of her reach. I cannot stop her visiting here, if Mrs. Jenkins wishes it, but…"

"I shan't be speaking to her again," declared Furness. "Unless to give her a piece of my mind, the spiteful creature."

"Better to ignore her," said Cates. "A cold greeting and nothing more. As if she was beneath our notice."

Furness nodded. "Don't give her the satisfaction. A good thought, Mr. Cates. Thank you."

"My pleasure."

Violet caught Cates's eye and almost thought she saw a twinkle. But it was gone before she could be sure. "Well...good. That's settled then."

"Yes, my lady," they said in unison. The concord surprised a smile from each. They left the room in an amity that Violet had despaired of ever seeing.

When the door closed behind them, Violet bared her teeth in triumph. She'd accomplished something, at least. She'd ended this small part of the dowager's game. Whether the old woman knew of Renshaw's machinations or not—most probably she did not—she was the cause of them.

Anger overwhelmed the glow of achievement. Other instances of interference and oppression came to mind, the legacy of a lifetime's deceit. And now the old woman loomed over her future like a storm cloud. It was insupportable. She had to think, to find a way to thwart her.

The afternoon passed into a restless evening without revealing an answer. As the hour grew late, Violet wondered what had become of Nathaniel. She had supposed he would be back by sunset. You couldn't hurl a carriage and four through narrow gates in the darkness. She was just beginning to worry when she heard the bell below, and then rushing footsteps on the stairs. She jumped up from the sofa, fearing an accident with the phaeton. But the figure who appeared in the doorway was not a messenger bearing bad news. Instead, Marianne stumbled into the parlor, pale as a ghost, her blue eyes wild. "Violet! Oh, Violet, you must help me!" she cried.

Shutting the door in the face of the curious housemaid, Violet took her friend's hands. They were icy. Her blond hair was disheveled. She led her over to the sofa and made her sit. "What is the matter? Are you hurt?"

"Not me. It's Anthony. He's been shot!"

"What?" Had she heard correctly?

Marianne began to moan. "Oh, God. Oh, God."

Violet squeezed her fingers. "Tell me what happened."

Her friend rocked back and forth on the cushions, moaning louder.

Violet gave her hands a little shake. "Marianne! How did Anthony come to be...?"

Marianne pulled her hands free and covered her face, bending over as if to curl into a ball. "What am I to do? Oh, God. Oh, God."

Violet went over to the sideboard and poured a small amount of brandy into a glass. She returned to put a hand on Marianne's shoulder and urge her upright. "Come. I cannot help you if I don't know what has occurred."

Her friend let her hands drop, but she remained bent over, staring at the carpet.

"Drink a bit of this," Violet urged, holding out the glass.

Marianne sat up, took it, and downed the liquor with startling speed. She coughed and sputtered, then sat panting as if she'd run a footrace.

Violet retrieved the glass before it could fall to the floor. "Now," she said. "Tell me."

Marianne struggled to control herself. After a while she was able to say, "Anthony was shot on the way home from a card party at the Regent's."

"Just now? Tonight?" Violet asked.

Her friend nodded. "I have only just... Oh, what am I going to?"

"He isn't dead!"

Marianne turned wild blue eyes on her. "No. No, only a ball through the shoulder. He...they...missed."

"But...how could this... Was it some sort of accident?"

Marianne buried her face in her hands once more. "Oh, God." She burst into choking sobs.

Violet put an arm around her, feeling both sympathetic and uncertain. Marianne's intense distress did not seem to gibe with her previous remarks about her husband. Yet perhaps the extreme circumstances explained it. She could only image how terrified she would be if Nathaniel was wounded. She held her friend until the storm of weeping subsided. When at last Marianne sat back on the sofa, exhausted, she handed her a handkerchief. "I'm sure he will recover if it is only..."

Marianne silenced her with a bleary-eyed stare. "You don't understand. It was Daniel."

"What was? Oh...oh no!"

"Daniel lay in wait behind a stack of barrels near a tavern and shot Anthony when he passed by."

She had said that Daniel would do anything for her, Violet remembered. "How do you know? Was he caught?" This would be a scandal like no other.

"No." Marianne's breath hitched on a sob. "He came to tell me. At our lodgings. Very proud of himself. The gentlemen who saw Anthony fall had only just carried him up to his bedchamber."

Imagining the scene, Violet was speechless.

Marianne nodded at her appalled expression. "I never wished him dead," she declared. "I swear I didn't!"

"Of course you did no—"

"I may have said some foolish things," her friend interrupted. "Well, I did, but I never meant for anything like this to happen. Or ask Daniel to…to do anything. I didn't, Violet!"

"Of course you did not."

"You believe me? Don't you?"

"Why should I doubt…?" Violet saw the fear in the other's eyes. "You haven't told me the whole, have you?"

Marianne clenched her fists. She closed her eyes briefly. "Daniel believes that he has proved his love for me by this…act, and that I must run away with him now. He is… I fear he has lost his mind."

"Where is he?" asked Violet sharply.

"I don't know." Marianne's voice shook. "I told him to go home, but I can't be sure he really heard me. He was… I think he's half-mad. Violet, what am I going to do?"

"You must break it off. Never see him again."

Marianne turned and reached out as if she might shake her. "You still don't understand! I told him that, and he swore that he would shoot me and him-self if I left him. I barely managed to get him away from the house."

Violet swallowed. This was far beyond anything she had ever experienced. "We…we must go to a magistrate."

Marianne grasped her arm with both hands, so tightly it hurt. "What do you imagine Daniel will say if he is taken into custody? He is convinced he did this thing for me." Violet pulled her arm free, and Marianne bent over again, as if she was in pain. "I only wanted a little pleasure, a bit of passion in my life. It didn't seem so much to ask. And this is how I am punished!"

This hit rather close to home for Violet.

"How could I have been such a fool? Whichever way I turn, I am ruined." She started to moan again.

"No one would believe that you asked him to…"

"Your grandmother said that people were talk-ing. How many will be delighted to credit such a juicy story?"

Violet was silenced. But her mind raced. In the stillness, the ticking of the mantel clock seemed loud. When she'd said nothing for several minutes, Marianne let out a long sigh. "I shouldn't have come here. This isn't your problem. You thought I was wrong all along. You warned me." She gave a humor-less laugh. "As my old nurse used to say, 'I have made my bed and now I must lie in it.' She must be turning in her grave to see her adage come so literally true." She rose. "I must go. The Regent is sending his own physician to tend Anthony."

"I want to help," Violet said.

Marianne smiled wearily down at her. "You are a good friend. Indeed, my best friend. Thank you for listening to my woes. But there is nothing you can do. I've made a complete hash of my life."

"Perhaps if I asked Nathaniel…"

"Asked him what?"

The words had come out of their own accord, simply because she'd never known anyone as trustworthy and capable as her husband. He was up to any challenge. But now that she'd said it, Violet was unsure. "Everyone in his family looks to him for help," she murmured.

"I don't think the Langfords have had difficulties like this."

And she did not wish to embroil him in this one, Violet realized. It was too much.

Marianne had caught a glimpse of herself in the mirror over the mantel. She adjusted her tilting bonnet. "If Hightower has any ideas, I would be happy to hear them. I'm so sorry I dragged you into this, Violet."

The dowager's words about Violet's choice of friends came roaring back to her. What would the old woman do if this terrible new development came out? She swallowed. "You're confident that Granchester will recover?" Murder couldn't be concealed, Violet thought. If it came to that, they'd have to expose Daniel Whalen, and wreck two families, or perhaps three.

"The doctor assured me that he would," Marianne said.

Violet's thoughts raced. "You must go home and sit with him."

"Hold his hand and play the ministering angel?" There was distaste in her friend's tone.

"Yes, Marianne. I think you owe it to Anthony. You did get him shot."

Marianne blinked. Finally, she nodded. "I really do not wish him to die, Violet."

"Then see that he doesn't. I will consult Nathaniel. And then we will make a plan."

Her friend looked dubious, but turned to go.

Violet realized it was nearly eleven o'clock. "Did you come alone? I'll get someone to escort you home."

What could be keeping Nathaniel? she wondered.

Seventeen

WHEN ROCHFORD HAD INSISTED ON A DRINK TO celebrate their successful afternoon, Nathaniel had never imagined that they'd end up at a brothel. He hadn't even known the place existed—several miles outside Brighton in a small manor house. The distance allowed visitors to be discreet, he supposed, but it made things damnably awkward for him. The hour was growing late, and he very much wanted to go home. He'd arrived behind Rochford's horses, however, and Rochford appeared to be well settled in, perhaps for the whole night. He'd brushed aside Nathaniel's objections as if he couldn't be serious. When their dispute had begun to attract the amused attention of the entire room, Nathaniel had given it up.

He couldn't walk back to town in the dark; he wasn't actually sure of the way. And this wasn't like London, where there were hackney cabs to be hailed at every corner. It was a ridiculous plight; he was well aware of that. But a real one, nonetheless.

One of the half-clad young ladies dropped into his lap and laced her arms about his neck. "Still all alone, lovey?" As he had done with several others, Nathaniel fended her off. She was pretty. All the females here were. The place was as luxurious as the most exclusive houses he'd seen in London, as a much younger man. One did, when first on the town, with rowdy groups of one's peers, released from the bonds of school and parental domiciles, eager to experience all life had to offer. But he'd never frequented brothels, even when he was green and stupid.

A dark-haired girl across the room threw her head back and laughed, long and loud. Nathaniel was suddenly reminded of the determined young opera dancer who'd appropriated him during his first season in London. She'd come up to him after a performance he'd attended and frankly offered herself. He was nineteen and hardly likely to refuse. It was weeks before he discovered that he was part of a careful plan to change her situation.

She didn't wish to be set up in a house or provided with a lavish wardrobe and a carriage. She wanted only gifts of money, or in a pinch, jewelry that could be sold. She liked him well enough, she said, but she intended to save up enough to leave England and begin again in a new country. In the end, he'd given her all she needed, and she'd set sail for America as a "respectable young lady." Her words. A single letter one year later informed him that she'd married a man of some wealth and become a pillar of their community in a place called "New Jersey." He'd wished her well. For her spirit as well as all she'd taught him about a woman's body.

Rochford returned from upstairs, his neckcloth rumpled and loose.

Thinking he'd gotten what he came for, Nathaniel went to speak to him again. "I should be getting back."

Rochford accepted a glass of brandy from one of the girls, pulling her to him and idly fondling an exposed breast. "It's early yet."

"I'm newly married," Nathaniel pointed out.

"Moreley's daughter must know what's what," was the careless reply.

It was true that the earl habitually kept a mistress, but Nathaniel didn't think Violet knew this. He hoped she did not. The girl across the room laughed again. She really did sound like Jean, he thought.

"You like the brunette? I can vouch for her... energy," Rochford said. He beckoned with the hand holding the glass.

"No," said Nathaniel. Fortunately, the girl had missed the signal.

"Come, come. Don't be prudish. Everyone knows men take their pleasures where they will."

It was true for many, perhaps most, Nathaniel acknowledged. Was he prudish? No, that wasn't it.

"And these girls are so much more fun than wives." Rochford gave the last word a contemptuous twist.

Nathaniel thought of Violet's determination to have fun. And her signal success. Rochford was definitely wrong there.

"He *can* smile," said the dark-haired girl. Rochford had managed to summon her to Nathaniel's side. She hung on his arm. "Come along upstairs, luv, and you'll be smiling like a loony for the rest of the night."

Nathaniel gently untangled her hands. "No, thank you." He turned away.

"Where the devil are you going?" asked Rochford.

He could hang about outside, Nathaniel thought. Someone driving back to town would give him a seat in their carriage.

"Hightower?"

"I'll see you on Thursday," he told Rochford with a wave. He didn't wish to offend him. The man could do what he liked. But he wasn't staying any longer.

❧

Violet asked Cates to accompany her to Rochford's lodgings, as the household kept no menservants. The valet argued that he should go alone to inquire, and she supposed he was right. Well, she knew he was. But she couldn't sit still waiting any longer. The events of the last few days had shaken her. Now, she couldn't stop imagining Nathaniel lying dead in a ditch next to his overturned phaeton. Though she knew someone would have brought word of an accident, she had to move, to find out for herself. She wanted to bring him home.

Cates carried a lantern and a stout cane as they walked the short distance through the dark streets. Brighton was not London. It was safe to go on foot. But Violet was very glad of the company nonetheless.

Cates used the cane to knock when they reached the house where Rochford was staying. For some minutes, there was no response. If Violet hadn't been so worried, she would have slipped away in embarrassment, for clearly the residents had gone to bed. At last, however, they heard the sound of bolts being shot back. A man of about forty opened the door, glaring at them. Violet couldn't help stepping back a bit into the dark.

"We are looking for Lord Hightower," said Cates before the man could voice the protest clearly on the tip of his tongue. "He and Lord Rochford went out driving today."

"I know that, don't I? And won't be back before morning, I expect." The man smirked in the lantern light.

"Morning?" said Cates before Violet could ask. "Why would that be?"

"Who the devil are you?" replied the man.

"Lord Hightower's valet," said Cates. "He was expected back some time ago."

"Valet, eh?" The man looked Cates up and down. "Well, I'm Lord Rochford's, and I can tell you that since it's got so late, they aren't like to be returning. His lordship likes to go to Mrs. Strathmore's after he's been out driving. Ready for a bit of an outlet, if you know what I mean." He smirked again.

"Mrs. Strathmore?" The question escaped Violet. She'd never heard the name.

At the sound of her refined accent, the man in the doorway frowned. "Who's that?"

Cates stepped in front of her, blocking her view. "Thank you for the information," he said. He backed up, forcing Violet to do the same.

Rochford's valet peered into the darkness. "Who's there?" he repeated.

Cates continued to herd Violet away from the house. Confused, Violet let him. After a bit, the door snapped shut behind them.

"I have never met anyone called Strathmore," said Violet. "I suppose she must be a friend of Lord Rochford's?"

Cates began to walk rapidly back the way they'd come. She had to hurry to catch up with him.

"Have you heard of anyone of that name?"

Cates seemed at a loss for words. Violet had never seen the self-contained valet so rattled.

"You have, haven't you?" She had a sinking feeling that there was more bad news coming. "Tell me."

"Mrs. Strathmore is"—Cates cleared his throat— "not anyone you should know, my lady."

"Shouldn't? I don't understand."

"I…I really can say no more." Cates walked even faster. They were practically trotting down the street.

Violet started to insist that he be clearer. Then the implications of his tone and discomfort, along with the attitude of Rochford's servant, sank in. They combined with the stories she'd heard about Rochford at the charity tea to tell her that Mrs. Strathmore must be a member of the demimonde.

She stopped short. Nathaniel had gone along to see this woman, and to spend the night? He could not have.

"My lady?" Cates was peering back, shining the lantern to light her way.

Violet made herself move. They walked back to the house in silence, and once there, she went directly to her bedchamber. She couldn't think. There had been too many shocks, one on top of another. But the one constant bulwark through it all had been Nathaniel. Could she have been mistaken in him, after all? She couldn't believe it. And yet, why hadn't he come home?

◈

Nathaniel found a few men setting off in the darkness of the summer night, and they were going short distances, not toward Brighton. Rochford had long since disappeared upstairs with another of the young ladies, obviously not intending to reappear before morning. His horses had been stabled behind the house, along with Nathaniel's phaeton.

Nathaniel was weary and annoyed and feeling a bit of a fool. His situation was ridiculous. He had no wish to attract more amused sidelong glances from the patrons of this place. He'd inquired about borrowing a mount from the stables and been told by one of the thugs watching over them that there was none to be had. He'd actually considered stealing a horse, but he gave up the idea at the thought of the uproar it would cause.

So here he was, hanging about the front door of a bawdy house, looking for transport—like a…well, not like anything he wished to be considered. It was straight out of a bad farce. A man went to a brothel or he didn't. Nathaniel didn't; he didn't wish to. And yet here he was, lurking. He could almost hear the laughter of his brothers, a raucous chorus. He would have laughed too, if he hadn't been conscious of how Violet must be worrying.

The first gray light of dawn was showing before he found a young man driving back to Brighton and willing to take him up. He then had to endure half an hour of braggadocio about the lad's amatory prowess, with far too much corroboratory detail. Fortunately, not much response was required. A few nods and the occasional appreciative sound sufficed. And the fellow's self-absorption was so complete that he evinced no curiosity about Nathaniel's situation. Nathaniel wasn't even certain that he'd retained his name.

His accidental benefactor set him down on the doorstep of their lodgings. Nathaniel used the key he'd been given to let himself in very quietly. But his bad luck held. The housemaid was already up and saw him enter. She gave him a sketchy curtsy, her eyes and mouth round with surprise as he strode up the stairs.

He hadn't intended to conceal his absence. He couldn't, of course. He had no need to; he'd done nothing shameful. But a few hours' rest were in order before explanations, a little time to marshal his thoughts and decide just what to say.

Nathaniel slipped into his bedchamber. Violet was lying on his bed, fully clothed, with one corner of the blue coverlet pulled over her feet. A shaft of sunlight speared through curtains inadequately closed and burnished the skin of her arm, her emerald gown. As he looked down at her, her hand twitched, and she muttered in her sleep. "No duchess…can't…never taught me French!" The last phrase had a curious vehemence, the product of some odd dream.

She looked anxious and vulnerable, even in sleep. Clearly, his absence had worried her. She had waited and paced about, and then dropped off here. Not his fault, but he was sorry. Let her rest, Nathaniel thought. He could ease into her room and sleep for a while there…

Violet opened her eyes. For a moment, they were blank and disoriented. Then they cleared and fixed on him. She sat up abruptly. "I was afraid you'd been killed in a carriage accident! There was no message or…"

Why hadn't he spent some of those tedious hours outside the brothel concocting a story that wouldn't distress her? But meeting that apprehensive gaze, Nathaniel realized he couldn't fob her off with some half-truth. He could, however, put the blame where it belonged. "It was Rochford's fault," he said.

Violet blinked as if struggling to full consciousness. "Is that supposed to reassure me?" she asked. She sat straighter. Her sandy hair fell in wild tendrils about her shoulders. "Rochford is a rake, a libertine, a—"

"Violet."

She pressed her lips together as if physically stemming the flow of words.

"Rochford's character is not the issue."

"It is if he corrupts you!" she interrupted.

"Corrupts? Do you have any idea how insulting that—?"

"I know you went to visit some woman," she accused. "Some…you needn't bother to deny it."

"How the dev…deuce do you know that?"

"You don't deny it?" She sounded forlorn.

"*Rochford* chose to go to a…place well outside town. As we were using his horses, I had no way to return until I could find someone to… How did you know?"

"I went to look for you at Rochford's lodgings. His valet said that Rochford had gone to seek some… relief. It was obvious what he meant," she finished with distaste.

A surge of annoyance flashed through Nathaniel. Not only was it humiliating that his wife had been traipsing about town inquiring into his movements, it would cause a storm of talk. Violet should have known that; she must know that. "Why did you go searching for me?" he said tightly.

"I was worried!" Violet cried.

"You might have trusted that I know what I'm doing. Someone would have ridden directly here if there'd been an accident, obviously." He could easily imagine people staring and whispering behind their hands. His parents might well hear. "At our station in life, we attract a greater degree of attention than others," he said. "A duchess cannot be seen sneaking about, questioning servants…"

"Well, I'm not a duchess!" she cried.

"Yet. You are—"

"Maybe I never will be!"

This was irrational, and Nathaniel was worn-out from a frustrating evening following an active day. "You are overwrought."

"Yes! I am! You don't know what's been happening." Violet wrung her hands. They were shaking.

The distress in her voice and posture moved Nathaniel. "There was no accident. I am home and well. You can rest easy."

"It isn't that."

He sat on the bed beside her, concern dissipating some of his annoyance. "Tell me what's wrong."

"I'm sure you're too busy with your dissipations to care!"

"Violet." He used the tone that always brought his brothers to heel, no matter what wild mood was upon them.

She put her hands to her cheeks as if to contain her emotions.

"Violet," he repeated.

She looked at him, wavering. And then a whole convoluted story began to pour out. She was some sentences into it before Nathaniel understood that the problem was her friend's, not his wife's. After that, relief let him listen more attentively. But it didn't prevent him from exclaiming, "Shot Granchester?!"

Violet nodded. "With a pistol, I think."

"What does the weapon—? You're telling me this young fool actually wounded him?"

"From behind a stack of barrels. He got away, though. No one else knows that it was—"

"And Granchester?" Nathaniel still didn't quite believe this. He wondered if Violet's friend had run a bit mad.

"Hit in the shoulder, Marianne said. The doctor promised her that he would recover. Of course that is the most important thing." She twisted her hands together again. "I would not ask you to help if he was dead."

"I don't know that I could. Or why I should, really. I hardly know this woman." At this moment, he wished Violet didn't either. What a thing to be faced with after a sleepless night. "What did you imagine I might do?"

"I'm not sure. I…I thought perhaps you'd know. You always know just what to do."

"Not in this case." His brothers always assumed the same, Nathaniel thought. Perhaps he gave that impression. He needed to know how he did that—so he could stop. "I don't think we should interfere," he said.

"But Marianne needs—"

"Despite what you believe, I get no pleasure from… involving myself in other people's business. And I have no desire take a hand in your friend's affairs."

"You won't help?"

It sounded like an accusation, nearly as impassioned as when she'd called him a busybody. "You want me to interfere now?"

"To help," she repeated. "Perhaps if you just talked to Mr. Whalen," she began.

"Who?"

"Marianne's…friend."

"The terrifying stripling who fired on Granchester?" There was a discussion that could not go well, he thought.

"I wouldn't call him a stripling. He looked to be more than twenty."

"Whatever his age, I do not intend to meet…" His mind caught up with her words. "Wait, you know him?"

"No. I saw him when…"

"When?"

"It was a…sort of…accident." She couldn't say that Marianne had tricked her. That would only make him angrier. Violet gazed up at her husband. He looked so tired. Which was his own fault, for going about with a man like Rochford. Surely he ought to have known… But she mustn't get diverted. "The thing is, I am somewhat…involved."

"You? How?"

"Marianne used me as a…an excuse for her meetings with Mr. Whalen."

"What?"

"I didn't know. I thought we were just going for

a walk. But she'd arranged to meet him in a church. When we arrived there, I was surprised—"

"So," Nathaniel interrupted, gazing at her. "You thought you were going on one kind of expedition, and you ended up on quite another? Through no fault of your own."

"Yes," replied Violet eagerly.

"Rather like I did tonight."

She stiffened. "I saw no reason to expect an illicit rendezvous. Marianne is not an infamous libertine."

"Neither is Rochford," replied Nathaniel wearily. He ran a hand through his hair. "Well, one walk is hardly—"

"Two," Violet had to admit. "And at a ball, I walked in on them. By mistake."

He sighed.

She hesitated, then went on in a rush, to get the worst of it out of the way. "Grandmamma has heard about it. She said everyone has. And that Granchester will do something…that he will 'crush' Marianne. If he brought an action for divorce, I…I fear I might be called to provide evidence." Violet clasped her hands tight at the anxiety this provoked.

"Ah."

Violet didn't know how to interpret his tone. "If there is a public scandal…"

"That would be one for the ages," Nathaniel agreed. "Very well. I will see what I can do."

"I'm sorry to drag you into this matter."

"It appears there is no choice," he replied. "I'd like to get some sleep now, before embarking on this… quest. I've been up all night."

He wanted her to go, Violet thought. He didn't

want her here in his bed. Her spirits sank further. She scooted to the edge, closer to him, yet feeling farther away. "What is that perfume on your coat?" Violet sniffed. "It's not a scent I use."

"Oh, some of the girls…" he began. And stopped.

"Girls? What girls?"

"Ah, perhaps I should say young women…that is…"

"Perhaps you should just say the truth." Violet remembered Rochford's smirking valet. "Oh. That sort of… How many of them *were* there?"

"I'm not accustomed to discussing…"

"I'm a married woman," she declared. "I'm allowed to know things." Fleetingly, she wondered if she would regret his answers as much as she did her interrogation of her mother. But no, this was entirely different. "And you're supposed to tell your wife everything," she concluded.

"Indeed? I hadn't heard that particular rule."

"Now you have." Violet sat up straighter and stared at him.

"Oh, very well, it's not as if… Rochford insisted on going for a drink when we'd finished driving, and he directed me to a bawdy house."

"A whole house of…" It was shocking and a bit fascinating.

"I had no idea that's where we were going," Nathaniel repeated. "Though I see now that he steered us in that direction during the afternoon."

"And how did the perfume get on your coat?"

"Some of them mauled me about, trying to get me to…" He closed his lips on the rest of that remark.

"A man can't be mauled about," Violet objected.

"Why not?"

"Well, it just sounds…odd."

"Men may do most of the mauling. Well, they do. But that doesn't mean we wish to be pawed by—"

"Young women." She drew the words out, still disturbed by the picture they represented.

"Complete strangers," Nathaniel corrected.

"But I thought men… I mean, the reason there are such houses in the first place…"

Nathaniel acknowledged this with a nod. "Especially young men. But eventually most of us realize that intimacies are much more gratifying with a…closer acquaintance."

"Like a wife," she ventured.

"Precisely like a wife. A woman of birth and breeding, with the sensitivity and intelligence to enter into all one's concerns as well as share the heat of passion." He held out a hand. "A wife like you."

It would have been everything Violet wanted to hear if not for that fateful word "birth." Her soaring emotions ran up against it like waves meeting the seawall down the street. They crashed and broke and made her eyes prick with tears. She felt like the foolish heroine of a fairy tale—the sort who had everything she ever wanted safe in her hands and yet could not resist taking the one forbidden step that ruined all. No one had warned her, an anguished inner voice exclaimed. No magical helper had said, do as you please, go where you will, but do not question your mother. Violet eased her hand out of his. "I'll let you sleep then," she said and went out before he noticed her renewed tears.

Eighteen

TWO DAYS LATER, VIOLET'S FRIEND MARIANNE CALLED at the Brighton lodgings of Viscount and Lady Hightower, at their request. She found them in their pleasant parlor, with the windows open to a warm sea breeze. It was a beautiful August afternoon, almost too beautiful for worries. But not quite.

Marianne's gown and shawl were of an uncharacteristically subdued brown. Violet supposed that she wanted to acknowledge Granchester's condition, but the hue had a suggestion of mourning, which did not seem the best choice. She waited along with her friend to hear what Nathaniel had to say. He hadn't yet shared the information with her, claiming he preferred to tell his tale only once. It was not unreasonable, yet she feared that the real explanation was the lingering distance between them. It wasn't large. A stranger wouldn't have noticed it at all. But she felt it like a weight on her heart.

Marianne was seated, refreshment offered, and the servants shut out of the room, the door securely latched. Marianne clasped her hands tightly in her lap.

"I finally tracked down your friend Mr. Whalen," Nathaniel said then. "It took some time, because he has left his home and is staying at an inn a few miles out of town. Since he was denied admittance to your house—"

"I couldn't let him in!" exclaimed Marianne. "What was he thinking to come?"

"No. So, we had a long, rather rambling talk, during which I learned a good deal about him. He is a third son, you know, and hasn't had much to occu—"

"Is he still threatening to shoot me?" Marianne interrupted.

It disturbed Violet that her friend didn't seem to care about the young man's life. Still, he had threatened to kill her. And perhaps she already knew the details of his story.

"He is not," Nathaniel replied dryly.

"Thank God." Marianne sagged back on the sofa. "Can you make him stay away from me?"

Violet watched Nathaniel look at Marianne. It seemed to her that there was sympathy as well as judgment in his gaze.

"I was able to point out that he had choices open to him," Nathaniel said. "Opportunities for advancement and…exotic adventure. Providing he did not ruin all by another rash act. Such as fomenting a scandal, or shooting someone else. Mr. Whalen was eventually moved by this argument. He has decided that he would like to try his luck in India."

"He will leave his life here behind?" Violet said.

As Nathaniel was speaking, Marianne had looked more and more cheerful. "I daresay he will have far better prospects there," she said. "Men are always making their fortunes in India. Look at all the nabobs."

In that moment, Violet felt that she didn't really know her friend. Her attitude toward the young man she'd recently claimed to love seemed callous. She exchanged a glance with Nathaniel and saw he felt the same.

Marianne noticed the look. Her eyes fell. "It might be the push he needed," she added. "To make a great success of his life. He was bored at home, and…constrained. He told me so. This could be a good thing."

"He is clearly unhappy now," Nathaniel replied.

Marianne's hands twisted in her lap. "I'm sorry for that. I truly am. I made a mistake."

There was a pause. There could be no answer other than, "Yes, you did." And Violet didn't wish to say it aloud.

"The thing is," Marianne continued, "Anthony is…he seems different. He was quite shaken by the shooting. The…the contemplation of death. And he really seems to be grateful for my nursing. Surprised that I… It may be that there is…that this truly regrettable…situation can help us make a change."

Violet searched for a reply. Finally, she said, "Well, that's good then."

Marianne nodded. She stood abruptly. "I should get back to him." She held out a hand to Nathaniel. "I am so very thankful for your help." When Nathaniel had clasped her hand politely and let go, she bent and embraced Violet. "You are such a good friend to me!" she exclaimed. In the next moment, she was gone.

They sat in silence, listening to her footsteps

hurrying down the stair. When they had died away, Violet said, "You gave him money, didn't you?"

Nathaniel turned to her, eyebrows raised.

"A third son of a country squire? How would he equip himself for a new start in India?"

He shrugged. "It seemed a small price to pay. Literally."

"It was kind of you." He was kind, she thought—kind bone deep.

"I felt a certain…sympathy for his plight." In response to her look, he added, "Not the entanglement with your friend, but what lay behind it. A young man's longing for something significant to do. Daring exploits, intensity."

"I thought females were supposed to be the dramatic sex?" Violet replied with a smile.

"Did you somehow avoid hearing of Byron?"

She laughed and enjoyed a moment of lightness and freedom. Nathaniel had solved her friend's problem so neatly, so perfectly. She truly believed that Daniel Whalen would be better off on his adventure than scraping for some occupation as a third son.

And then the moment passed, for she couldn't forget the much thornier dilemma still hanging over her. How happy she would be now, she thought wistfully, if only she had appreciated the contentment she'd already possessed.

❧

The day continued fine, declining into a lovely evening, with soft sea air and the promise of a glorious sunset. The Hightowers went out to stroll along the

Marine Parade, with all the rest of Brighton society, and enjoyed it. With his wife on his arm, nodding to acquaintances, pausing to speak to friends, Nathaniel regained a sense of well-being. He recalled Violet's admiring gaze at the way he'd handled young Whalen. Though the thing hadn't been that difficult in the end. He'd known just what to say to turn the fellow's ambitions in another direction, after years of advising his brothers. Still, he didn't mind if his wife thought him a hero. Didn't mind it at all. That look had taken all the sting from her earlier complaints about interference. Indeed, he expected it would add spice to their activities later tonight. Or, why later? Why shouldn't they turn back right now?

"Hightower."

He turned to find Rochford approaching, walking with a group of gentlemen whose red faces and loud laughter suggested they'd had a very convivial dinner.

"Got home safe the other night, did you?" Rochford added. He nudged the man next to him, drawing the group's attention.

Nathaniel had expected that the story of his exit from the brothel would make the rounds. He knew he would face a certain amount of chafing, and though he wished otherwise, he would endure it. But he hadn't expected Rochford to refer to it in front of Violet. That was beyond the line; Rochford had more finesse. He was thoroughly drunk, Nathaniel concluded, though he carried it well. "As you see," he said evenly.

Rochford gathered the gazes of his companions with a derisive look. "Always a sad thing to see a man living under the cat's foot, eh?"

He actually smirked at Violet. Nathaniel was abruptly furious. How dare the man bring her into this? In the street, where anyone might hear. He had to shield her...

"I'm quite partial to cats," Violet said before he could speak.

"Such sweet, furry creatures?" Rochford sneered. He looked at his friends again, enjoying his own cleverness, clearly implying that Violet was a ninny.

"Do you think so?" Violet responded, the epitome of well-bred surprise. "Have you never reached for a cat who did not wish to be patted and ended up scored with bloody scratches?"

Rochford blinked, suddenly looking more befuddled by drink.

"They're ruthless when they hunt too," she mused. "Have you seen a pampered house cat toy with a mouse? Letting it go, until the poor creature thinks it has escaped those sharp claws, and then sinking them in again?"

"Isn't it a splendid sunset?" interrupted Nathaniel. He'd been hiding amusement and admiration of Violet's pluck, but Rochford had begun to scowl. Whatever the man deserved, it wasn't wise to push him further.

Most of Rochford's companions turned to gaze at the western sky. Nathaniel wondered if they would even recall this exchange? Obviously, they'd all drunk deep.

"So, do you still intend to race, Hightower? Perhaps you will be sneaking out of that as well? If the...cat objects?"

It had been a mistake to renew his acquaintance with Rochford, Nathaniel realized. At first blush, the man seemed cordial and entertaining, but he was unsound at heart.

"Oh, no one tells Nathaniel what to do," said Violet, steel in her tone. "He makes up his own mind, on all things."

Pulling gently on her arm, Nathaniel urged her away. Much as she might enjoy twitting Rochford—as she obviously did—it was enough. Best to leave him before he had any real excuse to retaliate.

"What a tiresome man," Violet said when they were well out of earshot.

Nathaniel nodded. He was that, tonight at least.

"Will you still race his team?"

Part of him wanted to draw away from Rochford, letting the connection lapse into its former distance, yet the challenge and excitement of the race had gotten into his blood. He found he was reluctant to let that go.

"You want to," Violet said.

"Not because it is his team. Despite that."

"Well, then, you must. Although…" She smiled impishly up at him. "The cat insists that you be careful." She made a small clawing gesture with her free hand.

Nathaniel laughed. They strolled on, admiring the bands of warm color on the horizon. As the light faded, they turned and were heading for home when they encountered another familiar group. Violet's family stood before them, the earl and his wife overshadowed, as always, by the dowager countess. Nathaniel felt his wife tremble against his side.

She'd almost forgotten, for a little while, that she'd been ordered to go back to her old way of dressing and behaving, Violet thought. So much else had been happening. But now, face to face with her putative grandmother, her anxiety came flooding back. Confronting Rochford had been simple by comparison.

The dowager was looking her up and down. Her glances, her expression, catalogued a host of faults. When she met Violet's eyes, her gaze was absolutely unyielding. And then she shifted her attention to Nathaniel. "I will call on you tomorrow morning, Hightower," she said.

The words struck Violet like the knell of doom.

"On me?" he asked.

"I have something important to say to you," the old woman answered.

Violet tried to still her trembling, but she couldn't manage it. Nathaniel looked down at her, then back at the dowager. "I'm afraid that will not be convenient," he said. "I'm quite busy just now. I have a race coming up."

The dowager snorted her contempt of this activity.

"And so I shall be out most of the day. Perhaps when it is done—"

"Are you putting me off?" The old woman seemed unable to believe it.

"For a few days only." He was pleasant but unyielding. "I really have no time until then."

"I shall come early. Before you go out. You would not dare deny me."

The expressions of her son and Violet's mother showed that they certainly would not have dared.

"I'm sure you would not wish to push in when you have been informed the visit is unwelcome."

Violet's mother gasped audibly.

The dowager sputtered and fumed. She tried to stare Nathaniel down, and failed. So she glared at Violet as she said, "It seems I have no choice but to wait."

"It is kind of you to understand," said Nathaniel blandly. No one, hearing it, could miss the irony in his voice.

Violet had never admired anyone more in her life. Or been more relieved.

"Good evening," he added and led Violet away.

"That was...tremendous," she said. "It was beyond anything. You...you routed her."

He smiled. "We are each to have our victories tonight, it seems."

"I rate yours well above mine. Rochford may be annoying, but G–Grandmamma is...she is like one of those things in the Alps. What is it called? When the side of the mountain collapses?"

"An avalanche?"

"Those cascades of snow that roll right over whole villages and crush them to splinters?"

"That is what they call them. But I think you overrate—"

"That's what it feels like when she descends on you." Seeing that he was staring at her, Violet added, "Felt like, I mean. When I was younger. A child."

He regarded her with grave sympathy. "Is there anything you wish to tell me, Violet?"

In that moment, Violet wanted to tell him everything. She yearned to lay all her worries at his feet and have them swept off as handily as the dowager had been just now. His expression was so resolute, his voice so kind. It seemed as if she could confide anything, and he would accept it and stand by her and make it right. But a frightened inner voice reminded her of her husband's preoccupation with birth and lineage and the legacy of his noble family. He hated to appear less than the perfect duke's heir.

"I can't imagine anything you could say that would trouble me," he added.

Could he imagine that she was not the person she was supposed to be? Violet doubted that his imagination ran as far as that. Violet sighed. Her doom had only been postponed, not averted, and she still didn't know how she was going to stop it. But she knew in that moment that she had to do it herself.

"Violet?"

"There's nothing. It's...merely a disagreement between G-Grandmamma and me."

"I side with you," he declared.

He would, Violet realized, in public, before others, the dowager in particular. He would never act like Rochford or as the dowager had threatened Granchester would. He had too much pride, compassion.

But what about in private, in the inner sanctum of their marriage? Would he feel deceived, betrayed? Would that change everything between them? She simply could not take the risk. She would find her own way out of this tangle.

Nineteen

On the following day, the town of Brighton was gratified to learn that the Duke and Duchess of Langford had arrived to enjoy part of the summer season. The Regent, who was given a daily list of such illustrious additions to local society, immediately added them to the guest list for his next reception. Friends and acquaintances noted the address of their lodgings and made plans to call. Violet learned the news more personally, when their landlady's housemaid came scurrying into her parlor, goggle-eyed, and announced, "There's a duchess at the door, my lady!"

"A...?" The maid handed her a visiting card, and Violet read the name of Nathaniel's mother. She felt as if her heart had leapt onto her throat. She was alone; she had never received the duchess alone. Indeed, their previous meetings had been very formal occasions, supervised—indeed, fully orchestrated—by the dowager countess. Two formidable women facing each other over Violet's...person. It had felt rather like making her curtsy to the Queen at her court presentation. The gravity of each occasion was impressed upon her. She was warned not to offer her uninformed opinions, not to fidget or seem bored, and never, ever, to ask impertinent questions. Since the dowager's idea of impertinence was unpredictable, she'd made no inquiries at all. As a consequence, their exchanges had been bland and empty, and they could not be said to know each other at all. There was no question of refusing her admittance. But Violet would almost rather have had a visit from the dowager herself. "Of course, ask her to step upstairs," she said, her voice a bit higher than usual.

In the next moment the tall, striking figure of the duchess appeared. She looked, as she always did, alert and assured, as well as unostentatiously fashionable. She looked the way one would hope to look when past fifty, Violet thought. Probably a forlorn hope. She would never be so poised. Violet restrained her impulse to sink into a deep curtsy. She called upon her years of social tutelage and held out her hand instead. "How pleasant to see you. I didn't know you were coming to Brighton. I fear Nathaniel is out just now." It came out in a rush, as if she was nervous, which of course she was.

The duchess shook her head and smiled. "Practicing for this race tomorrow. I know. His father went to watch the contenders try to improve the speed of their turns."

Had they come to town because of the race? Violet wondered. Did they disapprove of it as much as the dowager did? Was Nathaniel's mother here to blame her for his escapade? That wasn't fair. "He bought a high-perch phaeton, and then he…" Was she trying to divert any scolding onto Nathaniel? Violet got hold of herself. She offered the sofa with a gesture and sat down.

The duchess joined her. "So we have heard. Did you have a hand in that? Well, you must have."

They *were* blaming her. "I didn't. He went up to town with…" Did they feel as others did about Rochford? She wouldn't mention him.

"Look at your lovely gown, for example," the duchess continued.

Confused, Violet looked down at her dress of amber silk embroidered with twining vines of green and black. What did it have to do with high-perch phaetons? Was she criticizing it as well? But she'd said lovely as if she meant it. She met the duchess's eyes, the same lustrous blue as Nathaniel's. She couldn't read them; she didn't know her. "Th-thank you." It seemed the safest response.

"You know, when Nathaniel announced that you had accepted his offer of marriage, I was doubtful."

"What?" replied Violet, stricken. The older woman's rueful expression was unfathomable. But the thought that both Nathaniel's mother and the dowager had been against her marriage made her stomach churn.

The duchess nodded. "I said nothing to him, of course, because I could see that he was determined. And in any case, it was settled. He couldn't draw back. But I thought you much too…staid for him. I feared you would pull him down a path that he had already traversed too far."

"Too far?" Violet told herself to concentrate and

keep up, but it felt as if the ground of this conversation kept shifting under her.

"Toward solemnity."

"Solemnity?" She must stop repeating words like a parrot, Violet thought. This didn't *sound* like something her grand—the dowager would say at the beginning of a thundering scold. But she still wasn't sure.

"Well, there is steady, and then there is starchy, yes?" The duchess smiled. She had a lovely smile. It gave her austere features a clear radiance. Violet couldn't help smiling back, even though she was hopelessly off balance. "So I must congratulate you."

"Congratulate…me?"

"I'm delighted that you've proved me quite wrong," Nathaniel's mother continued.

"Wrong about…?" She should know the answer to this. But one part of her was so agitated at the thought of being blamed that she couldn't quite comprehend.

"Your temperament." The duchess nodded, as if they were agreeing about something. "Your grandmother did not really…allow us to become well acquainted. I suppose all those pastels you used to wear were her idea?"

Violet nodded, not wishing to reveal her bewilderment by speaking.

"So unbecoming. But she is a woman of strong opinions."

Violet nodded again. This, at least, she could wholeheartedly endorse.

"It sometimes seemed to me," said the duchess more slowly, "that she did not wish… But perhaps she was jealous of a new relationship in your life, though I would never attempt to come between—"

"Jealous!" After all that had occurred in the last few weeks, the idea was absurd.

Nathaniel's mother cocked her head inquiringly.

"No," Violet said, finding her voice at last. "Gr-Grandmamma simply has to control any situation involving her…family."

"Ah." The duchess did not appear surprised by this information.

Thankful to have recovered a crumb of composure, Violet backtracked. "What did you mean, a path Nathaniel had traversed too far?"

The older woman nodded approvingly, as if she'd asked a proper question. "Nathaniel is an exemplary elder brother." Her tone was fond. "In the last five years, he has helped three of the other boys—at least three—out of serious scrapes. They think I don't know." She shrugged at the naïveté of this belief. "As if I wouldn't hear from some 'concerned' acquaintance. Those rescues led to confidences, and finally, Sebastian, Randolph, and Robert, in particular, began relying on him for every little thing. Trivialities. Matters they should certainly handle themselves." She looked at Violet. "Nathaniel is very kind."

Violet nodded, which seemed to be the correct response.

"But it seemed to me that…trifles had begun to take over his life. I told him that he should learn to say no, but he didn't really heed me. You, however, have succeeded where I failed. That is why I congratulate you." Her smile this time was impish. "Such complaints I've been receiving in the mail! 'What is wrong with Nathaniel? He has not replied to my letter. He has not found me a bishop or a book or a lute.' Whyever does Sebastian want such a thing?" She shook her head. "You would think that their lives were falling apart."

Violet's relief was mixed with lingering anxiety. "I didn't really... I wouldn't wish to come between Nathaniel and his brothers."

"No, no, it's all for the best, I assure you. My other sons are having to find their own solutions to life's little annoyances, which is exceedingly good for them."

Remembering some of the errands Nathaniel had been running for his brothers, Violet had to agree. She wondered if the games for girls had done the trick for Sebastian?

"They'll be the better for it, and Nathaniel... Well, I hope he is having a perfectly splendid time. I suspect he is. I might wish it did not involve careening around the countryside in a sporting vehicle."

"He drives very well," Violet put in.

The duchess nodded. "I trust him to make certain he has the skills to race. And I wanted to be sure to tell you how grateful I am that you have...put the reins in his hands, so to speak."

Violet gazed at her, overcome. She could feel the love that the duchess had for her sons. It was in her tone and expression, in the humor as well as the concern. Here was a mother who would take action for her children, who watched over them, even though they were grown men, and exerted herself to understand them. Not control them or...abandon them to their fate. And where had Nathaniel learned kindness, after all? Violet had to blink back tears.

"What is it?" asked the duchess. "What have I said?"

"Nothing. I beg your pardon."

The older woman examined her. "I have lived too many years as a mother not to see that something is distressing you. Is it this race?"

Violet's throat tightened. She swallowed, shaking her head. She could not break down like a blubbering fool in front of Nathaniel's mother.

"I know we are not yet friends," the duchess continued, "though I hope we will be. However, I would be glad to help you in any way I can."

She had Nathaniel's eyes—or he hers, Violet supposed. They were like…beacons of good will. It was a temptation. She shook her head again.

"I'm not one to pry." The duchess smiled. "Well, if I'm honest, I can be. A bit. But I promise you I can also be quite useful. The fruits of long experience, you know."

Violet didn't doubt it. If only her dilemma had been one of the ordinary problems of life, she would have taken the duchess up on her offer in an instant. But her plight was hardly ordinary. Still, she couldn't resist just skirting along its edges, testing the waters, as it were. "The…the Langfords are a very old family."

The duchess looked puzzled.

"With a…a truly distinguished lineage," Violet added. "They're descendents of the Plantagenets."

"One of the more ramshackle ones, if I recall," Nathaniel's mother replied.

Aristocrats said such self-deprecating things, Violet

thought. The man she'd been taught to call her father did so. But it was just an inverted sort of pride. If their listeners seemed to take such comments at face value, they'd soon point out that standards of behavior had been quite different hundreds of years ago. Then casually mention their connection to some ancient king. "You're the daughter of a marquess," she added.

The duchess did not reply, as another might have, "And you're the daughter of an earl." She watched Violet silently, her eyes alive with speculation.

"That sort of…heritage matters a great deal to… people. You…and the duke particularly, I suppose, must be…so glad that…" Violet ran down. She didn't know how to continue without exposing everything.

Nathaniel's mother waited to let her finish. When Violet said nothing more, she looked at her as if she posed a riddle to be solved. The duchess tapped a gloved finger on her knee, then said, "Are you worried, for some reason, about fitting in to the family? I assure you you're most welcome."

She was, in a way that was so much more sweeping than the duchess could imagine.

Nathaniel's mother waited a moment, then continued, "Have you become at all acquainted with Ariel?" When Violet looked confused, she added, "Alan's wife."

"Oh. I met her at the wedding. There was no time to talk really. She's very beautiful." As was the duchess, Violet thought, and Sebastian's intended, Lady Georgina. While she herself would never be more than passable. Why must she think about this right now?

"You know that Ariel is the daughter of an actress from the London stage."

Violet blinked in shock. She hadn't known. She couldn't recall Nathaniel ever mentioning it. She did remember that the dowager had made slighting remarks about that marriage. But one learned to ignore her continuous stream of criticism and complaint.

"Though it isn't much discussed, Ariel makes no secret of it. Her father is a gentleman, but her mother was a child of the slums. Nothing whatever is known of her 'lineage.'"

"And you let him marry her?" Violet searched the duchess's face for remorse or shame, but she showed no signs of such emotions.

"It's hardly a question of 'letting' once sons are grown," the older woman replied with a smile.

Violet wished someone would inform the dowager of this. "Lord Alan will not be the duke," she pointed out.

"It would be a tragedy indeed if he were to inherit." Nathaniel's mother shivered a little, as if contemplating the thought of all the others dead. "My point is that Ariel is welcome in the Langford family. By all of us. We find the person more important than the 'lineage.'"

But Ariel had not deceived them, Violet thought. She'd made no pretense of noble birth. "The duke also…?"

"Indeed." Seeing concern in Violet's expression, she added, "After more than thirty years, I'm certain of it. You need have no doubts."

How wonderful that must be, to have all those years together. Violet closed her hands into fists. She would not have that possibility taken from her.

The duchess laid a hand on her arm. "Violet. May I call you Violet?"

She nodded, near tears again at the concern in the other's voice.

"I don't understand what's troubling you, but I'll say again that I would be very glad to help."

"I want you to think well of me!" It popped out of Violet's mouth, a heartfelt cry. She'd wanted it from her own family, only to find that esteem—let alone love—was forever out of reach.

The duchess frowned at her. "Well, I am thought to be a good judge of character. And I do."

"You scarcely know me," Violet reminded her. "You said so."

She nodded. "I trust my instincts, however."

Violet gazed at her. She seemed to mean it. She seemed to be offering a true welcome into the Gresham family. Once again, the bitter irony of her situation chafed at Violet. If she'd let well enough alone, she'd be receiving a precious gift right now.

"It's obvious you need to confide in someone," the duchess went on. "Perhaps your own mother…" At Violet's quick negative gesture, she said, "Or another member of your family. Or Nathaniel."

"What if I were not what I seemed?" burst from Violet.

"Not levelheaded and intelligent and charming?" the duchess said with a smile.

Could she really be so accepting? Violet couldn't believe it. "How can you say that?"

"You have been very good for Nathaniel," the duchess declared. "That is what matters to me."

She said this, addressing the daughter of an earl,

Violet thought. She wondered if the family's acceptance of Alan's wife had been quite as simple as the duchess made it sound? She looked up to find Nathaniel's mother staring at her. Violet felt as if she'd put a keen foxhound onto a scent.

"What are we talking about?" the duchess asked. "Do you wish me to swear myself to secrecy?" She put a hand over her heart. "I do. I'm quite good at keeping secrets."

It was so tempting. Swayed by the sympathy in her voice, Violet came close to breaking down and telling her everything. But in the end, the years of being oppressed by the dowager, the earl's indifference, her mother's weakness, her despair about the future, all of them flooded her with fear. She couldn't risk it. Violet swallowed tears.

"I wish you would trust me," the duchess added.

She wanted it more than anything—well, anything except Nathaniel—a family she could trust. One where she had a secure and beloved place. It seemed this dream had been just within her grasp, and then slipped away.

"But perhaps it's too soon." The duchess examined Violet's face with compassion. "It's just distressing to see you so miserable."

This had gone too far. Violet sat straighter. She had to stop it. "I'm not. Miserable. I...I beg your pardon, but you've misunderstood me." It would be wrong, in any case, to reveal her secrets to Nathaniel's mother before telling him. How would he feel about that?

The duchess held up her hands. "My dear. Of course." She hesitated, then added, "Just...allow me to say that you are a Gresham now. And we take care of our own."

Violet's throat was too tight to say more than, "Thank you."

Nathaniel's mother examined her. She held out her hand. After a tiny hesitation, Violet took it. The squeeze of her fingers felt like redemption.

Then the mantel clock struck, and the duchess turned, surprised. "Oh, I must go. I promised to meet my husband." She looked back at Violet. "If you are all right?"

"Perfectly." Violet rose along with her guest. "And…I'm very grateful for your kindness. I wish I could repay it."

Nathaniel's mother gave her an impish smile. "Oh, I'm sure I shall find all sorts of ways to get my own back. There are my charitable endeavors and tenant visits and so much more."

Violet laughed, as she was meant to do, the mood lightened.

"You are making Nathaniel happy," the duchess added. "That is all I can ever ask."

"I hope I am, that I can," blurted Violet. "I…I want to so desperately."

"From what I hear, you're doing very well. Both of you."

Hear? What did she hear? But before Violet could beg her to elaborate on that statement, she was gone.

Twenty

WHEN SHE WAS ALONE AGAIN, VIOLET DECIDED THAT she couldn't sit any longer, waiting for the axe to fall. Something in the duchess's visit had made that intolerable—perhaps the promise of a real family if only she got out from under the dowager's thumb. It was like a prize dangling, tantalizing, just out of reach. She had to take the leap and grasp it.

But she still stood by the front window, staring unseeingly down into the street. It was so hard to fight someone who had been a parent figure all your life. There were so many memories of shame and failure. And so, again, she longed for the impossible—to return to the blissful days of ignorance and safety. Illusory safety, yes, all right. But she hadn't known that, had she? To see that there was no safety… The image of Nathaniel's mother rose in her mind, her assurance that Violet was a Gresham now. She wanted that to be true as much as she'd ever wanted anything. But it never would be unless she faced down the past. If she couldn't find the courage to do that, then perhaps she didn't deserve the reward.

Before she could waver, Violet fetched her bonnet and shawl and walked out into the street. It was only a short distance to Lady Dunstaple's house. Gathering her resolve as she went, she found herself wishing it was longer. But she didn't stop.

Taking a leaf from the dowager's book, she didn't wait to be announced. "I'm family," she told the maid who opened the door. The irony of the word made her jaw tight as she brushed past the girl to mount the stairs.

She nearly collided with the Earl of Moreley at the top. He held his hat and gloves and was obviously on his way out. "Hello, 'Papa,'" Violet said. "I've come to see you."

"Me?"

Violet might have found his startled look amusing in any other circumstances. "And the rest of my 'family,'" she replied. With a shooing motion and an expression borrowed from his formidable mother, she herded him toward the upper parlor.

There, she found her mother and the dowager countess sitting with their hostess. She edged the earl toward them. "Good afternoon, Lady Dunstaple," Violet said. "I must beg your indulgence. I've come to discuss some important family business."

"Violet!" exclaimed the dowager.

"I know it's terribly rude to eject you from your own parlor," Violet continued. "Please excuse me. I wouldn't ask it for anything trivial."

"You will do no such thing," said the dowager. "I cannot believe you would dare."

"But, *Grandmamma*, you know we have critical matters to settle."

"I do not see what we—"

"Well, you will in a moment."

The dowager's mouth hung a little open. Violet gazed limpidly at their hostess.

Very slowly, Lady Dunstaple rose. *Curious* did not begin to describe her expression, but in the face of Violet's insistence, she could not refuse. "Of course," she said. Violet followed as she moved reluctantly to the parlor door. After making sure it was firmly shut, she turned to face the remaining trio.

"That was unacceptable," began the dowager.

"A word that apparently describes my very existence, for you," Violet replied. Her mother looked frightened. The man she'd always thought of as her father was grim, the brim of his hat in clenched hands. The dowager's glare was all too familiar. "So, I've come for a family conference. As if we were a family. Though I understand now that we are not."

"Violet," moaned her mother.

"Sorry, Mama. Or, actually, I'm not sorry. Why should I be sorry? What have I done?"

"Your behavior is absolutely unacceptable," said the dowager.

"Is it? Well, what else can you expect from a misbegotten 'cuckoo in the nest'?" Now that she was actually doing it, daring to speak the truth to them, Violet's courage rose.

"You are insolent, girl," said the earl.

"Girl. You've never called me your daughter, have you? I didn't notice somehow. How could I have missed that? Too busy hoping to please you, I suppose. You speak of your sons quite often."

He glowered at her.

"As you never wanted me, and never pretended to, I don't see that I owe you any obedience. Particularly now that I no longer live under your roof."

"I paid for your keep and your—"

"Grudgingly," Violet allowed. "And as far as I can see, all the decisions were made by my dear 'grand-mamma.' So it's not as if you offered me charity, even. You simply did as you were told."

His scowl deepened.

"Do you mean to provoke me to do even more than I promised?" said the dowager. "Because I will."

"I mean to tell you what I will do unless you leave me alone." She surveyed the three people that she'd tried to respect and please and, yes, to love all her life. She had struggled so hard to love them, made so many excuses for inexcusable behavior. The earl was not a demonstrative man, she'd told herself. The dowager scrutinized every detail because she cared. She had to fight her way past a flash of pain in order to continue.

"If you do not give me your promises, your sacred word of honor, that you will never mention this matter again, I will go to the Langfords the moment I leave here. They are in Brighton, had you heard? I will tell them of your scheme to foist off a low-born imposter upon them."

"What?" exclaimed the earl.

Violet put a hand on her heart. "Me, that is." She shook her head as if deploring their actions. "I'll describe how much you enjoyed fooling them, how you hugged your secret to your bosoms and felt smug and superior—to a duke! I'll describe how shocked I was when I found out. Just aghast. I'll beg their pardons."

"You would never expose your mother to such a scandal," said the dowager. Her mother had put her head in her hands.

Violet felt a pang of sympathy, but drawing back now wouldn't save her mother from distress. "Why not? You threatened to tell Nathaniel your own version of the story. And do your best to ruin my marriage." She met the dowager's glare resolutely. "Believe me when I say I will do anything to prevent that."

The old woman looked her up and down, her eyes sharp with the usual contempt. "Brave talk, my girl. But you would never dare."

Violet stared at her, rebellious, as she'd given up being years ago. "Do you forget that I've been observing *you* all my life? I've had innumerable lessons in ruthlessness."

"Nonsense! You're as spineless as your mother."

A bolt of fury ran through Violet. She felt as if her bland gray eyes actually flamed. "I wouldn't count on it!"

The dowager's gaze actually faltered. "The Langfords would agree with me about what must be done." Belatedly, she added, "Even if they believed you."

"Not believe that you deceived them?" Violet surveyed the three people before her. The earl looked distinctly uneasy, the dowager irate. Her mother cowered on the sofa; if only she would get up, Violet thought, and stand beside her. They could weather this together. "But you did."

"Mama," said the earl.

"As for the other, my observations of the Langford family suggest that they do not agree with you about very much. Do you think they are fond of you? I don't. Indeed, I imagine that they will distance themselves from you, at the least."

"How will that look, Mama?" said the earl.

"People will wonder at it, even if they don't know the reasons." Violet had imagined that the Deveres' obsession with appearances would work in her favor. "They'll begin to invent some. I daresay they'll be interesting."

"And I would simply tell them about Harriett's… folly," retorted the dowager.

Her mother moaned, and Violet wished, again, that she could spare her this confrontation—even as a small, sad inner voice pointed out that Violet had never been spared. "If you wish to provide a field day for the gossips," she agreed. "I would be sorry to see my brothers—pardon me, my half brothers—subjected to such a trial."

"No," said the earl.

"Violet!" cried her mother at the same instant.

It took all her control not to flinch. And to endure the dowager's suddenly speculative stare. She had to convince the old woman that she would carry out her threats, even if the thought of her young brothers enduring whispers and mockery was distressing.

"We will not speak of this, to anyone," declared the earl, carefully not looking at his mother. With his customary craven unfairness, he glared at his wife. "It was very bad of you to reveal it."

Violet waited, all her muscles tight with tension.

"You think you've bested me," said the dowager, her wrinkled face grim.

"You forced me to fight for my life," Violet answered.

There was a silence. It stretched until Violet thought she would scream.

"I will not speak to Hightower," the old woman finally conceded.

"Or to any of his family. Or friends. None of society."

After a moment, the dowager gave a stiff nod.

"I have your word."

Looking as if she'd eaten something bitter, the old woman nodded again.

"I'm afraid I must ask you to say it," Violet told her.

"You…do you dare to question me?"

"You have offered me no reason, in all our years, to trust you," Violet declared.

The dowager's thin lips worked. Her hands clenched. Then, as if choking out the words, she said, "I give you my word."

"Good." Violet had to resist an impulse to collapse in relief. "You can all go home then."

The old woman bridled in outrage. "Insolence! You think to give me orders as well?"

"You came to Brighton only to harass me. You don't even like it here." Violet watched the woman she'd always thought of as her grandmother struggle to find a blistering retort. Her victory was satisfying, and cheerless.

"You are not welcome back at Moreley," the old woman spit out at last. "You will be turned away at the gate."

"As I never was welcome there, that is no real

change." Violet gazed at the dowager, the earl. She saw no softening or sympathy, and tried to deny that it hurt. "I don't care if I never see you again," she told them.

"Violet!" cried her mother.

She turned, tried to smile. "You may come and visit me whenever you like, Mama, for as long as you like. We will soon be settled in our new home, and there will always be a room for you there."

"Oh, I…" Violet's mother looked like a rabbit surrounded by foxes.

"I will send you money for a post chaise, anything you need. They cannot stop you, you know."

The doubt in her face did not lift.

"Unless you let them." Violet waited for a reaction, a spark of rebellion. None came. "I suppose you will let them, but I so wish you would not." She turned to go.

"You think you'll be happy now, my girl?" said the dowager. "You think it's so simple?"

"I mean to do my best," Violet replied without turning. And then—trembling and triumphant, hopeful and forlorn—she left the people she'd thought of as her family behind.

Twenty-one

THE DAY OF THE RACE DAWNED CLEAR AND WARM, and Nathaniel woke with it. Staring at a shaft of early light that speared through a gap in the draperies, he puzzled over why he had ever gotten involved in this…circus. He, who disliked being on show, would be the focus of countless stares and excited discussion for hours and hours.

Well, it hadn't started out as a spectacle, he told himself. In the beginning, the idea had been for a few gentlemen to try their skills and their teams in a friendly contest. A chance to challenge oneself. But somehow, it had expanded out of all proportion as time passed. Many people seemed intrigued that he was racing, he admitted, because he hadn't done such things before. And Rochford had talked of it, praising his team. A few more aspirants joined in; wagers began to pile up on the betting board at Raggett's Club. The Regent had declared his interest in observing the race, as one who knew the fine points of the sport, and suddenly the thing had become one of the chief events of the Brighton season.

This had never been his intention, Nathaniel thought as he threw back the coverlet and got out of bed. If he had known it would happen, would he ever have begun?

He started to ring for Cates, then realized his man wouldn't be awake yet. The sun was only just up. He pushed back the curtains and looked out at the quiet street. His dreams had been full of tight corners and narrow gateways. His head was full of advice and the plan of the course that had been set. He couldn't stop reviewing the twists and turns that would test the finest drivers, the two places where it would be safe to pass another vehicle. On top of all that, he would be taking out another man's team, which required extra care.

Standing at the window, he found himself moving along the route in his mind. He swayed slightly as he envisioned a tricky corner, tensed as he imagined the longest straight bit where you would have to go full out. The idea of the race still excited him, he realized, despite all the trappings it had acquired. He looked forward to pushing himself, seeing what he could do against the other drivers. Suddenly the hours till the start seemed long.

"I will certainly come to see the finish of the race," Violet said at the breakfast table. "Lydia Barnes has invited me to sit in her barouche. With a picnic hamper." Seeing her husband's grimace, she said, "Do you not wish me to go?" That would be a disappointment, but nothing could dampen Violet's mood today, after she had vanquished the dowager. She felt an impulse to giggle. She felt like the hero who has slain the dragon that long terrorized the countryside.

"You, absolutely," Nathaniel said. "The whole town, with refreshments, as if it was a raree-show, not really."

She laughed. She wanted to laugh at everything today. "With the Regent officiating…"

Nathaniel nodded. "It could hardly be anything else, I know."

"I shall be hoping for you to win. Oh! If only we had that banner from Langford, with the ducal coat of arms. I could wave it."

"You're in fine fettle today," he replied, smiling. "What happened?"

"What?"

"You've been a bit…gloomy lately."

"I…I have?" It sounded inane. But she hadn't realized that he'd noticed. Or, she had, but she'd been so wrapped up in her own misery. She needed a convincing lie. Something that would satisfy him without revealing too much.

And then, meeting his warm blue eyes, she understood that she had to tell him the truth. She'd been so preoccupied with her fears, and then gloating a bit, she admitted it. But now, sitting with her husband over their homely breakfast table, she knew that she couldn't keep such a huge secret from him. It wasn't the fact that the dowager might change her mind and repeat her threats, not even that. It was that such a secret would open a space between them. And over the years, it would grow, she saw. Small deceptions would build on one another; the distance would widen It would eat away at her, gradually devour her marriage.

"What's wrong?" said Nathaniel, reaching across the table to take her hand. "I was joking. Mainly."

She would tell him, Violet resolved. But not right before his race. That would be wrong. As soon as it was over, she would find an opportunity. "I...I'm worried about you," she answered. It was not a lie. "You will take care, won't you?" Wild young men—even staid older people—were injured or even killed in carriage spills.

He squeezed her hand. "Certainly. I have no urge to risk my neck just when life has become so sweet."

Violet's pulse fluttered. "Has it?"

"Unquestionably. Are you not happy?"

"More than I ever thought I would be," Violet blurted.

"As am I."

When she met his eyes, and saw the tenderness there, Violet flushed with joy. It was on the tip of her tongue to tell him how much she loved him, when the housemaid came in with a fresh pot of tea.

Nathaniel withdrew his hand. "We are fortunate," he said.

"Beyond anything," she replied. He smiled at her, and it melted her heart.

"I must go and prepare."

"I'll see you after the race. Right after." As he rose, she repeated, "Take care."

"I will."

❧

Six high-perch phaetons were lined up at the spot designated for the start of the race. It was the one place on the course wide enough for them all to stand side by side. The teams were all restive. They were bred to run, and they longed to leap away and go. The excitement of the crowd and the roar of conversation only increased their edginess. Some of the leaders tried to nip at each other or kick against the traces. Nathaniel pulled hard to hold his team in check.

The Prince Regent stepped forward, holding a pistol at his side. He had been only too pleased to fire the starting shot.

The jostling at the beginning would be fierce, Nathaniel reminded himself. It was vital to keep a cool head and remember your strategy. Full out along the straight bit, get ahead of as many of the others as possible, then line up for the first turn.

The Regent pointed the gun straight up. "Ready," he called. Nathaniel braced himself. The pistol went off.

Twenty-four powerful horses were lashed to speed. They sprang away. The pounding of hooves and the clatter of wheels rose in a ferocious cacophony. Clods of earth flew into the air. Phaetons bounced over ruts and slammed down again. The vehicle on Nathaniel's right came within inches of bumping his. His mouth went a bit dry as the two flying wheels veered apart again. Then his reins jerked, and he had no attention for anything but driving forward.

He was slightly ahead of four of the others. The fifth, on the far right, paced him as they approached the first turn. They would have to slacken the pace to make it. But who would slow first? Whose nerve would break? With a pounding heart, Nathaniel urged his team to greater efforts.

It was not enough. The other phaeton—it was Gibbons, he saw—surged ahead and got to the turning

before him. Then they all had to pull back to round
the sharp curve without overturning. Nathaniel heard
a loud crack behind him, as of wood striking wood,
but he couldn't look around.

Afterward, the six carriages were strung out along
the road in a close file, the lead horses' noses perilously
near the rear wheels of the one before. The drivers
would strive to hold or better their positions at any
place where they could pass. It was not unknown for
a racer to try to bump another into a ditch as they
sought to push by. There was some disagreement
about whether this was truly sporting.

A narrow gate came up before Nathaniel would
have thought it possible. He had driven this team rapidly during practice runs, but the race seemed so much
faster. He lined them up as carefully as one could at
such speeds and flew through the passage, knowing
there were only inches to spare. He was also acutely
aware that another turn, even sharper than the last, was
coming fast. One wheel of the phaeton left the ground
as he careened around it. He held his breath until it
dropped to the earth once more.

When they reached the first wider spot in the
course, Nathaniel was still in second place, and the
carriage behind him was pressing close. As soon as the
road widened, the trailing driver tried to edge up on
Nathaniel's left to get by. But Nathaniel had been preserving his horses for just this danger, and opportunity.
Now he flicked the whip over their heads and asked
for more speed. They obliged, and moved closed to
the leader of the race, even as the one behind pounded
up at his rear wheel. Nathaniel spared a quick glance,

and saw that a fourth racer was just behind the latter, pushing just as hard to overtake.

Hooves thundered over the ground as the bounding phaetons vied for position. Gibbons in front wove back and forth a bit to prevent the others from passing. But this cost him speed. Nathaniel had edged the first pair of his team past Gibbons's seat when the road narrowed again, and he had to slack off or tip into the ditch.

The horses didn't want to slow. They were wild to run by this time. It took all his strength on the reins to ease them back just enough to stay right on the tail of the leader. As they thundered on, he heard a crash. He stole an instant to glance back again. The two vehicles behind him had apparently misjudged the clearances. They'd collided, side to side, and careened off into opposite ditches. Fortunately, they hadn't overturned. The drivers remained in place, but they were clearly out of the race, frantically maneuvering across the shallow ditches and into adjacent fields.

Nathaniel saw the final two competitors come pounding up, and then he had to pay attention to the road ahead. A tricky stretch was coming up, where you had to manage a long left turn, and then line up immediately for a sharp right through a set of tall hedges.

He made the turns successfully and slid into a long, slanting curve that took the course back in the direction of the start. But he didn't gain much on the leader, and the two behind him lost no ground. The teams were tiring slightly by this time. The horses were still well able to run, even eager, but they were not so wild to go at top speed. The second half of the race was as much about tactics as sheer daring.

The second wider spot in the road was coming up. Nathaniel envisioned all the details in his head. The hedges drew back first on the left. He might be able to squeeze out a small advantage if he was lined up on that side. He had to move fast. There was, perhaps, just enough space to pass. It was his last chance to take the lead.

There it was, ahead. Nathaniel encouraged his team. They were sweet goers, with the hearts of winners, and they responded to his signal. His phaeton pounded up on the left, Nathaniel calculating the inches as the road gradually widened. Gibbons glanced quickly back. He tried to swing left to block Nathaniel, but his team reacted to the animals coming up fast beside them and refused.

Nathaniel leaned forward, all his focus on going faster, faster. The phaeton bounced in a rut, throwing him up from the seat and slamming him back down. It might have been frightening had he had any time to contemplate the danger. He was gaining, a few feet, a few more. He flicked a glance forward, to the side. He had just enough room to get by. Didn't he?

His seat came even with Gibbons's. They glanced at each other, jaws tight, expressions intent. For what seemed an endless time, they thundered along side by side, perilously close. And then Nathaniel pulled a little ahead, a little more.

The road narrowed in seconds. He had to coax more speed from his valiant team. He cracked the whip over their heads, and they leaned in and gave it to him. In the nick of time, as the hedges crowded in, scraping the varnished sides of the phaeton, scoring Nathaniel's coat sleeve, they flew past Gibbons's carriage and moved into the lead. Gibbons shouted something—probably curses—but Nathaniel didn't catch it.

Nathaniel found he was panting, as if he had been the one running. He couldn't believe he'd done it. If he hadn't passed precisely when he did, he would have plowed the team into the hedge. He'd have injured the horses and most likely been thrown clear over the branches to land in a broken heap in the field beyond. His heart shuddered at the thought of having been seconds from death.

He pulled in just slightly, to conserve the horses for the remainder of the race. It was simply a matter of taking the last turns now and staying on the road. There was nowhere to pass on the rest of the course.

Nowhere sane, that is. On the final straightaway, Gibbons tried to push forward, even though there was no space. He brought the noses of his horses right up to Nathaniel's spinning rear wheel, as if he imagined they might shoulder the phaeton off the road. Nathaniel heard the lead animal's squeal of protest as the whip cracked behind him. "Are you mad?" he shouted backward, though he knew the words would be lost in the thunder of hooves.

He urged his team on again, and once again they came through. Slowly, they pulled away from the idiot dogging him.

And then they were flying toward the crowd massed at the end of the course, past the first scatter of spectators, and across the finish line to a great roar of approval.

Abruptly exhausted, Nathaniel pulled in the reins. It still took all his strength to ease the horses down, slowing them gently. He'd won. By God, he'd won!

When his speed had slackened sufficiently, stablemen ran to the leaders' heads. They trotted along beside them, full of soothing phrases. The horses slowed to a walk. Nathaniel jumped down from the moving carriage. His legs trembled slightly from the strain. He went to the horses, walking alongside the stablemen as they continued to cool them down, to praise their great hearts. "Once they're cool, a good rubdown," he said to the ostlers. "And a good feed. The horses are the real heroes of these events."

"Not many says so," replied the stableman, with a salute. "No fear, m'lord, they'll be treated like kings. His lordship always does so." And then Rochford was there, slapping Nathaniel on the back, laughing at the triumph of his cattle. He chivvied Nathaniel back to face a sea of congratulations, the Regent first among them. Someone thrust a bottle of champagne into his hand, and he drank from it, terribly thirsty, though he would have preferred a pint of ale.

One by one, the other racers joined in. Nathaniel inquired about the two who had collided and learned they were all right, only shaken up. One horse had come up lame, and another was badly bruised. The animals took the brunt of these sports, he thought, as people jostled closer to stare at him. It wasn't worth that.

A total stranger pounded his back and told him he was a complete hand. Others began to rehearse the details of the race, looking to him to resolve their disputes. He would not be doing this again, Nathaniel thought, the exhilaration of the win fading. He would enjoy some lively spins in his phaeton—with Violet— but no more of this melee. Memories of the day they'd driven together surfaced. How much more pleasurable that had been! He looked for her, but couldn't spot her in the large crowd.

⁓

Should she push her way through the press of people to Nathaniel? Violet wondered. It would be a hot, jostling effort, and some of the men were becoming quite rowdy. Better to stay in her friend's barouche, sip champagne, and watch her husband being lionized. She was terribly proud of him, and happy to accept congratulations on his behalf. She was also still trembling a little at the way his phaeton had come careening into the finish, and over the fact that only four of the six racers had returned. But Nathaniel was fine, she told herself, her heart full of love.

There'd been no sign of the Earl of Moreley among the crowd, for which she was grateful. She'd never expected to see her mother or the dowager. She hoped they had, in fact, left Brighton. It would make everything easier.

Before the dramatic ending of the race, she had encountered Marianne, walking beside her husband, who was being pushed along in a Bath chair. It was clear from the brief conversation that followed that the Granchesters were reconciled. Violet was glad to see it, but the way Marianne avoided her eye told her that they would not be such close friends in the future. Violet's involvement in the Daniel episode, unwilling

as it had been, would color all their encounters from
now on. Which was not fair, she thought. But once
you knew gossip, you couldn't unknow it, she realized. Nor could the other people in the case forget that
you knew. Here was another unforeseen consequence
of greater freedom in society.

Violet sighed and took another bite of a really
excellent ham sandwich from Lydia's hamper. It was
sad about Marianne, though her opinion of her old
friend had changed a bit as well. Perhaps a little more
distance was for the best. Indeed, everything would
be practically perfect if it weren't for the confession
looming ahead of her.

Twenty-two

It was evening before Violet and Nathaniel were back in their snug parlor, with sea breezes wafting the curtains and a light supper set before them. "This is better," said Nathaniel, sitting back with a wineglass in his hand. Late-summer sun made the liquid glint like rubies. "If I'd had any notion that race would attract such mobs, I wouldn't have done it."

"You liked winning," Violet replied, teasing him.

He laughed. "I admit it. And passing Gibbons with an inch to spare was an undeniable thrill. But I'm also glad it's over. It's not a thing I shall do again. And I'm more than glad we didn't go out. Everyone is still talking of the race. A quiet dinner is exactly what I wished for." He raised his glass to her. "With a private celebration after?"

"Hot pursuit around the bedchamber?" Violet said.

Nathaniel choked on his wine.

As they laughed together, Violet thought how lovely it would be to put off telling him her secret. He was so happy tonight. She didn't wish to spoil it, or her own mood. But if she gave in to that impulse it would pop up again and again, she realized. Each time there would be a reason not to confide—preserving a mellow occasion, lightening a somber one. And the distance she'd feared would gradually increase between them.

"I have to speak to you," she said in an altered tone. There was no choice but to do it. "There's something I have to tell you."

Nathaniel put down his wine. "No. You don't."

Startled, Violet said, "What?" Had he heard somehow? Had the dowager broken her word? Or the earl? She examined his face for clues.

"I can tell from the tone of your voice that you would rather not speak. So I'm assuring you that you needn't. Whatever it is won't matter."

"You can't know—"

"I know you," Nathaniel interrupted. "I trust you. I love you."

Violet sat frozen in her chair for a long moment, not quite able to believe what she'd heard. Then her breath caught on a cascade of joy, rising through her chest, tightening her throat. She sprang up and went to throw her arms around him. "Oh, Nathaniel, I love you too. So much!"

He pulled her into his lap, the silk of her skirts slithering over his knees. "That's enough. That's everything," he said, and kissed her with such blazing tenderness that she could hardly bear it.

She put all of her love for Nathaniel in her responses to his lips and hands, in the caresses of her own, and vowed again, with all the strength of her being, that she would sustain this marriage, which had turned out to be so much more than she'd ever dreamed.

One kiss led to another. His hands wandered in delicious ways. Her senses swam, and she came within an inch of forgetting everything else. But then there was a sound downstairs, as of a door slamming, and it all came rushing back. She wanted to give herself to him without reservation, without any hidden snares. "I have to tell you," she said, breathless. She pulled away and then, reluctantly, returned to her own chair. "We can't hide...important things from each other. If we do, all will go wrong."

Nathaniel adjusted his neckcloth, which had become twisted. "Must it be now?" he asked, a bit breathless. At her quick gesture, he held up his hands in surrender. "Very well."

But when it came down to it, Violet found it hard to begin. The fearful parts of her roused up again and threatened disaster. "When I spoke to my mother," she began. And stalled.

At last, Nathaniel nodded. "She shared some confidences with you, which are difficult to contemplate."

He'd been angry at the time, Violet remembered, hurt that she wouldn't tell him what was said. This spurred her on. "She turned my life upside down." She drew in a breath. There was nothing for it but to plunge in. "Before she was married to my father—"

The parlor door crashed open, hitting the wall and bouncing partway back. Renshaw stood framed in the opening, funereal in her perennial black, her eyes burning with malice and triumph. "My lord," she declaimed, like an actress in a bad melodrama, "I have a piece of news for you!"

"What are you doing here?" said Violet, standing. Nathaniel rose as well.

"I've been sent," was the sneering reply. "To tell his lordship the truth about the imposter he married."

She had gotten the dowager's promise not to speak, Violet thought, and the earl's, but they had made no oaths about envoys. It was like the old woman to break the spirit of the agreement while following the letter. Still, she couldn't quite believe the dowager had shared the family's secret with a spiteful creature like Renshaw. It was so stupid, and dangerous.

Renshaw pointed at Violet, her arm extended to full length. "She's no more the daughter of an earl than I am," she intoned. "Her father was a foreign rogue who dallied with the countess and was murdered for his crimes. She's bad blood and not worthy of the position she's been called to occupy. All by my lady's charity."

Violet sank back in her chair. There was no argument to make. Renshaw might have put the story in the worst possible light, but it wasn't false. Well, except for the part about charity. The dowager had never been charitable in her life.

Nathaniel was looking at Renshaw, not at her. Was he shocked by the deception? Was he angry? Could he not bear the sight of her now? From the side, his face looked grim. The silence stretched until Violet thought she would scream.

Nathaniel's eyes narrowed. He did not stand, but when he spoke, his tone was utterly commanding. "You will never repeat this slander."

"You can't stop the truth," Violet's former maid replied smugly. "If you take me to the law, I'll tell the judges all about—"

"You will not be arrested," Nathaniel cut in. "You'll simply find yourself branded as a lunatic."

Renshaw sneered at him. "My lady would never allow—"

"If you are referring to the dowager countess," Nathaniel interrupted, "as I assume you are, I believe you will find her quite reluctant to oppose *me*."

Under his unwavering gaze, Renshaw quailed a little. "No. She sent me here."

"Which was a dangerous mistake, as she will soon discover." Now he stood. As he walked toward Renshaw, she backed up a few steps.

"Her ladyship—"

"Do you imagine she can prevail against me? And all the resources Langford can bring to bear?" He walked over to the open door, checked the hall, and then called down the stairs, "Send Cates to me, please."

Renshaw looked uneasy now, uncertain. "Perhaps you have not understood me, my lord. You have not married a Devere but a—"

"Quiet!"

His voice was like a whiplash. Violet had never heard her husband speak so. She trembled in her chair, wondering if it would be turned on her next.

Cates entered the parlor. He gave a small bow and waited.

"Miss Renshaw has been overtaken by a disorder of the senses," Nathaniel told him. "I fear her dismissal from our service has…overset her faculties and caused her to suffer delusions. You will escort her to the lodgings of the dowager countess…"

"My lady will make you pay for this," cried Renshaw.

"...along with a note I shall write," Nathaniel continued as if she hadn't spoken. "You are to give the note directly to the dowager. No one else."

"Yes, sir," said Cates.

"Will you see me treated so, Mister Cates?" Renshaw cried.

The look that the valet cast at his former colleague would have discouraged anyone, Violet thought. Renshaw had made a mistake here, fomenting quarrels.

Nathaniel sat at the writing desk and drew a sheet of notepaper toward him. He dipped a pen into the inkpot, thought a moment, then began to write. The parlor was silent except for the scratching of his pen.

He finished, waited a moment for the ink to dry, then sealed the missive. As he handed it to Cates, he looked at Renshaw. "I hope you understand that I am deadly serious. Keep on with this lunacy at your peril."

Renshaw quailed under his gaze. She said nothing more as Cates urged her from the room, closing the door firmly behind him.

Nathaniel drew in a deep breath, and Violet found herself echoing it. She watched his face as he returned to his chair. "It's true," she blurted out. "That's what I was about to tell you." Her hands were shaking. "Mama...she eloped with a French émigré before her marriage. He claimed to be the son of a marquis, but... They were nearly to Scotland when an enemy of his caught up to them and killed him right before her eyes."

"My God."

Was he appalled at the story or at her personal history? "The Deveres took her back because of her money," she added. "They wanted her fortune enough to bury the scandal."

"I assumed she had told you some secret, but I never imagined a story such as this."

Had he actually understood all of it? "When she married, Mama was already… I am the daughter of that Frenchman. Not a Devere, just as Renshaw told you." There, she'd said it. Her shame was revealed. Now she would discover whether the duchess's assurances, Nathaniel's professed love, would bear up under the truth.

"I would never have thought it of your mother," Nathaniel said.

Violet couldn't take it in at first. He didn't sound angry. Indeed, in any other circumstances, she would have thought he was amused.

"She actually fled to the border?"

"She was in love," whispered Violet, remembering her mother's face when she spoke of the Frenchman. She hadn't even told her his last name, she realized.

"Well, that is quite a heritage," Nathaniel said.

"What?" Violet gazed at him, still too shaken to comprehend. "What do you mean?"

"To come from a line of people who love so much that they risk everything," he replied.

She swallowed. When she met his eyes, she took another long breath.

"We might try to research your father's history," Nathaniel said. He sounded simply interested. "We should be able to find the son of a marquis if he—"

"He was a rogue," Violet told him. "He was the sort of man who would lure an heiress into an elopement. Does that sound like a nobleman?"

"Well, the émigrés had a hard time after the revolution, even the highest born. Their case was rather desperate. And he might have loved her. Also."

Violet couldn't quite believe it. "Nathaniel, you don't seem to care that I am…not what you were told. I'm not the daughter of an English earl."

"I do understand that."

"But my lineage is not… You are always saying I will make a perfect duchess."

"And so you will. It's you I admire and love, Violet, not your bloodline."

She was too moved to speak for several moments. "I thought you would be… Your family is so ancient."

"If it had come out before I got to know you better, perhaps I might have been…concerned. I can't tell. But Violet"—he came over to pull her from her chair and into his arms—"if your father was a rogue, well, perhaps I needed a little roguishness in my life. You have certainly made it happier in every way." He dropped a kiss on her nose. "You must always be my charming rogue."

She clung to him. "The dowager still may do something…"

"She can't put the story about after all these years," Nathaniel said. "Setting aside the scandal, it would make her and your—the earl look like cheats and fools. I said as much in my note."

"You did?" she marveled.

Nathaniel nodded. "Aren't you a little glad to find that you're no relation to the old dragon? I am!" He smiled down at her.

"There is that," Violet acknowledged.

"Now, I think we have better things to do than worry about the deplorable Deveres." He drew her closer.

Violet wasted no time in indicating her complete agreement.

Read on for a sneak peek at the next
in *The Duke's Sons* series

FAME AND FORTUNE FAVOR A LORD

LORD JAMES GRESHAM GAZED AT THE SPIRES OF Oxford University, visible above the trees at the edge of his brother's garden; at the early summer flowers in curving beds; at the fifteen people standing about chatting and drinking lemonade. It was a pretty scene, the sort of thing one dreamed of when tossed by a five-day tempest seven hundred miles from shore, or when repairing the ravages of a broadside that near as nothing took down the mainmast. Some poet had a bit about a lovely summer's day. Probably Shakespeare. Nine times out of ten it was Shakespeare. If Randolph was here, and not stuck in his parish in the far north, he'd know the lines, for certain. Randolph had been mad for poetry before he became a vicar, always spouting some sonnet or other. Well, he probably still did. No reason a parson couldn't, and he had a whole congregation for a captive audience now.

James had forgotten all the poetry they'd tried to make him memorize at school. He'd never taken to any subject except those that would help him onto a ship. For as long as he could remember, he'd been mad for the sea, haring off at sixteen to a midshipman's berth on a man-of-war. How green he'd been, and how thrilled. All he'd ever wanted to do was captain a navy ship.

And now he'd lost his vessel, only two years after he'd been given a command at last. The *Charis* had been small, yes, and years of war had left her battered and limping into port, but he still couldn't believe the Admiralty had decommissioned her. All their blathering about reduced requirements, with Napoleon beaten for good and all, and more efficient designs coming along in the shipyards was just so much noise, as far as he was concerned. Like condolences at a family funeral, the words hadn't penetrated his sorrow. But they'd towed the *Charis* off to some backwater and abandoned her. And after ten years of service, they'd shaken his hand, given him a medal, and told him to enjoy a bit of a well-deserved rest.

So here he was, stuck on shore, waiting for a new posting, like who knew how many other navy men. The most likely berth would be second or third officer on a bigger ship, and more years to wait for another command.

The prospect depressed his spirits. It had made him consider, seriously, whether it wasn't time to leave the navy and settle down. Had he, perhaps, had his fill of the sea? Which had brought him here, to this covey of chattering guests in their civilian clothes.

James eyed his hosts, his youngest brother Alan and Ariel, Alan's lively and lovely new wife. According to family gossip, Ariel was a wizard at promoting perfect matches. She'd greased the wheels of Nathaniel's marriage and helped Sebastian win a dazzling heiress. He hadn't been able to resist asking her to see what she could come up with for him. With his prize money from the war, he certainly had the means to support a wife.

James strolled over to a table under a spreading oak and helped himself to a couple of small sandwiches. When he'd left the *Charis* for the last time, and had the leisure to consider his future, he'd fully absorbed the fact that, although many senior naval officers were married, they didn't see their wives and families for years at a time. A tour of duty could take you halfway 'round the world, where even mail packets rarely reached. You were back for a few weeks or months, then off again. Such a life would be nothing like his parents' close partnership. And in that instant, he'd realized that his model for marital happiness was his father, the duke, and his beloved duchess.

Thus had begun the conflict within him, his love for the sea fighting his desire for the kinship he'd grown up observing. And living, as well, of course. As a boy, he'd been surrounded by a horde of brothers and cousins and aunts.

At times, the back and forth seemed almost like a true battle, ringing with the echo of gun barrages and beset by swinging cutlasses. He couldn't see a way to have both, and yet he wasn't prepared to give up either.

As he usually did at this point, James turned away from the inner argument. He'd never been one to brood, and he didn't intend to start now. He went to join a cluster of his brother's guests.

"*Chelonia mydas*," said an older man in the center of the group, "maintains the balance of its body fluids by excreting the excess salt from seawater."

A woman on James's left tittered with embarrassment, earning censorious glances from the others.

"Chel-what?" asked James, his interest caught by the mention of the sea.

"The green sea turtle," replied the professorial type.

In fact, he most likely was a professor, James thought. Alan's friends came from the Oxford faculties. His brother was very much at home here, performing his arcane experiments on the nature of light. And if James knew what that meant, he'd be…well, quite another sort of person. "You mean these turtles can drink down seawater and then…be rid of the salt, er, naturally?"

The older man nodded.

"There's many a sailor who would be glad of a skill like that," James said.

The woman tittered again, her hand in front of her mouth. The professor gave her a condescending glance, as if she were an errant child. "It is one of the elements that allows the species to live their lives far from land," he added.

James noticed Ariel approaching with a very pretty blond in tow, and he examined her with interest. Although his brother's wife had made it abundantly clear that he couldn't order up a bride to any particular specifications, there was no harm in wanting a handsome one, was there? It seemed to him that the woman one was going to be looking at for the rest of one's life ought to be easy on the eyes, and this girl certainly was.

He stepped forward to meet the two ladies, and was distracted by a flicker of movement at the edge of his vision. He turned in time to see a figure emerge from the shrubbery at the bottom of the garden and stride toward him. In one raking glance, James noted a loose shabby coat, a rough scarf pulled well up over the face, a slouching cloth cap shading it, and, riveting his attention, a pistol in the youth's right hand. It was primed and cocked and aimed right at him.

With reflexes honed by years of war, James was instantly in motion. He lunged low, his speed taking the assailant by surprise. He caught the intruder's gun hand in a crushing grip and forced it upward. The pistol went off harmlessly into the sky, the sound alarmingly loud in the peaceful garden, even as the weight of James's body smashed the lad to the ground.

The party erupted into a babble of screams and shouts and questions. Some people ran toward the house; some froze in place. Glasses of lemonade dropped to the grass. Sandwiches went flying. James scarcely noticed. He was preoccupied by the fact that the body under him was definitely not that of a stripling. There were tantalizing curves under his hands. The intruder was a woman, not a boy.

"Thief, murderer!" she cried, flailing at him with her free hand.

Blows landed on his shoulder, his cheek. "What? Stop it. Ow!" He tried to grab her other wrist, and missed.

"Let me go!"

She landed another good hit, making James wonder if she'd blacked his eye. He managed to get hold of her free arm, and pinned it above her head. Her body arched and writhed beneath him in the most distracting way. "Let go of the pistol first," he said, tightening his grip on that wrist.

With a sound like a growl, she released the gun. Using her own imprisoned hand, James managed to shove it out of her reach on the grass.

"What have you done now, James?" said his brother's voice from above. James craned his neck and discovered a circle of faces—appalled, curious, frightened, amazed—staring down at them.

"He's a thief and a murderer," repeated the shooter. "A blackguard of the worst stripe."

The eyes in the circle of observers focused on James. They were not universally filled with righteous indignation at the attack, he noticed. Indeed, a couple of the women gazed at him reproachfully. The professor was starting to scowl. It was a scene out of one of those nightmares where you faced an examination all unprepared.

Incensed and bewildered, James gathered himself and jumped up, keeping a secure hold on the girl's arms and pulling her along with him. Before she could get a solid footing on the lawn, he bent, threw her over his shoulder, and carried her off toward the house.

Her fists rained blows on his back. She kicked and squirmed like an eel in his grasp. She called him all sorts of names. It was like trying to carry a sack of maddened cats, and he nearly lost his footing a time or two. She must be some sort of lunatic, he decided. But why the devil had she set her disordered sights on him?

As he maneuvered his shouting burden through the open French doors at the rear of the house, he heard one of the guests say, "Your parties are always so invigorating, my dear."

But James couldn't spare a moment to wonder about the eccentricities of Ariel's hospitality. The girl had started to claw at his neck above his shirt collar, and it felt as if she might be drawing blood. He hurried into the back parlor and dumped her unceremoniously onto a sofa. The cap fell from her head as she landed, releasing a cascade of raven-black hair. "What the hell are you shouting about?" he asked.

"Thief! Murderer!"

"Will you stop?"

"Never!" Dark eyes burned in a face smudged with dirt and half obscured by swathes of dark hair. "I swore to make you pay, if nothing else!" Her hands crooked into claws.

She looked ready to fly at him and scratch his eyes out. James took a step backward. "Pay for what?"

"You know very well what you've done!"

"On the contrary, I have no idea who you are or what the devil you're talking about."

"Liar! Thief!"

"Why do you keep saying…?"

Ariel walked through the French doors, looking surprisingly composed. "Alan is seeing the guests out. What's this all about?"

"I think she must be an escaped lunatic," said James. "Is there a bedlam house near here?"

The girl sprang up from the sofa. Her dark hair reached almost to her waist, James noticed. She extended an arm to point at him, a picture of outraged virtue, if you were devoted to bad melodrama. "I came here for justice," she declared.

Ariel looked at James. "I have no idea what she's talking about," he said.

"Ha!" said their visitor, her full lower lip curling.

"Will you stop?" said James again. "If you're not mad, then you've made some sort of mistake. Got the wrong man."

The girl shook her head, fists and jaw clenched. But as they simply stared at her, her shoulders slumped a little.

"You're tired," said Ariel. "Are you hungry?"

Tears started in the girl's eyes. She blinked them away angrily.

"Come with me," Ariel went on. "We'll get you something…"

"Hold on there," James protested. "She tried to put a bullet in me!"

Ariel paused on her way to the inner doorway. "Do you have another pistol?" she asked the girl.

The intruder slumped a little more. She bent her head, and wings of raven hair fell over her cheeks. "No," she said. She did sound exhausted.

Ariel gave James a look that seemed to say, *See?* She went over and took the girl's arm. "Come."

"Get Mary to help you," said Alan from the doorway. "Eliza, too. She did fire a pistol in our garden."

With a wave of acknowledgment, Ariel took the stranger away.

"Are you just going to let her go off with that… assassin?" asked James.

Alan shrugged. "Once Ariel gets an idea in her head… But that's why I mentioned the housemaids. She'll have them with her."

"Oh, maids. That's all right then." When his brother ignored the sarcasm, James shook his head. "Where's the pistol?"

Alan took it from his coat pocket. "It's practically a relic, and not well cared for. I think it went off by accident, when you jostled her hand."

"Jostled?" James couldn't believe what he was hearing. "I saved your garden party from an armed attack. And do I get so much as a 'thank you'?"

"Thank you," Alan replied. "You were quite impressive. I've never seen anyone move so fast." He started to put the pistol back in his pocket.

"Shouldn't you lock that away somewhere?" James asked, somewhat mollified.

His brother looked at the shabby gun, nodded. "I will. Later. It's empty now." He slipped it away. "So what did you do to her?"

"What?"

"Why is she after you?"

"I've never seen her before in my life." James gazed at his brother, deeply aggrieved. "Why do you assume I did something?"

Alan raised an eyebrow. "A girl rushes in, waving a gun, calling you a…"

"And you believe *her*—clearly a lunatic—over me?"

"No, but…" Alan shrugged. "You tend to be the one of us who goes just that step too far, James," he said. "You locked Nathaniel's valet in the garden shed on the day of his wedding."

"I thought that was part of the prank!" James protested. "Sebastian took his clothes. Robert cut the bell rope."

Alan conceded with a nod. "That jape did get rather out of hand…"

"And the shed did the fellow no harm," James pointed out. "It was all part of a joke, nothing like this…female is calling me a thief and murderer."

"And you're sure you don't know…?"

"I swear I have no idea who she is or what she's talking about."

"How…odd."

"You are a master of understatement," James replied.

The two brothers stood, perplexed, in the comfortable parlor, shafts of afternoon sun illuminating pale cream walls and blue and yellow chintz. Somewhere in the house a bell rang. Female voices were audible for a moment, then were cut off by the sound of a closing door. "Perhaps a glass of wine?" Alan suggested.

"Excellent idea."

The men had drunk their wine and run through a number of improbable theories about the uninvited guest before Ariel at last returned. They sprang up when she entered the room, and James opened his mouth to ask a question. Then he caught sight of the figure behind her.

His brother's wife was a lovely woman—small and curvy, with glossy brown hair, skin like ripe peaches, and entrancing hazel eyes. But this newcomer very nearly cast her in the shade. She was certainly a far different, far more unusual type.

The cascade of jet-black hair had been tied back with a blue ribbon. It tumbled down the back of a simple blue gown, one of Ariel's, James assumed, and framed an absolutely exquisite face. Broad forehead, jutting cheekbones, a pointed chin, full lips pink as rose petals, skin the color of honey. Huge dark eyes with sooty lashes stared at him, burning with the fire of an avenging angel. No wonder she'd smudged herself with dirt and hid her features with a scarf and cap. She'd have been mobbed otherwise, and God knew what else.

"This is Kawena," said Ariel.

James realized his mouth was hanging open. He closed it.

"I promised that she would have the chance to tell her story," his brother's wife went on. "She believes that James…"

"He killed my father!" the girl interrupted.

"That's rot," said James. "I've never killed any… or…was he a French sailor?"

"No! My father was an English gentleman!" She glared at him.

Then I didn't kill him. Unless he'd signed onto one of Boney's fighting ships. And if he did, then he deserved…"

"You stole everything he had and broke his spirit so that he died," Kawena accused.

"I did no such thing." James had never been more certain. "You have the wrong man."

"Liar!"

It seemed as if she would fly at him again. Who would think that dark eyes could burn like that?

"We're getting nowhere," said Alan, with a crisp authority that made Ariel smile. "We must begin at the beginning if we are to untangle this riddle. You… Miss…Kawena, sit there." He pointed to the sofa.

"James, over there." He indicated an armchair well out of reach, then drew Ariel to a pair of seats between them. "Now, give us your tale."

"It's not a 'tale,'" the girl responded. "It's the truth!"

"He only meant your story," Ariel put in. "What happened to bring you here."

The visitor sat back. James thought she might be trembling, but she was doing all she could to hide it.

"I come from the island of Valatu, very far from here."

"Far? That's on the other side of the world," James interjected.

"You admit you know it!" Kawena accused.

"My ship called there for supplies once or twice," he replied. "It's in the middle of the Pacific Ocean," he told Alan and Ariel. "Or, well, not the middle, but a thousand miles or more from the coast of Australia." He turned back to Kawena. "But I never saw you…"

"My father never let me near the harbor when ships were in."

James could easily see the wisdom of that. "Your father, the English gentleman," he said. "I don't remember meeting any…"

"He didn't work in the trade house. He was not a shopkeeper!"

"The beginning," Alan reminded her. "And if you could stop interrupting, James."

"Me? I'm not the one who—"

Alan held up a hand to silence him. James subsided with a frown.

Under three pairs of eyes, Kawena hesitated briefly. Then she put back her shoulders, seeming to gather herself, and said, "My father was the son of a rich

English merchant. When he was young, he was sent out on a long voyage, so that he could learn how the trading was done. But when his ship was blown off course by a great storm, and he came to Valatu, he was…much taken with the place. And he met my mother. And so he chose not to go on with his ship, but to stay there."

Her voice has a wonderful lilt, James thought. *She doesn't sound like anyone else I know.*

"He understood what ships needed so far away from their homes," Kawena continued. "And so he made a place where they could trade for island things. Fruit and other food, fresh water, things that people on the island made. He took in trade items desired by other ships. Rope and metalwork and sailcloth. My father was very wise and…and canny. He built a fortune in this way." Sadness in her face shifted to anger. "And then you stole it from him!" she said to James.

About the Author

Jane Ashford discovered Georgette Heyer in junior high school and was captivated by the glittering world and witty language of Regency England. That delight was part of what led her to study English literature and travel widely in Britain and Europe. She has written historical and contemporary romances, and her books have been published in Sweden, Italy, England, Denmark, France, Russia, Latvia, Slovenia, and Spain, as well as the United States. Jane has been nominated for a Career Achievement Award by *RT Book Reviews*. She lives in Los Angeles.

A Gentleman's Game

Romance of the Turf
by Theresa Romain

---— ❦ —---

How far will a man go

Talented but troubled, the Chandler family seems cursed by bad luck—and so Nathaniel Chandler has learned to trade on his charm. He can broker a deal with anyone from a turf-mad English noble to an Irish horse breeder. But Nathaniel's skills are tested when his stable of trained Thoroughbreds become suspiciously ill just before the Epsom Derby, and he begins to suspect his father's new secretary is not as innocent as she seems.

To win a woman's secretive heart?

Nathaniel would be very surprised if he knew why Rosalind Agate was really helping his family in their quest for a Derby victory. But for the sake of both their livelihoods, Rosalind and Nathaniel must set aside their suspicions. As Derby Day draws near, her wit and his charm make for a successful investigative team…and light the fires of growing desire. But Rosalind's life is built on secrets and Nathaniel's on charisma, and neither defense will serve them once they lose their hearts…

---— ❦ —---

For more Theresa Romain, visit:
www.sourcebooks.com

Will's True Wish

True Gentlemen

by Grace Burrowes

New York Times and *USA Today* Bestselling Author

--- ⊷ ---

It's a dog's life...

Will Dorning, as an earl's spare, has accepted the thankless duty of managing his rambunctious younger siblings, though Will's only true companions are the dogs he's treasured since boyhood. When aristocratic London is plagued with a series of dognappings, Will's brothers are convinced that he's the only person who can save the stolen canines from an awful fate.

But the lady's choice...

Shy, bookish Lady Susannah Haddonfield has no patience with loud, smelly beasts of any species, but must appear to like dogs so as not to offend her sister's only marital prospect. Susannah turns to Will, an acquaintance from her most awkward adolescent years, to teach her how to impersonate a dog fancier. Will has long admired Susannah, though he lacks the means to offer for her. Yet as they work together to rescue the purloined pets, it's loyal, dashing Will who steals Susannah's heart.

--- ⊷ ---

For more Grace Burrowes, visit:
www.sourcebooks.com